Praise for
HARLAN COB

"Harlan's a great thriller writer. . . . ~~~~ ~~ ~~~ favorites."
—John Grisham

"Coben is simply one of the all-time greats—pick up any one of his thrillers and you'll find a riveting, twisty, surprising story with a big, beating heart at its core."
—Gillian Flynn

"Coben never, ever lets you down."
—Lee Child

"Harlan Coben is the modern master of the hook-and-twist."
—Dan Brown

"Don't let Coben's wry observations fool you: They gift wrap keen insights into our society."
—*The Washington Post Book World*

"What sets Harlan Coben above the crowd are wit and wicked nonchalance."
—*Los Angeles Times Book Review*

"Coben has melded sly humor, sophisticated plotting, and solid storytelling with bizarre yet believable characters."
—*Chicago Tribune*

Praise for
DROP SHOT

"Engaging . . . hilarious."
—*Los Angeles Times Book Review*

"A fast-paced plot, witty dialogue, more than a few surprises, and a you'll-never-guess-whodunit denouement."
—*Armchair Detective*

"Superb writing . . . Harlan Coben serves up an ace with *Drop Shot*."
—John Lutz, author of *Death by Jury*

BY HARLAN COBEN

THE MYRON BOLITAR SERIES

Deal Breaker
Drop Shot
Fade Away
Back Spin
One False Move
The Final Detail

Darkest Fear
Promise Me
Long Lost
Live Wire
Home
Think Twice

STANDALONE NOVELS

Play Dead
Miracle Cure
Tell No One
Gone for Good
No Second Chance
Just One Look
The Innocent
The Woods
Hold Tight
Caught

Stay Close
Six Years
Missing You
The Stranger
Fool Me Once
Don't Let Go
Run Away
The Boy from the Woods
The Match
I Will Find You

WINDSOR HORNE LOCKWOOD III

Win

BOOKS FOR YOUNG READERS

THE MICKEY BOLITAR SERIES

Shelter
Seconds Away
Found

DROP SHOT

DROP SHOT

A Myron Bolitar Novel

Harlan Coben

DELL

NEW YORK

2024 Dell Trade Paperback Edition

Copyright © 1996 by Harlan Coben
Excerpt from *Fade Away* by Harlan Coben
copyright © 1996 by Harlan Coben

Published in the United States by Dell, an imprint of Random House,
a division of Penguin Random House LLC, New York.

DELL and the D colophon are registered trademarks of
Penguin Random House LLC.

Originally published in the United States by Dell,
an imprint of Random House, a division of Penguin Random House LLC,
in 1996.

ISBN 978-0-593-97452-0
Ebook ISBN 978-0-440-33812-3

Printed in the United States of America on acid-free paper

randomhousebooks.com

1st Printing

Book design by Virginia Norey

For Anne and Charlotte,
from the luckiest man in the whole world

DROP SHOT

1

"**C**ESAR ROMERO," MYRON SAID.

Win looked at him. "You're not serious."

"I'm starting off with an easy one."

On Stadium Court the players were changing sides. Myron's client, Duane Richwood, was shellacking the number-fifteen seed Ivan Something-okov, leading 5–0 in the third set after winning the first two sets 6–0, 6–2. An impressive U.S. Open debut for the unseeded twenty-one-year-old upstart from the streets (literally) of New York.

"Cesar Romero," Myron repeated. "Unless you don't know."

Win sighed. "The Joker."

"Frank Gorshin."

"The Riddler."

Ninety-second commercial break. Myron and Win were keeping themselves busy with a scintillating game of Name the *Batman* Criminal. The TV *Batman*. The *Batman* starring Adam West and Burt Ward and all those Pow, Bam, Slam balloons. The *real* Batman.

"Who played the second one?" Myron asked.

"The second Riddler?"

Myron nodded.

From across the court Duane Richwood flashed them a cocky smile. He sported garish aviator sunglasses with loud fluorescent green frames. The latest style from Ray•Ban. Duane was never without them. He had become not only identified by the shades but defined by them. Ray•Ban was rather pleased.

Myron and Win sat in one of the two players' boxes reserved for celebrities and players' entourages. For most matches every seat in the box was filled. When Agassi played the night before, the box had overflowed with his family, friends, suck-ups, young lasses, environmentally correct movie stars, hair weaves—like an Aerosmith backstage party. But Duane had only three people in the box: agent Myron, financial consultant Win, and Duane's coach, Henry Hobman. Wanda, the love of Duane's life, got too nervous and preferred to stay home.

"John Astin," Win answered.

Myron nodded. "How about Shelley Winters."

"Ma Parker."

"Milton Berle."

"Louie the Lilac."

"Liberace."

"Chandell the Great."

"And?"

Win looked puzzled. "And what?"

"What other criminal did Liberace play?"

"What are you talking about? Liberace only appeared in that one episode."

Myron leaned back and smiled. "Are you sure?"

In his seat next to the umpire's chair Duane happily chugged down a bottle of Evian. He held the bottle so that the sponsor's name could be clearly seen by the television cameras. Smart kid. Knew how to please the sponsor. Myron had recently signed Duane to a simple deal with the natural water giant: during the U.S. Open Duane drank Evian in marked bottles. In return Evian paid him ten grand. That was water rights. Myron was negotiating Duane's soda rights with Pepsi and his electrolyte rights with Gatorade.

Ah, tennis.

"Liberace only appeared in that one episode," Win announced.

"Is that your final answer?"

"Yes. Liberace only appeared in that one episode."

Henry Hobman continued to study the court, scrutinizing with intense concentration, his line of vision swinging back and forth. Too bad no one was playing.

"Henry, you want to take a guess?"

Henry ignored them. Nothing new there.

"Liberace only appeared in that one episode," Win repeated, his nose in the air.

Myron made a soft buzzing sound. "Sorry, that answer is incorrect. What do we have for our player, Don? Well, Myron, Windsor gets the home version of our game plus a year's supply of Turtle Wax. And thank you for playing our game!"

Win was unmoved. "Liberace only appeared in that one episode."

"That your new mantra?"

"Until you prove otherwise."

Win—full name: Windsor Horne Lockwood III—steepled his manicured fingers. He did that a lot, steepling. Steepling fit him. Win looked liked his name. The poster boy for the quintessential WASP. Everything about his appearance reeked arrogance, elitism, *Town and Country* Parties Page, debutantes dressed in monogrammed sweaters and pearls with names like Babs, dry martinis at the clubhouse, stuffy old money—his fine blond hair, his pretty-boy patrician face, his lily-white complexion, his snotty Exeter accent. Except in Win's case some sort of chromosomal abnormality had slipped through the generations of careful breeding. In some ways Win was exactly what he appeared to be. But in many more ways—sometimes very frightening ways—Win was not.

"I'm waiting," Win said.

"You remember Liberace playing Chandell the Great?" Myron asked.

"Of course."

"But you forgot that Liberace also played Chandell's evil twin brother, Harry. In the same episode."

Win made a face. "You cannot be serious."

"What?"

"That doesn't count. Evil twin brothers."

"Where in the rule book does it say that?"

Win set his jutting jaw in that certain way.

The humidity was thick enough to wear as undergarments, especially in Flushing Meadows' windless stadium court. The stadium, named strangely enough for Louis Armstrong, was basically a giant billboard that also happened to have a tennis court in the middle. IBM had a sign above the speedometer that clocked the velocity of each player's serve. Citizen kept both the real time and how long the match had been going on. Visa had its name printed behind the service line. Reebok, Infiniti, Fuji Film, Clairol had their names plastered wherever there was a free spot. So did Heineken.

Heineken, the official beer of the U.S. Open.

The crowd was a complete mix. Down low—in the good

seats—people had money. But anything went in the dress department. Some wore full suits and ties (like Win), some wore more casual Banana Republic–type clothes (like Myron), some wore jeans, some wore shorts. But Myron's personal favorite were the fans who came in full tennis gear—shirt, shorts, socks, tennis shoes, warm-up jacket, sweatbands, and tennis racket. Tennis racket. Like they might get called on to play. Like Sampras or Steffi or someone might suddenly point into the stands and say, "Hey, you with the racket. I need a doubles partner."

Win's turn. "Roddy McDowall," he began.

"The Bookworm."

"Vincent Price."

"Egghead."

"Joan Collins."

Myron hesitated. "Joan Collins? As in *Dynasty*?"

"I refuse to offer hints."

Myron ran episodes through his mind. On the court the umpire announced, "Time." The ninety-second commercial break was over. The players rose. Myron couldn't swear to it, but he thought he saw Henry blink.

"Give up?" Win asked.

"Shhh. They're about to play."

"And you call yourself a *Batman* fan."

The players took the court. They too were billboards, only smaller. Duane wore Nike sneakers and clothes. He used a Head tennis racket. Logos for McDonald's and Sony adorned his sleeves. His opponent wore Reebok. His logos featured Sharp electronics and Bic. Bic. The pen and razor company. Like someone was going to watch a tennis match, see the logo, and buy a pen.

Myron leaned toward Win. "Okay, I give," he whispered. "What criminal did Joan Collins play?"

Win shrugged. "I don't remember."

"What?"

"I know she was in an episode. But I don't remember her character's name."

"You can't do that."

Win smiled with perfect white teeth. "Where in the rule book does it say that?"

"You have to know the answer."

"Why?" Win countered. "Does Pat Sajak have to know every puzzle on *Wheel of Fortune*? Does Alex Trebek have to know every question on *Jeopardy!*?"

Pause. "Nice analogy, Win. Really."

"Thank you."

Then another voice said, "The Siren."

Myron and Win looked around. It seemed to have come from Henry.

"Did you say something?"

Henry's mouth did not appear to be moving. "The Siren," he repeated, his eyes still pasted to the court. "Joan Collins played the Siren. On *Batman*."

Myron and Win exchanged a glance.

"Nobody likes a know-it-all, Henry."

Henry's mouth might have moved. Might have been a smile.

On the court Duane opened the game with an ace that nearly bore a hole through a ball boy. The IBM speedometer clocked it at 128 mph. Myron shook his head in disbelief. So did Ivan What's-his-name. Duane was lining up for the second point when Myron's cell phone rang.

Myron quickly picked it up. He was not the only person in

the stands who was talking on a cell phone. He was, however, the only one in a front row. Myron was about to disconnect the power when he realized it might be Jessica. Jessica. Just the thought quickened his pulse a little.

"Hello."

"It's not Jessica." It was Esperanza, his associate.

"I didn't think it was."

"Right," she said. "You always sound like a whimpering puppy when you answer the phone."

Myron gripped the receiver. The match continued without interruption, but sour faces spun to seek out the origin of the offending ring. "What do you want?" he whispered. "I'm in the stadium."

"I know. Bet you look like a pretentious asshole. Talking on a cell phone at the match."

Now that she mentioned it . . .

The sour faces were glaring daggers now. In their eyes Myron had committed an unpardonable sin. Like molesting a child. Or using the salad fork on the entree. "What do you want?"

"They're showing you on TV right now. Jesus, it's true."

"What?"

"The TV does make you look heavier."

"What do you want?"

"Nothing much. I thought you might want to know I got you a meeting with Eddie Crane."

"You're kidding." Eddie Crane, one of the hottest tennis juniors in the country. He was seeing only the big-four agencies. ICM, TruPro, Advantage International, ProServ.

"No joke. Meet him and his parents by court sixteen after Duane's match."

"I love you, you know."

"Then pay me more," she said.

Duane hit a crosscourt forehand winner. Thirty–love.

"Anything else?" Myron asked.

"Nothing important. Valerie Simpson. She's called three times."

"What did she want?"

"She wouldn't say. But the Ice Queen sounded ruffled."

"Don't call her that."

"Yeah, whatever."

Myron hung up. Win looked at him. "Problem?"

Valerie Simpson. A weird, albeit sad case. The former tennis wunderkind had visited Myron's office two days ago looking for someone—anyone—to represent her. "Don't think so."

Duane was up forty–love. Triple match point. Bud Collins, tennis columnist extraordinaire, was already waiting in the gangway for the postmatch interview. Bud's pants, always a Technicolor fashion risk, were particularly hideous today.

Duane took two balls from the ball boy and approached the line. Duane was a rare commodity in tennis. A black man. Not from India or Africa or even France. Duane was from New York City. Unlike just about every other player on the tour, Duane had not spent his life preparing for this moment. He hadn't been pushed by ambitious, carpooling parents. He hadn't worked with the world's top coaches in Florida or California since he was old enough to hold a racket. Duane was on the opposite end of the spectrum: a street kid who had run away at age fifteen and somehow survived on his own. He had learned tennis from the public courts, hanging around all day and challenging anyone who could hold a racket.

He was on the verge of winning his first Grand Slam match when the gunshot sounded.

The sound had been muffled, coming from outside the stadium. Most people did not panic, assuming the sound had come from a firecracker or car backfire. But Myron and Win had heard the sound too often. They were up and moving before the screams. Inside the stadium the crowd began to mumble. More screams ensued. Loud, hysterical screams. The court umpire in his infinite wisdom impatiently shouted "Quiet, please!" into his microphone.

Myron and Win sprinted up the metallic stairway. They leaped over the white chain, put out by the ushers so that no one could enter or leave the court until the players switched sides, and ran outside. A small crowd was beginning to gather in what was generously dubbed the "Food Court." With a lot of work and patience the Food Court hoped to one day reach the gastronomic levels of, say, its mall brethren.

They pushed through the crowd. Some people were indeed hysterical but others hadn't moved at all. This was, after all, New York. The lines for refreshments were long. No one wanted to lose their place.

The girl was lying facedown in front of a stand serving Moët champagne at $7.50 a glass. Myron recognized her immediately, even before he bent down and turned her over. But when he saw her face, when he saw the icy blue eyes stare back at him in a final, unbreakable death gaze, his heart plummeted. He looked back at Win. Win, as usual, had no expression on his face.

"So much," Win said, "for her comeback."

2

"**M**AYBE YOU SHOULD JUST LET IT GO," WIN said.

He whipped his Jaguar XJR onto the FDR Drive and headed south. The radio was tuned to WMXV, 105.1 FM. They played something called "Soft Rock." Michael Bolton was on. He was doing a remake of an old Four Tops classic. Painful. Like Bea Arthur doing a remake of a Marilyn Monroe film.

Maybe Soft Rock meant Really Bad Rock.

"Mind if I put on a cassette?" Myron said.

"Please."

Win swerved into a lane change. Win's driving could most kindly be described as creative. Myron tried not to look. He pushed in a cassette from the original production of *How to Succeed in Business Without Really Trying*. Like Myron, Win had a huge collection of old Broadway musicals. Robert Morse sang about a girl named Rosemary. But Myron's mind remained fixed on a girl named Valerie Simpson.

Valerie was dead. One bullet to the chest. Someone had shot her in the Food Court of the United States Tennis Association National Tennis Center during the opening round of America's sole Grand Slam event. Yet no one had seen a thing. Or at least no one was talking.

"You're making that face," Win said.

"What face?"

"The I-want-to-help-the-world face," Win said. "She wasn't a client."

"She was going to be."

"A large distinction. Her fate does not concern you."

"She called me three times today," Myron said. "When she couldn't reach me, she showed up at the tennis center. And then she was gunned down."

"A sad tale," Win said. "But one that does not concern you."

The speedometer hovered about eighty. "Uh, Win?"

"Yes."

"The left side of the road. It's for oncoming traffic."

Win spun the wheel, cut across two lanes, and swerved onto a ramp. Minutes later the Jag veered into the Kinney lot on Fifty-second Street. They gave the keys to Mario, the parking attendant. Manhattan was hot. City hot. The sidewalk scorched your feet right through your shoes. Exhaust fumes got stuck in the humidity, hanging in the air like fruit on a tree. Breathing was a chore. Sweating was not. The secret was to keep the sweat to a minimum while walking, hoping that the air-conditioning would dry off your clothes without giving you pneumonia.

Myron and Win walked south down Park Avenue toward the high-rise of Lock-Horne Investments & Securities. Win's family owned the building. The elevator stopped on the twelfth floor. Myron stepped out. Win stayed inside. His office at Lock-Horne was two floors up.

Before the elevator closed Win said, "I knew her."

"Who?"

"Valerie Simpson. I sent her to you."

"Why didn't you say anything?"

"No reason to."

"Were you close?"

"Depends on your definition. She's old money Philadelphia. Like my family. We were members of the same clubs, the same charities, that sort of thing. Our families occasionally summered together when we were kids. But I hadn't heard from her in years."

"She just called you out of the blue?" Myron asked.

"You could say that."

"What would you say?"

"Is this an interrogation?"

"No. Do you have any thoughts on who killed her?"

Win stood perfectly still. "We'll chat later," he said. "I have some business matters I must attend to first."

The elevator door slid closed. Myron waited for a moment, as though expecting the elevator to open again. Then he crossed the corridor and opened a door that read MB SportsReps Inc.

Esperanza looked up from her desk. "Jesus, you look like hell."

"You heard about Valerie?"

She nodded. If she felt guilty about calling her the Ice Queen moments before the murder, she didn't show it. "You have blood on your jacket."

"I know."

"Ned Tunwell from Nike is in the conference room."

"I guess I'll see him," Myron said. "No use moping around."

Esperanza looked at him. No expression.

"Don't get so upset," he continued. "I'm okay."

"I'm putting on a brave front," she said.

Ms. Compassion.

When Myron opened the conference room door, Ned Tunwell charged like a happy puppy. He smiled brightly, shook hands, slapped Myron on the back. Myron half expected him to jump in his lap and lick his face.

Ned Tunwell looked to be in his early thirties, around Myron's age. His entire persona was always upbeat, like a Hare Krishna on speed—or worse, a *Family Feud* contestant. He wore a blue blazer, white shirt, khaki pants, loud tie, and of course, Nike tennis shoes. The new Duane Richwood line. His hair was yellow-blond and he had one of those milk-stain mustaches.

Ned finally calmed down enough to hold up a videotape. "Wait till you see this!" he raved. "Myron, you are going to love it. It's fantastic."

"Let's take a look."

"I'm telling you, Myron, it's fantastic. Just fantastic. Incredible. It came out better than I ever thought. Blows away the stuff we did with Courier and Agassi. You're gonna love it. It's fantastic. Fantastic, I tell you."

The key word here: *fantastic.*

Tunwell flipped the television on and put the tape in the VCR. Myron sat down and tried to push away the image of Valerie Simpson's corpse. He needed to concentrate. This— Duane's first national television commercial—was crucial. Truth was, an athlete's image was made more by these commercials than anything else—including how well he played or how he was portrayed by the media. Athletes became defined by the commercials. Everyone knew Michael Jordan as Air Jordan. Most fans couldn't tell you Larry Johnson played for the

Charlotte Hornets, but they knew all about his Grandmama character. The right campaign made you. The wrong one could destroy you.

"When is it going to air?" Myron asked.

"During the quarter finals. We're gonna blitz the networks in a very big way."

The tape finished rewinding. Duane was on the verge of becoming one of the most highly paid tennis players in the world. Not from winning matches, though that would help. But from endorsements. In most sports, the big-name athletes made more money from sponsors than from their teams. In the case of tennis, a lot more. A hell of a lot more. The top ten players made maybe fifteen percent of the money from winning matches. The bulk was from endorsements, exhibition matches, and guarantees—money paid big names to show up at a given tournament no matter how they fared.

Tennis needed new blood, and Duane Richwood was the most exhilarating transfusion to come along in years. Courier and Sampras were about as exciting as dry dog food. The Swedish players were always a snooze-a-thon. Agassi's act was growing wearisome. McEnroe and Connors were history.

So enter Duane Richwood. Colorful, funny, slightly controversial, but not yet hated. He was black and he was from the streets, but he was perceived as "safe" street, "safe" black, the kind of guy even racists could get behind to show they are not really racists.

"Just check this baby out, Myron. This spot, I'm telling you, it's . . . it's just . . ." Tunwell looked up, as though searching for the word.

"Fantastic?" Myron tried.

Ned snapped his fingers and pointed. "Just wait till you see.

I get hard watching it. Shit, I get hard just *thinking* about it. Swear to Christ, it's that good."

He pressed the PLAY button.

Two days ago Valerie Simpson had sat in this very room, coming in on the heels of his meeting with Duane Richwood. The contrast was striking. Both were in their twenties, but while one career was just blossoming, the other had already dried up and blown away. Twenty-four years old and Valerie had long been labeled a "has-been" or "never-was." Her behavior had been cold and arrogant (ergo Esperanza's Ice Queen comment), or perhaps she'd just been distant and distracted. Hard to know for sure. And yes, Valerie had been young, but she had not exactly been—to quote a cliché—full of life. Eerie to say it now, but her eyes seemed to have more life in death— more animated while frozen and staring—than when she'd sat across from him in this very room.

Why, Myron wondered, would someone want to kill Valerie Simpson? Why had she tried so desperately to reach him? Why had she gone to the tennis center? To check out the competition? Or to find Myron?

"Watch this, Myron," Tunwell repeated yet again. "It's so fantastic, I came. Really, swear to God. Right in my pants."

"Sorry I missed that," Myron said.

Ned whooped with pleasure.

The commercial finally began. Duane appeared, wearing his sunglasses, dashing back and forth on a tennis court. Lots of quick cuts, especially to his sneakers. Lots of bright colors. Pounding beat, mixed in with the sound of tennis balls being blasted across the net. Very MTV-like. Could have been a rock video. Then Duane's voice came on:

"Come to my court . . ."

A few more hard ground strokes, a few more quick cuts. Then everything suddenly stopped. Duane vanished. The color faded to black and white. Silence. Scene change. A stern-looking judge glared down from his bench. Duane's voice returned:

". . . and stay away from his court."

The rock music started up again. The color returned. The screen cut back to Duane hitting the ball, smiling through his sweat, his sunglasses reflecting the light. A Nike symbol appeared with the words COME TO DUANE'S COURT below them.

Fade to black.

Ned Tunwell groaned—actually groaned—in satisfaction.

"You want a cigarette?" Myron asked.

Tunwell's smile doubled in wattage. "What did I tell you, Myron? Huh? Fantastic or what?"

Myron nodded. It was good. Very good. Hip, well-made, responsible message but not too preachy. "I like it," he said.

"I told you. Didn't I tell you? I'm hard again. Swear to God, that's how much I like it. I might just come again. Right here, right now. As we speak."

"Good to know."

Tunwell broke into a seizurelike fit of laughter. He slapped Myron's shoulder.

"Ned?"

Tunwell's laughter faded away like the end of a song. He wiped his eyes. "You kill me, Myron. I can't stop laughing. You really kill me."

"Yeah, I'm a scream. Did you hear about Valerie Simpson's murder?"

"Sure. It was on the radio. I used to work with her, you know." He was still smiling, his eyes wide and bright.

"She was with Nike?" Myron asked.

"Yep. And let me tell you, she cost us a bundle. I mean, Valerie seemed like a sure thing. She was only sixteen years old when we signed her and she'd already reached the finals of the French Open. Plus she was good-looking, all-American, the works. And she was already developed, if you know what I mean. She wasn't a cute little kid who might turn into a beast when she got a little older. Like Capriati. Valerie was a babe."

"So what happened?"

Ned Tunwell shrugged. "She had a breakdown. Shit, it was in all the papers."

"What caused it?"

"Hell if I know. Lot of rumors."

"Like?"

He opened his mouth, then closed it. "I forget."

"You forget?"

"Look, Myron, most people thought it was just too much, you know? All that pressure. Valerie couldn't hack it. Most of these kids can't. They get it all, you know, reach such big heights and then poof, it's gone. You can't imagine what it's like to lose everything like . . . uh . . ." Ned stammered to a stop. Then he lowered his head. "Ah, shit."

Myron remained silent.

"I can't believe I said that, Myron. To you of all people."

"Forget it."

"No. I mean, look, I can pretend I didn't just put my foot in my mouth like that, but . . ."

Myron waved him off. "A knee injury isn't a mental breakdown, Ned."

"Yeah, I know but still . . ." He stopped again. "When the Celts drafted you, were you a Nike guy?"

"No. Converse."

"They dump you? I mean, right away?"

"I have no complaints."

Esperanza opened the door without knocking. Nothing new there. She never knocked. Ned Tunwell's smile quickly returned. Hard to keep the man down. He stared at Esperanza. Appreciatively. Most men did.

"Can I see you for a second, Myron?"

Ned waved. "Hi, Esperanza."

She turned and looked right through him. One of her many talents.

Myron excused himself and followed her out. Esperanza's desk was bare except for two photographs. One was of her dog, an adorable shaggy pooch named Chloe, winning a dog show. Esperanza was into dog shows—a sport not exactly dominated by inner-city Latinos, though she seemed to do pretty well. The desk's other picture showed Esperanza wrestling another woman. Professionally wrestling, that is. The lovely and lithe Esperanza had once wrestled professionally under the name Little Pocahontas, the Indian Princess. For three years Little Pocahontas had been a crowd favorite of the Fabulous Ladies of Wrestling organization, popularly known as FLOW (someone had once suggested calling it the Beautiful Ladies of Wrestling, but the acronym was a problem for the networks). Esperanza's Little Pocahontas was a scantily clad (basically a suede bikini) sexpot whom fans cheered and leered at as she bravely took on enormous evil, cheating nemeses every week. A morality play, some called it. A classic reenactment of Good vs. Evil. But to Myron the weekly action was more like those women-in-prison films. Esperanza played the beautiful, naive prisoner stuck in cell block C. Her opponent was Olga, the sadistic prison matron.

"It's Duane," Esperanza said.

Myron took the call at her desk. "Hey, Duane. What's up?"

His voice came fast. "Get over here, man. Like now."

"What's the matter?"

"The cops are in my face. They're asking me all kinds of shit."

"About what?"

"That girl who got shot today. They think I got something to do with it."

3

"**L**ET ME SPEAK TO THE POLICE OFFICER," MYRON told Duane.

Another voice came on the line. "This is homicide detective Roland Dimonte," the voice barked with pure cop impatience. "Who the hell is this?"

"I'm Myron Bolitar. Mr. Richwood's attorney."

"Attorney, huh? I thought you were his agent."

"I'm both," Myron said.

"That a fact?"

"Yes."

"You got a law degree?"

"It's hanging on my wall. But I can bring it if you'd like."

Dimonte made a noise. Might have been a snicker. "Ex-jock. Ex-fed. And now you tell me you're a goddamn lawyer?"

"I'm what you might call a Renaissance man," Myron said.

"Yeah? Tell me, Bolitar, what law school would let in someone like you?"

"Harvard," Myron said.

"Whoa, aren't we a big shot."

"You asked."

"Well, you got half an hour to get here. Then I drag your boy to the precinct. Got me?"

"I've really enjoyed this little chat, Rolly."

"You got twenty-nine minutes. And don't call me Rolly."

"I don't want my client questioned until I'm present. Understood?"

Roland Dimonte didn't answer.

"Understood?" Myron repeated.

Pause. Then: "Must be a bad connection, Bolitar." Dimonte hung up.

Pleasant guy.

Myron handed the phone back to Esperanza. "Mind getting rid of Ned for me?"

"Done."

Myron took the elevator to the ground floor and sprinted toward the Kinney lot. Someone shouted, "Go, O.J.!" at him. In New York everyone's a comedian. Mario tossed Myron the keys without glancing up from his newspaper.

Myron's car was parked on the ground floor. Unlike Win, Myron was not what one would label a "car guy." A car was a mode of transportation, nothing more. Myron drove a Ford Taurus. A gray Ford Taurus. When he cruised down the street, chicks did not exactly swarm.

He'd driven about twenty blocks when he spotted a powder-blue Cadillac with a canary-yellow roof. Something about it bothered Myron. The color maybe. Powder blue with a yellow roof? In Manhattan? A retirement community in Boca Raton, okay, driven by some guy named Sid who always had his left blinker on. Myron could see that. But not in Manhattan. And more to the point, Myron remembered sprinting past the exact same car on his way to the garage.

Was he being followed?

A possibility, though not a great one. This was midtown Manhattan and Myron was heading straight down Seventh Avenue. About a million other cars were doing the same. Could be nothing. Probably was. Myron made a quick mental note and proceeded.

Duane had recently rented a place on the corner of Twelfth Street and Sixth Avenue. The John Adams Building, on the fringe of Greenwich Village. Myron illegally parked in front of a Chinese restaurant on Sixth, got passed through by the doorman, and took the elevator to Apartment 7G.

A man who had to be Detective Roland Dimonte answered the door. He was dressed in jeans, paisley green shirt, black leather vest. He also had on the ugliest pair of snakeskin boots—snow-white with flecks of purple—Myron had ever seen. His hair was greasy. Several strands were matted to his forehead like to flypaper. A toothpick—an actual toothpick—was jutting out of his mouth. His eyes were set deep in a pudgy face, like someone had stuck two brown pebbles in at the last minute.

Myron smiled. "Hi, Rolly."

"Let's get one thing straight, Bolitar. I know all about you. I know all about your glory days with the feds. I know all about how you like to play cop now. But I don't give a shit about none of that. Nor do I give a shit that your client is a public figure. I gotta job to do. You hear what I'm saying?"

Myron put his hand to his ear. "Must be a bad connection."

Roland Dimonte crossed his arms and gave Myron his most withering glare. The snakeskin boots had a high platform of some sort, pushing his height over six foot, but Myron still had a good three or four inches on him. A minute passed. Roland still glared. Then another minute. Roland gnawed on the toothpick. The glare persisted without a blink.

"On the inside," Myron said, "I'm quaking in fear."

"Go fuck yourself, Bolitar."

"Chewing the toothpick is a nice touch. A little cliché perhaps, but it works for you."

"Just keep it up, smart-ass."

"Mind if I come in," Myron said, "before I wet my pants?"

Dimonte moved out of the way. Slowly. The death glare was still locked on autopilot.

Myron found Duane sitting on the couch. He was wearing his Ray•Bans, but that was not surprising. He stroked his closely cropped beard with his left hand. Wanda, Duane's girlfriend, stood by the kitchen. She was tall, five-ten or so. Her figure was what was commonly referred to as tight or hard rather than muscular, and she was a stunner. Her eyes kept darting about like birds moving from branch to branch.

It was not a huge apartment. The decor was standard New York rental. Duane and Wanda had moved in only a few weeks ago. Month-to-month lease. No reason to fix the place up. With the money Duane was about to start making they could live anywhere they wanted to soon.

"Did you say anything to them?" Myron asked.

Duane shook his head. "Not yet."

"Want to tell me what's going on?"

Duane shook his head again. "I don't know."

There was another cop in the room. A younger guy. Much younger. He looked to be about twelve. Probably just made detective. He had his pad out, his pen at the ready.

Myron turned to Roland Dimonte. Dimonte had his hands on his hips, emanating self-importance from every pore. "What's this all about?" Myron asked.

"We just want to ask your client a few questions."

"About what?"

"The murder of Valerie Simpson."

Myron looked over at Duane. "I don't know nothing," Duane said.

Dimonte sat down, making a big production out of it. King Lear. "Then you won't mind answering a few questions?"

Duane said, "No." But he didn't sound very confident about it.

"Where were you when the shooting occurred?"

Duane glanced at Myron. Myron nodded. "I was on Stadium Court."

"What were you doing?"

"Playing tennis."

"Who was your opponent?"

Myron nodded. "You're good, Rolly."

"Shut the fuck up, Bolitar."

Duane said, "Ivan Restovich."

"Did the match continue after the shooting?"

"Yeah. It was match point anyway."

"Did you hear the gunshot?"

"Yeah."

"What did you do?"

"Do?"

"When you heard the shot?"

Duane shrugged. "Nothing. I just stood there until the umpire told us to keep playing."

"You never left the court?"

"No."

The young cop kept scribbling, never looking up.

"Then what did you do?" Dimonte asked.

"When?"

"After the match."

"I did an interview."

"Who interviewed you?"

"Bud Collins and Tim Mayotte."

The young cop looked up for a moment, confused.

"Mayotte," Myron said. "M-A-Y-O-T-T-E."

He nodded and resumed his scribbling.

"What did you talk about?" Roland asked him.

"Huh?"

"During the interview. What did they ask you about?"

Dimonte shot a challenging glare at Myron. Myron responded with his warmest nod and a pilotlike thumbs up.

"I'm not going to tell you again, Bolitar. Cut the shit."

"Just admiring your technique."

"You'll admire it from a jail cell in a minute."

"Gasp!"

Another death glare from Roland Dimonte before he turned back to Duane. "Do you know Valerie Simpson?"

"Personally?"

"Yes."

Duane shook his head. "No."

"But you've met?"

"No."

"You don't know her at all?"

"That's right."

"You've never had any contact with her?"

"Never."

Roland Dimonte crossed his legs, resting his boot on his knee. His fingers caressed—actually caressed—the white-and-purple snakeskin. Like it was a pet dog. "How about you, miss?"

Wanda seemed startled. "Pardon me?"

"Have you ever met Valerie Simpson?"

"No." Her voice was barely audible.

Dimonte turned back to Duane. "Had you ever heard of Valerie Simpson before today?"

Myron rolled his eyes. But for once he kept his mouth shut. He didn't want to push it too far. Dimonte was not as dumb as he appeared. No one was. He was trying to lull Duane before the big whammy. Myron's job was to disrupt his rhythm with a few choice interruptions. But not too many.

Myron Bolitar, darling of the tightrope.

Duane said with a shrug, "Yeah, I heard of her."

"In what capacity?"

"She used to be on the circuit. Couple years back, I think."

"The tennis circuit?"

"No, the nightclub circuit," Myron interjected. "She used to open for Anthony Newley in Vegas."

So much for Mr. Restraint.

The glare was back. "Bolitar, you're really starting to piss me off."

"Are you going to get to the point already?"

"I take my time with interrogations. I don't like to rush."

"Should do the same," Myron said, "when purchasing footwear."

Dimonte's face reddened. Still glaring at Myron, he said, "Mr. Richwood, how long have you been on the circuit?"

"Six months."

"And in those six months you never saw Valerie Simpson?"

"That's right."

"Fine. Now let me see if I got this right: You were playing a match when the gun went off. You finished the match. You shook hands with your opponent. I assume you shook hands with your opponent?"

Duane nodded.

"Then you did an interview."

"Right."

"Did you shower before or after the interview?"

Myron held up his hands. "Okay, that's enough."

"You got a problem, Bolitar?"

"Yeah. Your questions are beyond idiotic. I'm now advising my client to stop answering them."

"Why? Your client got something to hide?"

"Yeah, Rolly, you're too clever for us. Duane killed her. Several million people were watching him on national television during the shooting. Several thousand more were watching him in person. But that wasn't him playing. It was really his identical twin, lost since birth. You're just too smart for us, Rolly. We confess."

"I haven't ruled that out," Dimonte countered.

"Haven't ruled what out?"

"That 'we' stuff. Maybe you had something to do with it. You and that psycho-yuppie friend of yours."

He meant Win. Lot of cops knew Win. None liked him. The feeling was mutual.

"We were in the stadium at the time of the shooting," Myron said. "A dozen witnesses will back that up. And if you really knew anything about Win, you'd know he'd never use a weapon that close up."

That made Dimonte hesitate. He nodded. Agreeing, for once.

"Are you through with Mr. Richwood?" Myron asked.

Dimonte suddenly smiled. It was a happy, expectant smile, like a schoolkid sitting by the radio on a snow day. Myron didn't like the smile.

"If you'll just humor me for another moment," he said with syrupy phoniness. He rose and moved toward his partner, the Pad. The Pad kept scribbling.

"Your client claims he didn't know Valerie Simpson."

"So?"

The Pad finally looked up. His eyes were as vacant as a court stenographer's. Dimonte nodded at him. The Pad handed him a small leather book encased in plastic.

"This is Valerie's calendar book," Dimonte said. "The last entry was made yesterday." His smile widened. His head was held high. His chest puffed out like a rooster about to get laid.

"Okay, poker face," Myron said. "What's it say?"

He handed Myron a photocopy. Yesterday's entry was fairly simple. Sprawled across the entire page it read:

D.R. 555-8705. Call!

555-8705. Duane's phone number. D.R. Duane Richwood. Dimonte appeared gleeful.

"I'd like to talk to my client," Myron said. "Alone."

"No."

"Excuse me?"

"You're not going to duck away now that I have you on the ropes."

"I'm his attorney—"

"I don't give a rat's ass if you're the Chief Justice of the Supreme Court. You take him away, I take him downtown in cuffs."

"You don't have anything," Myron said. "His phone number is in her book. Means nothing."

Dimonte nodded. "But how would it look? To the press, for example. Or the fans. Duane Richwood, tennis's newest hero, being dragged into the station with handcuffs on. Bet that would be hard to explain to the sponsors."

"Are you threatening us?"

Dimonte put his hand to his chest. "Heavens no. Would I do something like that, Krinsky?"

The Pad did not look up. "Nope."

"There. You see?"

"I'll sue your ass for wrongful arrest," Myron said.

"And you might even win, Bolitar. Years from now, when the courts actually hear the case. Lot of good that's going to do you."

Dimonte looked a lot less stupid now.

Duane quickly stood and crossed the room. He snapped off the Ray•Bans, then, thinking better of it, put them back on. "Look, man, I don't know why my number is in her book. I don't know her. I never spoke to her on the phone."

"Your phone is unlisted. Is that correct, Mr. Richwood?"

"Yeah."

"And you just moved in. Your phone's only been hooked up, what, two weeks?"

Wanda said, "Three." She was hugging herself now, as though she were cold.

"Three," Roland Dimonte repeated. "So how did Valerie get your number, Duane? How come some woman you don't know has your brand-new, unlisted number in her date book?"

"I don't know."

Roland skipped skeptical and moved directly to absolute disbelief. For the next hour he continued to hammer Duane, but Duane stuck to his story. He never met her, he said. He didn't know her. He never spoke to her. He had no idea how she could have gotten his phone number. Myron watched in silence. The sunglasses made it harder to read Duane, but his body language was all wrong. So was Wanda's.

With an angry sigh Roland Dimonte finally stood up. "Krin-sky?"

The Pad looked up.

"Let's get the hell out of here."

The Pad closed the pad, joined his partner.

"I'll be back," Dimonte barked. Then pointing at no one in particular he added, "You hear me, Bolitar?"

"You'll be back," Myron said.

"Count on it, asshole."

"Aren't you going to warn us not to leave town? I love it when you cops do that."

Dimonte made a gun with his hand. He pointed it at Myron and lowered the thumb/hammer. Then he and the Pad disappeared out the door.

For several minutes no one said anything. Myron was about to break the silence when Duane started laughing. "You sure showed him, Myron. Tore him a whole new asshole—"

"Duane, we need—"

"I'm tired, Myron." He feigned a yawn. "I really need to get some sleep."

"We need to talk about this."

"About what?"

Myron looked at him.

Duane said, "Pretty weird coincidence, huh?"

Myron turned toward Wanda. She looked away, still hugging herself. "Duane, if you're in some kind of trouble—"

"Hey, tell me about the commercial," Duane interrupted. "How did it come out?"

"Good."

Duane smiled. "How did I look?"

"Too handsome. I'll be fighting off the movie offers."

Duane laughed too hard. Much too hard. Wanda did not laugh. Neither did Myron. Then Duane feigned another yawn, stretched and stood. "I really need to get some rest," he said. "Big match coming up. Hate to let all this bullshit distract me."

He showed Myron to the door. Wanda still had not moved from her spot by the kitchen door. She finally met Myron's eye.

"Good-bye, Myron," Wanda said.

The door closed. Myron took the elevator back down and walked to his car. A ticket was nestled between the windshield and the wiper. He grabbed it and started the car.

Three blocks away Myron spotted the same powder-blue Cadillac with the canary-yellow top.

4

YUPPIEVILLE.

The fourteenth floor of Lock-Horne Investments & Securities reminded Myron of a medieval fortress. There was the vast space in the middle, and a thick, formidable wall—the big producers' offices—safeguarding the perimeter. The open area housed hundreds of mostly men, young men, combat soldiers easily sacrificed and replaced, a seemingly endless sea of them, bobbing and blending into the corporate-gray carpet, the identical desks, the identical rolling chairs, the computer terminals, the telephones, the fax machines. Like soldiers they wore uniforms—white button-down shirts, suspenders, bright ties strangling carotid arteries, suit jackets draped across the backs of the identical rolling chairs. There were loud noises, screams, rings, even something that sounded like death cries. Everyone was in motion. Everyone was scattering, panicked, under constant attack.

Yes, for here was one of the final strongholds of true yuppie-ism, a place where man was free to practice the religion of eighties greed, greed at all costs, without pretense of doing otherwise. No hypocrisy here. Investment houses were not about helping the world. They were not about providing a service to mankind or doing what was best for all. This haven had a simple, clear-cut, basic goal. Making money. Period.

Win had a spacious corner office overlooking Park and Fifty-second Street. A prime-time view for the company's number one producer. Myron knocked on the door.

"Enter," Win called out.

He was sitting in a full lotus on the floor, his expression serene, his thumbs and forefingers forming circles in each hand. Meditation. Win did it every day without fail. Usually more than once.

But as with most things with Win, his moments of inner solitude were a tad unconventional. For one, he liked to keep his eyes open when meditating, while most practitioners kept them closed. For another, he didn't imagine idyllic scenes of waterfalls or does in the forest; rather, Win opted for watching home videotapes—videos of himself and an interesting potpourri of lady friends in assorted throes of passion.

Myron made a face. "You mind turning that off?"

"Lisa Goldstein," Win said, motioning toward a mound of writhing flesh on the screen.

"Charmed, I'm sure."

"I don't think you ever met her."

"Hard to tell," Myron said. "I mean, I'm not even sure where her face is."

"Lovely lass. Jewish, you know."

"Lisa Goldstein? You're kidding."

Win smiled. He uncrossed his legs and stood in one fluid motion. He switched off the television, hit the EJECT button, put the tape back in a box marked *L.G.* He filed the box under the *G*'s in an oak cabinet. There were a lot of tapes already there.

"You realize," Myron said, "that you're quite deranged."

Win locked the cabinet with a key. Dr. Discretion. "Every man needs a hobby."

"You're a scratch golfer. You're a champion martial artist. Those are hobbies. This is deranged. Hobbies; deranged. See the difference?"

"Moralizing," Win said. "How nice."

Myron did not respond. They had been down this road many times since they were freshmen at Duke. It never led anywhere.

Win's office was pure, elitist WASP. Paintings of a fox hunt adorned paneled walls. Burgundy leather chairs ideally complemented the deep forest-green carpeting. An antique wooden globe stood next to an oak desk that could double as a squash court. The effect—not a subtle one, at that—could be summed up in two words: Serious. Cash.

Myron sat in one of the leather chairs. "You got a minute?"

"Of course." Win opened a cabinet in the bar behind his desk, revealing a small refrigerator. He took out a cold Yoo-Hoo and tossed it to Myron. Myron shook the can as per the instructions (*Shake! It's Great!*) while Win mixed himself a very dry martini.

Myron started off by telling Win about the police visit to Duane Richwood. Win remained impassive, allowing himself a small smile when he heard how Dimonte had called him a psycho-yuppie. Then Myron told him about the powder-blue Cadillac. Win sat back and steepled. He listened without interrupting. When Myron finished, Win rose from his seat and picked up a putter.

"So our friend Mr. Richwood is holding something back."

"We can't be sure."

Win raised a skeptical eyebrow. "Do you have any thoughts as to how Duane Richwood and Valerie Simpson are connected?"

"Nope. I was hoping you might."

"*Moi?*"

"You knew her," Myron said.

"She was an acquaintance."

"But you have a thought."

"About a connection between Duane and Valerie? No."

"Then what?"

Win strolled to a corner. A dozen golf balls were all in a line. He began to putt. "Are you really intent on pursuing this? Valerie's murder, I mean?"

"Yep."

"It might be none of your business."

"Might be," Myron agreed.

"Or you might unearth something unpleasant. Something you would rather not find."

"A distinct possibility."

Win nodded, checked the carpet's lie. "Wouldn't be the first time."

"No. Not the first time. Are you in?"

"There is nothing in this for us," Win said.

"Maybe not," Myron agreed.

"No financial gain."

"None at all."

"In fact there is never any profit in your holy crusades."

Myron waited.

Win lined up another putt. "Stop making that face," he said. "I'm in."

"Good. Now tell me what you know about this."

"Nothing really. It's just a thought."

"I'm listening."

"You know, of course, about Valerie's breakdown," Win said.

"Yes."

"It was six years ago. She was only eighteen. The official word was that she collapsed under the pressure."

"The official word?"

"It may be the truth. The pressure on her was indeed awesome. Her rise had been nothing short of meteoric—but nowhere near as meteoric as the tennis world's expectations of her. Her subsequent fall—at least, up until the time of the breakdown—was slow and painful. Not at all like yours. Your fall, if you don't mind me using that word, was far swifter. Guillotine-like. One minute you were the Celtics' number one draft pick. The next minute you were finished. The end. But unlike Valerie, you had a freak injury and were thereby blameless. You were pitied. You cut a sympathetic figure. Valerie's demise, on the other hand, seemed to be of her own doing. She was a failure, ridiculed, but still no more than a child. To the world at large, the fickle finger of fate had ended the career of Myron Bolitar. But in the case of Valerie Simpson, she alone was culpable. In the eyes of the public she did not possess enough mental fortitude. Her fall, thus, was slow, torturous, brutal."

"So what does this have to do with the murder?"

"Perhaps nothing. But I always found the circumstances surrounding Valerie's mental collapse a bit disturbing."

"Why?"

"Her game had slipped, that much was true. Her coach— that famous gentleman who plays with all the celebrities . . ."

"Pavel Menansi."

"Whatever. He still believed Valerie could come back and win again. He said it all the time."

"Thereby putting more pressure on her."

Win hesitated. "Perhaps," he said slowly. "But there is another factor. Do you remember the murder of Alexander Cross?"

"The senator's son?"

"The senator from Pennsylvania," Win added.

"He was killed by robbers at his country club. Five, six years ago."

"Six. And it was a tennis club."

"You knew him?"

"Of course," Win said. "The Hornes have known every important Pennsylvania politician since William Penn. I grew up with Alexander Cross. We went to Exeter together."

"So what does he have to do with Valerie Simpson?"

"Alexander and Valerie were, shall we say, an item."

"A serious item?"

"Quite. They were about to announce their engagement when Alexander was killed. That night, as a matter of fact."

Myron did some quick mathematics in his head. Six years ago. Valerie would have been eighteen. "Let me guess. Valerie's breakdown took place right after his murder."

"Precisely."

"But I don't get something. The Cross murder was on the news every day for weeks. How come I never heard Valerie's name mentioned?"

"That," Win said, nailing another putt, "is why I find the circumstances disturbing."

Silence.

"We need to talk to Valerie's family," Myron said. "Maybe the senator's as well."

"Yes."

"You live in that world. You're one of them. They'd be more apt to talk to you."

Win shook his head. "They'll never talk to me. Being 'one of them,' as you put it, is a severe handicap. Their guard will be up with someone like me. But with you they won't be so concerned about facades. They'll perceive you as someone who doesn't matter, as someone inferior, as someone beneath them. A nobody."

"Gee, that's flattering."

Win smiled. "The way of the world, my friend. Many things change, but these people still consider themselves the true, original Americans. You and your kind are just hired help, shipped in from Russia or Eastern Europe or from whatever gulag or ghetto your people originated."

"I hope they don't hurt my feelings," Myron said.

"I'll arrange a meeting for you with Valerie's mother for tomorrow morning."

"You think she'll see me?"

"If I request it, yes."

"Groovy."

"Indeed." Win put down his putter. "In the meantime what do you suggest we do?"

Myron checked his watch. "One of Pavel Menansi's protégées is playing on Stadium Court in about an hour. I figured I'd pay him a visit."

"And *pour moi*?"

"Valerie spent the past week at the Plaza Hotel," Myron said. "I'd like you to look around, see if anybody remembers anything. Check her phone calls."

"See if she did indeed call Duane Richwood?"

"Yes."

"And if she did?"

"Then we have to look into that too," Myron said.

5

THE U.S.T.A. NATIONAL TENNIS CENTER IS neatly snuggled into the bosom of Queens' top attractions: Shea Stadium (home of the New York Mets), Flushing Meadows Park (home of the 1964–65 World's Fair) and La Guardia Airport (home of, uh, delays).

Players used to complain about the La Guardia planes flying overhead, for the very simple reason that it made Stadium Court sound like a launchpad during an Apollo liftoff. Then-mayor David Dinkins, never one to let a terrible injustice go unheeded, immediately sprang into action. Using all his political might, the former mayor of New York City—who in a fascinating and almost eerie coincidence was also an enormous tennis fan—had La Guardia's offending runway halt operations for the duration of the Open. Tennis millionaires were grateful. In a show of mutual respect and admiration Mayor David Dinkins returned their gratitude by showing up at the matches every day for the two weeks of play, except—in yet another eerie coincidence—during election years.

Only two courts were used for the night sessions: Stadium Court and the adjacent Grandstand Court. The day sessions,

Myron thought, were much more fun. Fifteen or sixteen matches might be going on at the same time. You could cruise around, catch a great five-set match on some obscure court, discover an up-and-coming player, see singles, doubles, and mixed doubles matches all in the glorious sunshine. But at night you basically sat in one seat and watched a match under lights. During the Open's first couple of days this match usually featured a top-seed mercilessly decapitating a qualifier.

Myron parked in the Shea Stadium lot and crossed the walking bridge over the No. 7 train. Someone had set up a booth with a radar gun where spectators could measure the speed of their own serve. Business was brisk. Ticket scalpers were also busy. So were the guys selling knockoff U.S. Open T-shirts. The knockoff T-shirts sold for five dollars, as opposed to the ones inside the gates that went for twenty-five dollars. Not a bad deal on the surface. Of course, after one wash the knockoff T-shirt could only be worn by a Barbie doll. But still.

Pavel Menansi was in one of the players' boxes, the same one Myron and Win had sat in earlier in the day. It was 6:45 P.M. The final day match was over. The first night match, featuring Pavel's latest protégée, fourteen-year old Janet Koffman, would not begin until 7:15 P.M. People were milling around during the day-to-night cusp. Myron spotted the usher from the day session.

"How ya doing, Mr. Bolitar?" the usher said.

"Fine, Bill. Just wanted to say a quick hello to a friend."

"Sure, no prob, go right ahead."

Myron headed down the steps. Without warning a man wearing a blue blazer and aviator sunglasses stepped in front of him. He was a big guy—six-four, two-twenty—just about Myron's size. His neatly combed hair sat above a pleasant though unyielding face. He expanded his chest into a paddleball wall, blocking Myron's path.

His voice said, "Can I help you, sir?" But his tone said, *Take a hike, bub.*

Myron looked at him. "Anyone ever tell you you look like Jack Lord?"

No reaction.

"You know," Myron said. "Jack Lord? *Hawaii Five-O?*"

"I'll have to ask you to leave, sir."

"It's not an insult. Many people find Jack Lord very attractive."

"Sir, this is the last time I'm going to ask nicely."

Myron studied his face. "You even have that Jack Lord surly grin. Remember it?" Myron imitated the grin for him, in case he'd never seen the show.

The face twitched. "Okay, buddy, you're out of here."

"I just want to speak to Mr. Menansi for a moment."

"I'm afraid that won't be possible at this time."

"Oh, okay." He spoke a little louder. "Just tell Mr. Menansi that Duane Richwood's agent wanted to discuss something very important with him. But if he's not interested I'll go elsewhere."

Pavel Menansi's head jerked around as though pulled by a string. His smile flicked on like a cigarette lighter. He rose, his eyes half open, his whole persona oozing that foreign charm that some women find irresistible and others find nauseating beyond words. Pavel was Romanian, one of tennis's original Bad Boys, the former doubles partner of Ilie "Nasty" Nastase. He was nearing fifty, his face tanned to the point of leathery. When he smiled, the leather cracked almost audibly.

"Pardon me," he said. His voice was smooth—part Roma-

nian, part American, part Ricardo Montalban discussing Co-
rinthian leather. "You are Myron Bolitar, are you not?"

"I am."

He dismissed Jack Lord with a nod. Big Jack was not happy
about it, but he moved out of the way. His body swung to the
side like a metal gate, allowing only Myron to enter. Pavel
Menansi held out a hand. For a moment Myron thought he
wanted him to kiss it, but it ended in a brief handshake.

"Please," Pavel said. "Sit here. Next to me."

Whoever was in the seat quickly made himself scarce.
Myron sat. Pavel did likewise. "I apologize for my guard's zeal,
but you must understand. People, they want autographs. Parents, they want to discuss their child's play. But here"—he
spread his hands—"this is not the time or place."

"I understand," Myron said.

"I've heard quite a bit about you, Mr. Bolitar."

"Please call me Myron."

Pavel had the smile of a lifelong smoker, *sans* proper dental
hygiene. "Only if you call me Pavel."

"Deal."

"Fine then. You discovered Duane Richwood, did you not?"

"Somebody pointed him out to me."

"But you saw the potential first," Pavel insisted. "He never
played in the juniors, never went to college. That's why all the
big agencies missed him, am I right?"

"I guess so."

"So now you have a top tennis contender. You are now competing with the big boys, yes?"

Myron knew that Pavel Menansi worked with TruPro, one
of the country's largest sports agencies. Working with TruPro
didn't automatically make you a sleazeball, but it brought you

awfully close. Pavel was worth millions to them—not because of what he made as much as the young talent he brought in. Pavel got a Svengali-like hold on prodigies at the age of eight or ten, giving TruPro a hell of an advantage in getting them signed. TruPro had never been a reputable agency—almost a contradiction in terms anyway—but over the last year it had become mob-controlled, run by the appropriately named Ache brothers of New York City. The Ache brothers were into all the top mob favorites: drugs, numbers, prostitution, extortion, gambling. Sweethearts, those Aches.

"Your Duane Richwood," Pavel continued. "He played a fine match today. Fine match indeed. His potential is quite limit-less. You agree?"

"He works very hard," Myron said.

"I'm sure he does. Tell me, Myron, who is Duane's present coach?" He said *present,* but it came out more like *former.*

"Henry Hobson."

"Ah." Pavel nodded with vigor, as though this response ex-plained something very complex. He, of course, already knew who coached Duane. Pavel probably knew who coached every player on the circuit. "Henry Hobson is a fine man. A compe-tent coach." He said *competent,* but it came out more like *crappy.*

"But I believe I can help him, Myron."

"I'm not here to talk about Duane," Myron said.

A shadow crossed his face. "Oh?"

"I want to discuss another client. Or should I say a once-potential client."

"And who would that be?"

"Valerie Simpson."

Myron looked for a reaction. He got one. Pavel lowered his head into his hands. "Oh, my God."

The box rumbled with overwrought concern. Comforting hands found their way to Pavel's shoulders, uttering his name in low voices. But Pavel pushed them away. Very brave.

"Valerie came to me a few days ago," Myron continued. "She wanted to make a comeback."

Pavel took a deep breath. He made a show of putting himself together a piece at a time. When he was able to continue, he said, "The poor child. I can't believe it. I just can't...." He stopped. Overwhelmed again. Then: "I was her coach, you know. During her glory years."

Myron nodded.

"To be shot down like that. Like a dog." He shook his head dramatically.

"When was the last time you saw Valerie?"

"Several years ago," he said.

"Have you seen her since the breakdown?"

"No. Not since she went into the hospital."

"Spoken to her? On the phone maybe?"

Pavel shook his head again. Then he lowered it. "I blame myself for what happened to her. I should have looked out for her better."

"What do you mean?"

"When you coach one so young, you have responsibilities that go beyond her life on the court. She was a child—a child growing up in the spotlight. The media, they are savages, no? They don't understand what they do to sell papers. I tried to cushion some of their blows. I tried to protect her, to not let it eat her up inside. In the end, I failed."

He sounded genuine, but Myron knew that meant nothing. People were amazing liars. The more sincere they sounded— the more they held your gaze and looked truthful—the more sociopathic they were. "Do you have any idea who would have wanted her dead?"

He looked puzzled by the question. "Why are you asking these questions, Myron?"

"I'm looking into something."

"Into what? If I may ask."

"It's kind of personal."

He studied Myron for a few seconds. The stench of tobacco was heavy on his breath. Myron was forced to inhale through his mouth. "I will tell you the same thing I told the police," Pavel said. "In my opinion Valerie's breakdown was not just from the usual tennis pressures."

Myron nodded, encouraging him to continue.

Pavel turned his palms toward the sky, as though seeking divine intervention. "Perhaps I am wrong. Perhaps I want to believe that to—how do you say?—soothe my own guilt. I don't know anymore. But I've had a lot of young people in my camp and never have I experienced anything like what happened to Valerie. No, Myron, her problems were caused by more than the pressures of big-time tennis."

"What then?"

"I'm not a medical doctor, you understand. I cannot say for sure. But you must remember that Valerie was being menaced."

Myron waited for him to elaborate. When he didn't, Myron said, "Menaced?" Probing interrogatories—one of Myron's strong suits.

"Stalked," he said with a finger snap. "That's the word they use nowadays. Valerie was being stalked."

"By whom?"

"A very sick man, Myron. A terrible man. After all these years I still remember his name. Roger Quincy. Crazy animal. He wrote her love letters. He called all the time. He hung around her house, by her hotel, at every match she played."

"When was this?"

"When she was on the tour, of course. It began—I don't know—six months before she was hospitalized."

"Did you try to stop him?"

"Of course. We went to the police. They could do nothing. We tried to get a court order, but this Quincy never actually threatened her. He would say 'I love you, I want to be with you,' things like that. We did our best. We changed hotels, signed in under different aliases. But you have to remember, Valerie was just a child. She became paranoid. The pressure on her was already tremendous. But now she had to look over her shoulder all the time. This Roger Quincy, he was a crazy beast. That's what he was. He was the one who should have been gunned down."

Myron nodded, waiting a beat. "How did Alexander Cross react to Roger Quincy?"

The question stunned Pavel like a surprise left hook. Lennox Lewis vs. Frank Bruno. He hesitated, trying to regain his footing. The players came out of the tunnel. Applause began to build. The distraction worked like a standing eight count, giving Pavel time to recover.

"Why would you ask that?" he asked.

"Weren't Alexander Cross and Valerie Simpson involved?"

"I guess you could say that."

"Seriously?"

"She was away a lot. Traveling. But they seemed fond of each other."

"And I assume their relationship was going on at the same time Quincy was stalking Valerie?"

"I believe the time periods overlapped, yes."

"So it's a natural question," Myron said. "How did Valerie's boyfriend react?"

"Natural, perhaps," he said. "But you must admit it is also a bizarre question. Alexander Cross has been dead for several years now. How is his reaction relevant to what happened to Valerie today?"

"For one, they were both murdered."

"You're not suggesting a connection?"

"I'm not suggesting anything," Myron said. "But I don't understand why you don't want to answer my question."

"It's not a matter of wanting or not wanting," Pavel replied. "It's a matter of doing what is right. You are delving into places where you do not belong. Personal places. Places that cannot possibly have any relevance in today's world. I feel like I am betraying confidences. You see?"

"No."

Pavel looked back at Jack Lord. Jack's mouth twitched. He stood again. The chest self-inflated.

"The match is about to begin," Pavel said. "I hate to be rude, but I really must ask you to leave now."

"Hit a raw nerve, did I?"

"Yes. I cared for Valerie very deeply."

"That wasn't what I meant."

"Please leave. I must concentrate on this match."

Myron did not move. Jack Lord put a big mitt on Myron's shoulder. "You heard the man," he said. "Move out."

"Let go of my shoulder," Myron said.

Jack shook his head. "No more games, pal. It's time for you to get lost."

"If you don't move your hand," Myron explained calmly, "I'll hurt you. Maybe severely."

From behind his sunglasses Big Jack finally smiled. His grip on Myron's shoulder tightened. Myron quickly reached up with his right hand and grabbed the man's thumb. He locked the joint and pulled it back the wrong way. Jack dropped to one knee.

Myron lowered his mouth toward Jack's ear. "I don't want to make a scene, so I'm going to let you go," he whispered. "If you do anything but smile I will hurt you. Definitely severely. Nod if you understand."

He nodded, his face pale.

Myron let the thumb go. "Later, Pavel."

Pavel said nothing.

Myron walked past Jack. As ordered, Jack was smiling.

"Book 'em, Dann-o," Myron said.

6

A STALKER.

Could it be that simple? Could some deranged fan have put a bullet into Valerie Simpson because a voice told him to? Doesn't explain Duane Richwood's connection. But maybe there was no connection. Or maybe the connection had nothing to do with the murder and, more important, was none of Myron's business.

Myron turned onto Hobart Gap Road. He was only a mile from his home in Livingston, New Jersey. The powder-blue Caddy with the canary-yellow roof finally turned off, jumping on the JFK Parkway. Whoever it was must have figured Myron was going home for the night, and hence there was no reason to keep the tail. But if the Caddy was around tomorrow, Myron would have to take care of it—unmask the true identity of Mr. Miami Gin Tournament.

Right now he needed to concentrate on this whole stalker possibility.

If Valerie had been killed by Roger Quincy, then why had ol' Pavel gotten so antsy when Myron mentioned Alexander Cross? Or was it just like Pavel said—he didn't want to betray confidences? When you thought about it, wasn't it a hell of a lot more probable that Pavel just felt it was in his best interest to keep quiet? Senator Cross was an awfully powerful man. Spreading stories about his murdered son wasn't necessarily the wisest course of action. So there could be nothing there. Then again it could be something big. Or something small.

Thoughts like these are what made Myron a brilliant detective.

He parked in the driveway. His mom's car was in the garage. His dad's was nowhere in sight. He opened the door with his key.

"Myron?"

Myron. God, what a name. You'd think he'd be used to it by now, but occasionally the horror hit him anew. He had been dubbed Myron. A last-second decision, his parents claimed. Something Mom came up with at the hospital. But to name a kid Myron Bolitar? Was that fair? Was that ethical?

As a youngster Myron tried giving himself nicknames: Mike, Mickey, even Sweet J, for his famous jumpshot. Okay, maybe it was a good thing that Sweet J didn't stick. But still.

Warning to parents naming children: Let's be careful out there.

His mother called out, "Myron? Is that you?"

"Yeah, Mom."

"I'm in the den." She was wearing an exercise outfit, watching some kind of workout tape. She stood on one leg, crane stance à la *The Karate Kid*. On the television a familiar voice crooned, "Now flow-step to the left. . . ."

David Carradine's T'ai Chi Workout. Wonderful.

"Hi, Mom."

"You're late," she said.

"I didn't realize I had a curfew."

"You said you'd be home by seven. It's past nine."

"Your point being?"

"I was worried. I saw on the news about that girl getting shot at the Open. How did I know you weren't killed?"

Myron held back a sigh. "Did the news say I was killed? Did the news say anything about unidentified bodies? Or did they say only one girl named Valerie Simpson was shot?"

"They could have been lying."

"Excuse me?"

"Happens all the time. The police lie to the reporters until they notify the next of kin."

"Weren't you home all day?"

"What, the police have my phone number?"

"But they could . . ." He stopped. What was the point? "Next time a murder takes place within a three-mile radius of my being I'll be sure to call home."

"Good." She snapped off the tape. Then she placed a pillow in a corner and stood on her head.

"Mom?"

"What?"

"What are you doing?"

"What's it look like? I'm standing on my head. It's good exercise. Makes the blood flow. Makes me look my best. You know who used to stand on his head every day?"

Myron shook his head.

"David Ben-Gurion."

"And everyone knows what a looker he was," Myron said.

"Smart-mouth."

Mom was a major paradox. On the one hand she'd been a practicing attorney for the past twenty years. She was the first generation born in the United States, her parents coming over from Minsk or somewhere like that, living lives that as near as Myron could tell paralleled *Fiddler on the Roof*. She became a sixties radical, an original bra burner, and experimented with various mind-altering drugs (hence naming a child Myron). She did not cook. Ever. She had no idea where the vacuum cleaner was stored. She did not know what an iron looked like, never mind whether or not she owned one. In the courtroom her crosses were legendary. She breakfasted on star witnesses. She was bright, frighteningly shrewd, and very modern.

On the other hand, all of this went out the window when it came to her son. She completely decompensated. She became her mother. And her mother before her. Only worse. Murphy Brown became Grandma Tzietl.

"Your father is picking up some Chinese food. I ordered enough for you."

"I'm not hungry, thanks."

"Spareribs, Myron. Sesame chicken." Meaningful pause. "Shrimp with lobster sauce."

"I'm really not hungry."

"Shrimp with lobster sauce," she repeated.

"Mom . . ."

"From Fong's Dragon House."

"No thanks."

"What? You love Fong's shrimp in lobster sauce. You're crazy about it."

"Maybe a little then." Easier.

She was still standing on her head. She began to whistle. Very casual-like. "So," she said in that strain-to-sound-aloof voice, "how's Jessica?"

"Butt out, Mom."

"Who's butting? I just asked a simple question."

"And I gave you a simple answer. Butt out."

"Fine. But don't go crying to me if something goes wrong."

Like that happens.

"Why has she been away so long anyway? What's she doing over there?"

"Thanks for butting out."

"I'm concerned," Mom said. "I just hope she's not up to something."

"Butt out."

"Is that all you can say? Butt out? What are you, a parrot? Where is she anyway?"

Myron opened his mouth, wrestled it closed, and stormed into the basement. His dwelling. He was almost thirty-two years old and still lived at home. He hadn't been here much the past few months. Most nights he'd spent at Jessica's place in the city. They had even talked about moving in together but decided to take it slow. Very slow. Easier said than done. The heart don't know from slow. At least Myron's didn't. As usual Mom had drilled into exposed nerve endings. Jessica was in Europe right now, but Myron had no idea where. He hadn't heard from her in two weeks. He missed her. And he was wondering too.

The doorbell rang.

"Your father," Mom called down. "Probably forgot his key again. I swear that man is getting senile."

A few seconds later he heard the basement door open. His mother's feet appeared. Then the rest of her. She beckoned him forward.

"What?"

"There's a young lady here to see you," she said. Then in a whisper, "She's black."

"Gasp!" Myron put his hand to his heart. "Hope the neighbors don't call the police."

"That's not what I meant, smart-mouth, and you know it. We have black families in the neighborhood now. The Wilsons. Lovely people. They live on Coventry Drive. In the old Dechtman home."

"I know, Mom."

"I was just describing her for you. Like I might say she has blond hair. Or a nice smile. Or a harelip."

"Uh-huh."

"Or limp. Or she's tall. Or short. Or fat. Or—"

"I think I get the drift, Mom. Did you ask her name?"

She shook her head. "I didn't want to pry."

Right.

Myron headed up the stairs. It was Wanda, Duane's girlfriend. For some reason Myron was not surprised. She smiled nervously, waved quickly.

"I'm sorry to disturb you at home," she said.

"No problem. Please come in."

They headed down to the basement. Myron had subdivided it into two rooms. One, a small sitting room he basically never used. Hence it was presentable and clean. The inside room, his living quarters, resembled a frat house after a major kegger.

Wanda's eyes darted around again, like they had when Dimonte had been at the apartment. "You live down here?"

"Only since I was sixteen."

"I think that's sweet. Living with your parents."

From upstairs: "If only you knew."

"Close the door, Mom."

Slam.

"Please," Myron said. "Sit down."

Wanda looked unsure but finally settled into a chair. She was wringing her hands nonstop. "I feel a little foolish," she said.

Myron gave her an understanding, encouraging smile—the Phil Donahue smile. *Caller, are you there?*

"Duane likes you," she said. "A lot."

"The feeling is mutual."

"The other agents, they call Duane all the time. All the big ones. They keep saying how you're too small-time to represent Duane. They keep saying they can help him make a lot more money."

"They might be right," Myron said.

She shook her head. "Duane doesn't think so. I don't think so either."

"That's nice of you to say."

"You know why Duane won't meet with those other agents?"

"Because he doesn't want to see me weep?"

She smiled at that one. The Master of Levity strikes again. Señor Self-Deprecation. "No," she said. "Duane trusts you."

"I'm glad."

"You're not just in it for the money."

"That nice of you to say, Wanda, but Duane is making me a lot of money. There's no denying that."

"I know," she said. "I don't want to sound naive here, but you put him first. Before the money. You look out for Duane Rich-wood the human being. You care about him."

Myron said nothing.

"Duane doesn't have many people," she continued. "He doesn't have any family. He lived on the streets since he was fifteen, scraping by. He wasn't an angel that whole time. He did some things he'd rather forget. But he never hurt anybody, never did anything serious. His whole life he never had anyone he could rely on. He had to take care of himself."

Silence.

"Does Duane know you're here?" Myron asked.

"No."

"Where is he?"

"I don't know. He just took off. He does that sometimes."

More silence.

"So anyway, like I said, Duane doesn't have anybody else. He trusts you. He trusts Win, too, but only because he's your best friend."

"Wanda, what you're saying is very nice, but I'm hardly driven by altruism. I'm well paid for what I do."

"But you care."

"Henry Hobson cares."

"Maybe. But his wagon is hitched to Duane's star. Duane is his ticket back to the bigs."

"Many would say the same for me," Myron countered. "Except that part about 'back,' since I've never been to the bigs. Duane's my only big tennis player. In fact Duane is the only player I've got in the U.S. Open."

She considered this for a moment, nodding. "Maybe that's all true," she said. "But when push came to shove—when trouble hit today—Duane came to you. And when push came to shove for me tonight, I came to you too. That's the bottom line."

The basement door opened.

"Would you kids like something to drink?"

"Got any Kool-Aid, Mom?"

Wanda laughed.

"Listen, smart-mouth, maybe your company is hungry."

"No, thank you, Mrs. Bolitar," Wanda shouted up.

"You sure, hon? Coffee maybe? A Coke?"

"Nothing, really, thank you."

"How about some Danish? I just bought some fresh at the Swiss House. Myron's favorite."

"Mom . . ."

"Okay, okay, I can take a hint."

Right. The Mistress of the Subtle Signal. The basement door closed.

"She's sweet," Wanda said.

"Yeah, adorable." Myron leaned forward. "Why don't you tell me why you're here?"

She started wringing her hands again. "I'm worried about Duane."

"If it's about Dimonte's visit, don't let him get to you. Being a horse's ass is part of his job."

"It's not that," she said. "Duane wouldn't hurt anybody. I know that. But something isn't right with him. He's tense all the time. He paces around the apartment. He flies off the handle at the littlest things."

"He's under a lot of pressure right now. It could just be nerves."

She shook her head. "Duane thrives on pressure. He loves competing, you know that. But the last day or two it's different. Something is really bothering him."

"Any idea what?"

"No."

Myron leaned forward. "Let me ask you the obvious question: Did Duane get a call from Valerie Simpson?"

She thought for a moment. "I don't know."

"Does he know her?"

"I don't know that either. But I know Duane. We've been together for three years, since we were both eighteen. He was still on the streets when we met. My father freaked out when he heard. He's a chiropractor. He makes a good living, worked hard to keep the bad element away from us. And here I was, dating a street kid, a runaway."

She chuckled at the memory. Myron sat and waited.

"No one thought it would last," she continued. "I left college and got a job so he could pursue tennis. Now he's putting me through NYU. We love each other. We loved each other before all this tennis stuff started and we'll love each other long after he puts down the racket for good. But for the first time he's shutting me out."

"And you think Valerie Simpson is somehow connected?"

She hesitated. "I guess I do."

"How?"

"I have no idea."

"What do you want me to do?"

She stood, paced in the small room. "I heard those policemen talking. They said you used to be a big deal with the government. You and Win. Something secretive with the FBI—after you recovered from the knee injury. Is that true?"

"Yes."

"I thought maybe you could, I don't know, look into it?"

"You want me to investigate Duane?"

"He's hiding something, Myron. It has to come out."

"You might not like what I find," he said, echoing Win's earlier words.

"I'm more afraid of going on like this." Wanda looked up at him. "Will you help him?"

He nodded. "I'll do what I can."

7

THE PHONE RANG.

Myron reached out blindly, swimming back to consciousness. He grabbed the receiver and croaked, "Hello?"

"Is this the Rent-a-Stud hotline?"

Her voice hit him like a jolt. "Jess?"

"Oh shit," Jessica said. "You were sleeping, right?"

"Sleeping?" Myron squinted at his digital. "At four-thirteen in the morning? Captain Midnight? Surely you jest."

"Sorry. I forgot about the time difference."

He sat up. "Where are you?"

"Greece," she said. "I miss you."

"You're just horny."

"Well, there's that."

"Captain Midnight is willing to help," he said.

"My fearless hero. I suppose you're not even a little horny."

"Captain Midnight lives chastely."

"Part of his image?"

"Exactly," he said.

"It's no fun," she said. "Being away from you."

His heart soared. "So come home."

"I am."

"When?"

"Soon." Jessica Culver, Miss Specific USA. "Tell me what's been going on," she said.

"You hear about the shooting at the Open?"

"Sure. The hotel has CNN."

Myron told her about Valerie Simpson. When he finished, her first comment was, "You didn't have to bend that clod's thumb back."

"But it was all very macho," Myron said.

"A real turn-on, I'm sure."

"Guess you had to be there," he said.

"Guess so. So are you going to find the killer?"

"I'm going to try."

"For Valerie's sake? Or for Wanda and Duane?"

"For all of them, I guess. But mostly Valerie. You should have seen her, Jess. She tried so hard to be sullen and unpleasant. A girl that young shouldn't have to try that hard."

"Do you have a plan?"

"Of course. First, I'm going to visit Valerie's mother tomorrow morning. In Philadelphia."

"And then?"

"Well, the plan isn't really that well developed. But I'm working on it."

"Please be careful."

"Captain Midnight is always careful."

"It's not just Captain Midnight I'm worried about it. It's his alter ego."

"And who might that be?"

"My Love Muffin."

Myron grinned into the receiver. "Hey, Jess, did you know Joan Collins was on *Batman*?"

"Of course," Jessica said. "She played the Siren."

"Oh yeah? Well, who did Liberace play?"

8

MYRON SPENT THE REST OF THE NIGHT DREAMing about Jessica, though as usual he could only remember meaningless scraps in the morning. Jessica was in his life again, but it was still new to him. Too new. He needed to hold back, to tread gently. He was afraid of being crushed under her heel again, of having his heart slammed in the door of love.

Door of love. Christ. He sounded like a bad country song.

He motored south on the famed New Jersey Turnpike. The powder-blue Cadillac with the canary-yellow top was four cars behind him. More than anything else, this stretch of roadway had made New Jersey the butt of so many jokes. He passed Newark Airport. Kind of ugly, but what airport isn't? Then he drove by the turnpike's pièce de résistance, its cause célèbre if you will—an enormous industrial power plant between exits 12 and 13 that closely resembled the futuristic nightmare world in the beginning of the *Terminator* movies. Thick smoke sprung from every orifice. Even in the bright sunshine the place looked dark, metallic, menacing, foreboding.

On the radio a rock group called the Motels were repeatedly singing the ingenious line *Take the L out of lover, and it's over.* Deep. Literal, but still deep. The Motels. Whatever happened to them?

Myron picked up the cellular phone and dialed. A familiar voice answered.

"Sheriff Courter speaking."

"Hey, Jake, it's Myron."

"I'm sorry. You must have the wrong number. Bye."

"Good one," Myron said. "Guess those night-school comedy courses are finally starting to pay off."

"What do you want, Myron?"

"Can't a friend just call and say hello?"

"So this is just a social call?" Jake said.

"Yes."

"I feel so blessed."

"Wait. It gets better. I'm going to be in your neck of the woods in a couple of hours."

"Be still my heart."

"I thought maybe we could meet for lunch. I'm buying."

"Uh-huh. You bringing Win?"

"No."

"Then okay. Guy gives me the creeps."

"You don't even know him."

"Cool by me. Now what do you want, Myron? This may be a surprise to you, but I work for a living."

"You still have friends on the Philadelphia force?"

"Sure."

"Can you get someone to fax you a homicide file?"

"Recent homicide?"

"Er, not exactly."

"How old?"

"Six years," Myron said.

"You're kidding, right?"

"It gets worse. The victim was Alexander Cross."

"The senator's kid?"

"Right."

"What the hell do you want that for?"

"I'll tell you about it when I get there."

"Someone is going to want to know why."

"Make something up."

Jake chewed on something that sounded like tree bark. "Yeah, all right. What time will you be here?"

"Probably around one. I'll call you."

"You're going to owe me, Myron. Owe me big."

"Didn't I mention I was buying lunch?"

Jake hung up.

Myron headed off at exit 6. The toll was almost four dollars. He was tempted to pay the Caddy's toll, but four dollars was a bit steep for the gesture. Myron handed the clerk the money. "I only wanted to drive on the road," Myron said. "Not buy it."

Not even a sympathetic smile. Complaining about toll prices. One of those signs you're becoming your father. Next thing you know Myron'd be screaming at someone for turning up the thermostat.

Altogether the trip to Philadelphia's wealthiest suburb took two hours. Gladwynne was old money. Plymouth Rock old money. Bloodlines were as important as credit lines. The house Valerie Simpson had grown up in was Gatsbyesque with signs of fray. The lawn was not quite manicured. The shrubbery was slightly overgrown. The paint was chipped in certain places. The ivy crawling along the walls seemed a tad too thick.

Still, the estate was huge. Myron parked so far away he almost waited for shuttle service. As he approached the front door Detectives Dimonte and Krinsky came out. In a major shock, Dimonte did not appear happy to see him. He put his hands on his hips. Important, impatient.

"What the fuck are you doing here?" he barked.

"Do you know what happened to the Motels?" Myron asked.

"The what?"

Myron shook his head. "How quickly they forget."

"Goddamn it, Bolitar, I asked you a question. What do you want here?"

"You left your underpants at my house last night," Myron said. "Jockey shorts. Size thirty-eight. Little bunny design."

Dimonte's face grew red. Most cops were homophobes. Best way to needle them was to play on it. "You better not be playing fucking Hardy Boys with my case, asshole. You and your pal Psycho-yuppie."

Krinsky laughed at that one. Psycho-yuppie. When ol' Rolly got hold of a good one he didn't let it go.

"Doesn't matter," Dimonte continued. "The case is just about wrapped up."

"And I'll be able to say I knew you when."

"You'll be happy to know your client is no longer my main suspect."

Myron nodded. "Roger Quincy the stalker is."

That didn't please Dimonte. "How the fuck do you know about that?"

"I am all-seeing, all-knowing."

"Doesn't mean your boy is fully in the clear. He's still lying about something. You know it. I know it. Krinsky here knows it."

Krinsky sort of nodded. Mr. Sidekick.

"But now we just figure your boy was porking her. You know, on the side."

"You have any evidence?"

"Don't need none. Don't give a shit. I want her killer, not her porker."

"Poetically put, Rolly."

"Ah screw it, I don't have time for your wit."

As they passed, Myron gave a little wave. "Nice talking to you, Krinsky."

Krinsky nodded.

Myron rang the doorbell. It rang dramatically. Sounded like an orchestra. Tchaikovsky maybe. Maybe not. A man of about thirty came to the door. He was dressed in a pink oxford shirt open at the neck. Ralph Lauren. Big dimple on chin. Hair so black it was almost blue, like Superman's.

He looked at Myron like he was a vagrant urinating on the steps. "Yes?"

"I'm here to see Mrs. Van Slyke." Valerie's mother had remarried.

"Now is not a good time," he said.

"I have an appointment."

"Perhaps you didn't hear me," he said in that haughty, Win-like accent. "Now is not a good time."

"Please tell Mrs. Van Slyke that Myron Bolitar is here," Myron persisted. "She is expecting me. Windsor Lockwood spoke with her last night."

"Mrs. Van Slyke isn't seeing anybody today. Her daughter was murdered yesterday."

"I'm aware of that."

"Then you'll understand—"

"Kenneth?"

A woman's voice.

"It's okay, Helen," the man said. "I'm handling the situation."

"Who is it, Kenneth?"

"No one."

Myron said, "Myron Bolitar."

Kenneth shot Myron a look. Myron held back the temptation to stick out his tongue. It wasn't easy.

She appeared in the foyer. All in black. Her eyes were red with equally red rims. She was an attractive woman, though Myron ventured to guess she was probably a lot more attractive twenty-four hours ago. Late forties. Blond hair, softly colored. Nicely coiffed. Not too bleachy.

"Please come in, Mr. Bolitar."

Kenneth said, "I don't think that's such a good idea, Helen."

"It's okay, Kenneth."

"You need your rest."

She took Myron's arm. "Please forgive my husband, Mr. Bolitar. He is just trying to protect me."

Husband? Did she say husband?

"Please follow me."

She led him into a room slightly larger than the Acropolis. Over the fireplace hung a gigantic portrait of a man with long sideburns and a walrus mustache. Kinda scary. The room was lit by a half dozen of those fixtures that look like candles. The furniture, while old-world tasteful, seemed a tad too worn. There wasn't a silver tea set, but there should have been. Myron sat in an antique chair about as comfortable as an iron lung. Kenneth kept his eye on Myron. Making sure he didn't pocket an ashtray or something.

Helen sat on the couch across from him. Kenneth stood behind her, hands on her shoulders. Would have made a nice photograph. Very regal. A little girl, no more than three or four, toddled into the room. "This is Cassie," Helen Van Slyke said. "Valerie's sister."

Myron smiled widely and leaned toward the little girl. "Hello, Cassie."

The little girl responded by bawling like she'd just been stabbed.

Helen Van Slyke comforted her daughter, and after a few more wails Cassie stopped. She peeked out behind balled-up fists every once in a while to study Myron. Maybe she too feared for the safety of the ashtrays.

"Windsor tells me you're a sports agent," Helen Van Slyke said.

"Yes."

"Were you going to represent my daughter?"

"We were discussing the possibility."

Kenneth said, "I don't see why this conversation can't wait, Helen."

She ignored him. "So why did you want to see me, Mr. Bolitar?"

"I'd just like to ask you a few questions."

"What kind of questions?" Kenneth asked. Sneering suspicion.

Helen silenced him with her hand. "Please go ahead, Mr. Bolitar."

"I understand Valerie was hospitalized about six years ago."

"What does that have to do with anything?" Kenneth again.

"Kenneth, please leave us alone."

"But Helen—"

"Please. Take Cassie for a walk."

"Are you sure?"

"Yes."

He protested, but he was no match for her. She closed her eyes, signaling the argument's end. Grudgingly Kenneth took his daughter's hand. When they were out of earshot, she said, "He is a bit overprotective."

"It's understandable," Myron said. "Under the circumstances."

"Why do you want to know about Valerie's hospitalization?"

"I'm trying to put some loose ends together."

She studied his face for a moment. "You're trying to find my daughter's killer, aren't you?"

"Yes."

"May I ask why?"

"There are several reasons."

"I'll accept one."

"Valerie tried to reach me before the murder," Myron said. "She called my office three times."

"That hardly makes you responsible."

Myron said nothing.

Helen Van Slyke took a deep breath. "And you think her murder has something to do with her breakdown?"

"I don't know."

"The police feel quite certain the killer is a man who stalked Valerie."

"What do you think?"

She stayed perfectly still. "I don't know. Roger Quincy seemed harmless enough. But I guess they all seem harmless until something like this happens. He used to write her love letters all the time. They were sort of sweet, in a kooky kind of way."

"Do you still have them?"

"I just gave them to the police."

"Do you remember what they said?"

"They vacillated between almost normal courting words and outright obsession. Sometimes he would simply ask her on a date. Other times he would write about eternal love and how they were destined to be together forever."

"How did Valerie react?"

"Sometimes it scared her. Sometimes it amused her. But mostly she ignored it. We all did. No one took it too seriously."

"What about Pavel? Was he concerned?"

"Not overly."

"Did he hire a bodyguard for Valerie?"

"No. He was dead set against the idea. He thought a bodyguard might spook her."

Myron paused. Valerie hadn't needed a bodyguard against a stalker, yet Pavel needs one against pestering parents and autograph hounds. It made one wonder. "I'd like to talk about Valerie's breakdown, if that's all right."

Helen Van Slyke stiffened slightly. "I think it's best to leave that alone, Mr. Bolitar."

"Why?"

"It was painful. You have no idea how painful. My daughter had a mental collapse, Mr. Bolitar. She was only eighteen years old. Beautiful. Talented. A professional athlete. Successful by any rational measure. And she had a breakdown. It was stressful on all of us. We tried our best to help her get well, to keep it from getting in the papers and becoming public. We tried our best to keep it under wraps."

She stopped then and closed her eyes.

"Mrs. Van Slyke."

"I'm fine," she said.

Silence.

"You were saying how you tried to keep it under wraps," Myron prompted.

The eyes reopened. She smiled and sort of smoothed her skirt. "Yes, well, I didn't want this episode ruining her life. You know how people talk. For the rest of her life people would point and whisper. I didn't want that. And yes, I was embarrassed too. I was younger, Mr. Bolitar. I was afraid of how her breakdown would reflect on the Brentman family name."

"Brentman?"

"My maiden name. This estate is known as Brentman Hall. My first husband was named Simpson. A mistake. A social climber. Kenneth is my second husband. I know tongues wag about our age differences, but the Van Slykes are an old family. His great-great-grandfather and my great-grandfather were partners."

Good reason to get married. "How long have you and Kenneth been married?"

"Six years last April."

"I see. So you got married around the same time Valerie was hospitalized."

Her eyes narrowed and her words came slower now. "What exactly are you implying, Mr. Bolitar?"

"Nothing," Myron said. "I wasn't implying anything. Really." Well, maybe a little. "Tell me about Alexander Cross."

She stiffened again, almost like a spasm. "What about him?" She sounded annoyed now.

"He and Valerie were serious?"

"Mr. Bolitar"—impatience creeping in—"Windsor Lockwood is an old family friend. He is the reason I agreed to see you. You earlier portrayed yourself as a man concerned with finding my daughter's killer."

"I am."

"Then please tell me what Alexander Cross or Valerie's breakdown or my own marriage has to do with your task?"

"I am making an assumption, Mrs. Van Slyke. I am assuming that this was not a random killing, that the person who shot your daughter was not a stranger. That means I have to know about her life. All of it. I don't ask these questions to amuse myself. I need to know who would have feared Valerie or hated her or had a lot to gain by her death. That means digging into all the unpleasantries of her life."

She held his gaze a beat too long and then looked away. "Just what do you know about my daughter, Mr. Bolitar?"

"The basics," Myron said. "Valerie became tennis's next wunderkind at the French Open when she was only sixteen. Expectations ran wild, but her play quickly leveled off. Then it grew worse. She was stalked by an obsessive fan named Roger Quincy. She had a relationship with the son of a prominent politician, who was later murdered. Then she had a mental collapse. Now I need to fill in—and illuminate—more pieces of this puzzle."

"It's very difficult to talk about all this."

"I understand that," Myron said gently. He opted now for the Alan Alda smile over the Phil Donahue. More teeth, moister eyes.

"There's nothing more I can tell you, Mr. Bolitar. I don't know why anyone would want to kill her."

"Perhaps you can tell me about the last few months," Myron said. "How was Valerie feeling? Did anything unusual happen?"

Helen fiddled with her strand of pearls, twisting them around her fingers until they made a red mark around her neck. "She finally started getting better," she said, her voice more of a choke now. "I think tennis helped. For years she wouldn't touch a racket. Then she started playing. A little at first. Just for fun."

The facade collapsed then. Helen Van Slyke lost it. The tears came hard. Myron took her hand. Her grip was both strong and shaky.

"I'm sorry," Myron said.

She shook her head, forcing the words out. "Valerie started playing every day. It made her stronger. Physically, emotionally. She finally seemed to be putting it all behind her. And then . . ." She stopped again, her eyes suddenly flat. "That bastard."

She might have been talking about the unknown killer. But somehow the anger seemed more specific.

"Who?" Myron tried.

"Helen?"

Kenneth was back. He quickly crossed the room and took his wife in his arms. Myron thought he saw her back away at his touch, but he couldn't be sure.

Kenneth looked over her shoulder at Myron. "See what you've done," he hissed. "Get out."

"Mrs. Van Slyke?"

She nodded. "Please leave, Mr. Bolitar. It's for the best."

"Are you sure?"

Kenneth bellowed again. "Get out! Now! Before I throw you out!"

Myron looked at him. Not the time or the place. "I'm sorry for the intrusion, Mrs. Van Slyke. My most sincere condolences."

Myron showed himself out.

9

When Myron entered the small police station Jake's chin was coated with something red and sticky. Might have been from a jelly doughnut. Might have been from a small farm animal. Hard to tell with Jake.

Jake Courter had been elected sheriff of Reston, New Jersey two years before. In view of the fact that Jake was black in an almost entirely white community, most people considered the election result an upset. But not Jake. Reston was a college town. College towns were filled with liberal intellectuals who wanted to lift a black man up. Jake figured his skin color had been enough of a disadvantage over the years, might as well turn the tide. White guilt, he told Myron. The best vote-getter this side of Willie Horton ads.

Jake was in his early fifties. He'd been a cop in a half-dozen major cities over the years—New York, Philadelphia, Boston, to name a few. Tired of chasing city scum, he'd moved out to the happy suburbs to chase suburban scum. Myron and Jake met a year ago, investigating the disappearance of Kathy Culver, Jessica's sister, a student at Reston University.

"Hey, Myron."

"Jake."

Jake looked, as always, rumpled. Everything about him. His hair. His clothes. Even his desk looked rumpled, like a cotton shirt kept in the bottom of a laundry hamper. The desk also had an assortment of goodies. A Pizza Hut box. A Wendy's bag. A Carvel ice-cream cup. A half-eaten sandwich from Blimpie. And, of course, a tin of Slim-Fast diet powder. Jake was closing in on two hundred and seventy-five pounds. His pants never fit right. They were too small for his stomach, too large for his waist. He was constantly adjusting them, searching for that one elusive point where they'd actually stay in place. The search required a team of top scientists and a really powerful microscope.

"Let's go grab a couple burgers," Jake said, wiping his face with a moist towelette. "I'm starving."

Myron picked up the Slim-Fast can and smiled sweetly. "'A delicious shake for breakfast. Another for lunch. And then a sensible dinner.'"

"Bullshit. I gave it a try. The shit doesn't work."

"How long were you on it?"

"Almost a day. Zip, nothing. Not a pound gone."

"You should sue."

"Plus the stuff tastes like used gunpowder."

"You get the file on Alexander Cross?"

"Yeah, right here. Let's go."

Myron followed Jake down the street. They stopped at a place very generously dubbed the Royal Court Diner. A pit. If it were totally renovated, it might reach the sanitary status of an interstate public toilet.

Jake smiled. "Nice, huh?"

"My arteries are hardening from the smell," Myron said.

"For chrissake, man, don't inhale."

The table had one of those diner jukeboxes. The records hadn't been changed in a long time. The current number one single, according to the little advertisement, was Elton John's *Crocodile Rock*.

The waitress was standard diner issue. She was grumpy, mid-fifties, her hair a purplish tint not found anywhere in the state of nature.

"Hey, Millie," Jake said.

She tossed them menus, not speaking, barely breaking stride.

"That's Millie," Jake said.

"She seems great," Myron said. "Can I see the file?"

"Let's order first."

Myron picked up the menu. Vinyl. And sticky. Very sticky. Like someone had poured maple syrup on it. There were also bits of coagulated scrambled eggs in the crease. Myron was losing his appetite in a hurry.

Three seconds later Millie returned, sighed. "What'll it be?"

"Give me a cheeseburger deluxe," Jake said. "Double order of fries instead of the coleslaw. And a diet Coke."

Millie looked toward Myron. Impatiently.

Myron smiled at her. "Do you have a vegetarian menu?"

"A what?"

"Stop being an asshole," Jake said.

"A grilled cheese will be fine," Myron said.

"Fries with that?"

"No."

"To drink?"

"A Diet Coke. Like my low-cal buddy."

Millie eyed Myron, looked him up and down. "You're kinda cute."

Myron gave her the modest smile. The one that said, *Aw, shucks.*

"You also look familiar."

"I have that kind of face," Myron said. "Cute yet familiar."

"You date one of my daughters once? Gloria maybe. She works the night shift."

"I don't think so."

She looked him over again. "You married?"

"I'm involved with someone."

"Not what I asked you," she said. "You married?"

"No."

"All right then." She turned and left.

"What was that all about?"

Jake shrugged. "Hope she's not getting Gloria."

"Why?"

"She kinda looks like a white version of me," Jake said. "Only with a heavier beard."

"Sounds enticing."

"You still with Jessica Culver?"

"Guess so."

Jake shook his head. "Man, she's something else. I've never seen nothing that looked that good in real life."

Myron tried not to grin. "Hard to argue."

"She also got you wrapped around her finger."

"Hard to argue."

"Lots of worse places for a man to be wrapped around."

"Hard to argue."

Millie came back with the two Diet Cokes. This time she

almost managed to smile at Myron. "Good-looking man like you shouldn't be single," she said.

"I'm wanted in several states," Myron said.

Millie did not seem discouraged. She shrugged, left. Myron turned back to Jake.

"All right," Myron said. "Where's the file?"

Jake flipped it open. He handed Myron a picture of a handsome, healthy man. Tan, fit, wearing tennis shorts. Myron had seen the picture in the paper after the murder.

"Meet Alexander Cross," Jake began. "Age twenty-four at the time of the murder. Wharton graduate. Son of United States senator Bradley Cross of Pennsylvania. On the night of July twenty-four, six years ago, he was attending a party at a tennis club called Old Oaks in Wayne, Pennsylvania. The esteemed senator was there. It's a pretty ritzy place—fancy food, indoor and outdoor courts, hard court, clay, lit, unlit, the works. Even grass courts."

"Okay."

"What happened next is a bit fuzzy, but here's what we have. Alexander Cross and three buddies were taking a walk around the grounds."

"At night? During a party?"

"Not unheard of."

"Not common either."

Jake shrugged. "Anyway, they heard a noise coming from the western end of the club. They went to check it out. They ran into two suspicious-looking youths."

"Suspicious-looking?"

"The youths were—what are they calling us today?—African American."

"Ah," Myron said. "Is it safe to assume that Old Oaks did not have a lot of African American members?"

"Like none. It's exclusive."

"So you and I could never be members."

"Real shame," Jake said. "I bet we'd have loved that party."

"So what happened next?"

"According to the witnesses, the white youths approached the black youths. One of the black youths—later identified as one Errol Swade—reacted by whipping out a switchblade."

Myron made a face. "A switchblade?"

"Yeah, I know. Such a cliché. No imagination. Anyway, an incident ensued. Alexander Cross was stabbed. The two youths ran. A few hours later the police caught up with them in north Philadelphia, not far from where the youths lived. During the apprehension, one of the punks pulled out a gun. A Curtis Yeller. Sixteen years old. A police officer shot him. Yeller's mother was at the scene, from what I understand. She was cradling the kid in her arms when he died."

"She saw him being shot?"

Jake shrugged. "Doesn't say."

"So what happened to Errol Swade?"

"He escaped. A nationwide manhunt began. His mug shot was in all the papers, sent to all the stations. Lot of cops on it, of course—the victim being the son of a U.S. senator and all. But here's where things get interesting."

Myron sipped the Diet Coke. Flat.

"They never found Errol Swade," Jake said.

Myron felt his heart sink. "Never?"

Jake shook his head.

"Are you telling me Swade escaped?"

"Appears so."

"How old was he?"

"Nineteen at the time of the incident."

Myron mulled that over a moment. "That would make him twenty-five now."

"Whoa. A math major."

Myron did not smile. Millie brought the food. She made another comment, but Myron did not hear it. Twenty-five years old. Myron couldn't help but wonder. It was a dumb thought. Unforgivable. And maybe even racist. But there it was. Twenty-five years old. Duane claimed to be twenty-one, but who knew for sure?

But no. It can't be.

Myron took another sip of the flat soda. "What do you know about Errol Swade?" he asked.

"A pedigree punk. He had already been in jail three times. First offense was stealing a car. He was twelve. Assorted felonies followed. Muggings, assaults, car thefts, armed robberies, drugs. Also a member of an ultraviolent street gang. Guess what the gang was called."

Myron shrugged. "Josie and the Pussycats?"

"Close. The Stains. Short for Bloodstains. They always wear a shirt dipped in a victim's blood. Kinda like a Boy Scout badge."

"Charming."

"Errol Swade and Curtis Yeller were also cousins. Swade had been living with the Yellers since his release a month earlier. Let's see what else. Swade was a dropout. Big surprise. A coke addict. Another shocker. And a major-league moron."

"So how has he eluded the police for so long?"

Jake picked up his burger and took a bite. A big bite. Half the burger vanished. "He couldn't have," he said.

"Excuse me?"

"No way he could have stayed out of trouble this long. Impossible."

"Hold up. Did I miss something here?"

"Officially the police are still looking," Jake said. "But unofficially they're sure he's dead. The kid was a dumb punk. He couldn't find his ass with both hands, never mind hide from a nationwide dragnet."

"So what happened?"

"Rumor has it the senator got a favor from the mob. They knocked him off."

"Senator Cross put out a hit on him?"

"What, that surprises you? The guy's a politician. That's like a step below child molester."

"Weren't you *elected* sheriff?"

Jake nodded. "There you go."

Myron risked a bite of his sandwich. Tasted a bit like a sink sponge. "Do you have a physical description of Errol Swade?" he asked, almost hoping the answer was no.

"I got better. I got Swade's mug shot." Jake dusted his hands off, rubbed them on his shirt for good measure. Then he reached into the folder and withdrew a photograph. He handed it to Myron. Myron tried not to appear too eager.

It wasn't Duane.

Not even close. Not even with plastic surgery. For one, Errol Swade was much lighter skinned. Swade's head was shaped like a block, completely different from Duane's. His eyes were spaced too far apart. Everything was different. His height was listed as six-four, three inches taller than Duane. Can't fake being shorter.

Myron almost sighed with relief. "Does the name Valerie Simpson pop up in that file?" he asked.

Jake's eyes caught a little fire. "Who?"

"You heard me."

"Golly, Myron, that wouldn't be the same Valerie Simpson who was murdered yesterday?"

"By coincidence it is. Is her name in there?"

He handed Myron half the file. "Hell if I know. Help me look."

They went through it. Valerie's name was only on one sheet. A party guest list. Her name along with a hundred others. Myron jotted down the names and addresses of the witnesses to the murder—three friends of Alexander Cross's. Nothing else of much interest in the file.

"So," Jake said, "what does the lovely and dead Valerie Simpson have to do with this?"

"I don't know."

"Jesus Christ." Jake shook his head. "You still yanking my chain?"

"I'm not yanking anything."

"What have you got so far?"

"Less than nothing."

"That's what you said about Kathy Culver."

"But this isn't your case, Jake."

"Maybe I can help."

"I really don't have anything. Valerie Simpson visited my office a few days ago. She wanted to make a comeback, but somebody killed her instead. I want to know who, that's all."

"You're full of shit."

Myron shrugged.

"The TV said something about a stalker doing the job," Jake said.

"Might be him. Probably is."

Silence.

"You're holding back again," Jake said. "Just like with Kathy Culver."

"It's confidential."

"You're not going to tell me?"

"Nope. It's confidential."

"Protecting someone again?"

"Confidential," Myron said. "As in not to be divulged. Communicated in the strictest of confidence. A secret."

"Fine, be that way," Jake said. "So how's your sandwich?"

Myron nodded. "Maybe the ambience isn't so good, but at least the food stinks."

Jake laughed. "Hey, you got tickets to the Open?"

"Yeah."

"How about getting me two?"

"For when?"

"The last Saturday."

The men's semis and women's finals. "Tough day," Myron said.

"But not for a big-time agent like yourself."

"Then we'll be even?"

"Yeah."

"I'll leave them at the on-call window."

"Make sure they're good seats."

"Who you taking?"

"My son Gerard."

Myron had played ball against Gerard in college. Gerard

was a bull. No finesse about his game. "He still working homicide in New York?"

"Yep."

"Can he do me a little favor?"

"Shit. Like what?"

"The cop on Valerie's murder is a devout asshole."

"And you want to know what they have."

"Yeah."

"All right. I'll ask Gerard to give you a call."

10

"**M**ESSAGES?**"

Esperanza nodded. "About a million of them."

Myron fingered through the pile. "Any word on Eddie Crane?"

"You're having dinner with him and his folks."

He looked up. "When?"

"Tonight. Seven-thirty. At La Reserve. I already made a reservation. Make sure you use Win's name."

Win's name carried weight at many of New York's finest restaurants. "You realize, of course, that you're a genius."

She nodded. "Yeah."

"I want you to come too."

"Can't. School." Esperanza went to law school at night.

"Is Eddie still being coached by Pavel Menansi?" Myron asked.

"Yeah, why?"

"He and I had a discussion last night at the Open."

"What about?"

"He used to coach Valerie."

"And you two 'discussed' that?"

Myron nodded.

"May I assume you wowed him with your usual charm?"

"Something like that."

"So we don't have a chance with Eddie," she said.

"Not necessarily. If Eddie was really close to Pavel, then Tru-Pro would have him signed by now. Maybe there's some friction there."

"Almost forgot." Esperanza picked up a small stack of papers. "This just came in by fax. They want it signed right away."

A contract for a baseball prospect named Sandy Repo. A pitcher. The Houston Astros had taken him in the first round. Myron scanned it over. The contract had been orally finalized yesterday morning, but Myron spotted the new paragraph right away. Sandwiched it in on the second-to-last page.

"Cute," he said.

"Who?"

"The Astros. Get me Bob Wasson on the line." The Astros' general manager.

Esperanza picked up the phone. "You're supposed to meet with Burger City tomorrow afternoon."

"Same time as Duane's match?"

She nodded.

"You mind handling it?" he asked.

"They're not going to like dealing with a receptionist," she said.

"You're an associate," Myron corrected. "A valued associate."

"Still not the main man. Still not Myron Bolitar."

"Ah, but who is?"

She rolled her eyes, picked up the phone, began dialing. She purposely did not look at him. "You really think I'm ready?"

The tone was hard to read. Myron couldn't tell if it signaled sarcasm or insecurity. Probably both.

"They're going to want Duane for their new promo," he said. "But Duane wants to wait for a national deal. Try to push someone else on them."

"Okay."

Myron went into his office. Home. Tara. He had a nice view of the Manhattan skyline. Not a corner office view like Win's, but not shabby either. On one wall he had movie stills. Everything from Bogie and Bacall to Woody and Diane. Another wall featured Broadway posters. Musicals mostly. Everything from Rodgers and Hammerstein to Andrew Lloyd Webber. The final wall was his client wall. Action photos of each player. He studied the picture of Duane, his body arched in a serving motion.

"What's going on, Duane?" Myron said out loud. "What are you hiding?"

The photo did not answer. Photos rarely did.

His phone buzzed. Esperanza came on the speaker. "I have Bob Wasson on the line."

"Okay."

"I can put him on hold. Until you're finished talking to your wall."

"No, I think I'll take it now." Wiseass. He hit the speakerphone. "Bob?"

"Goddamn it, Bolitar, take me off the speaker. You're not that goddamn important."

Myron picked up the receiver. "That better?"

"Yeah, great. What do you want?"

"I got the contract today."

"Well, yippee for you. Now, here's what you do next. Step

one: Sign it where the X is. You know how to do that, don't you? I had your name typed under the X in case you're unsure of the spelling. And use a pen, Myron. Blue or black ink, please. No crayons. Step two: Put the contract in the enclosed self-addressed envelope. Moisten the flap. With me so far?"

Good ol' Bob. Funny as a case of head lice. "There's a problem," Myron said.

"A what?"

"A problem."

"Look, Bolitar, if you're trying to squeeze me for more dough, you can fuck yourself from behind."

"Point thirty-seven. Paragraph C."

"What about it?"

Myron read it out loud. "'The player agrees that he will not engage in sports endangering his health or safety including, but not limited to, professional boxing or wrestling, motorcycling, moped riding, auto racing, skydiving, hang gliding, hunting, et cetera, et cetera.'"

"Yeah, so? It's a prohibited activities clause. We got it from the NBA."

"The NBA's contract says nothing about hunting."

"What?"

"Please, Bob, let's try to pretend I don't have a learning disability. You threw in the word *hunting*. Sneaked it in, if you will."

"So what's the big deal? Your boy hunts. He hurt himself in a hunting incident two years ago and missed half his junior year. We want to make sure that doesn't happen again."

"Then you have to compensate him for it," Myron said.

"What? Don't bust my balls, Bolitar. You want us to pay the kid if he gets hurt, right?"

"Right."

"So we don't want him hunting. Suppose he shoots himself. Or suppose some other asshole mistakes him for a deer and shoots him. You know what that's going to cost us?"

"Your concern," Myron said, "is touching."

"Oh excuse me. A thousand pardons. I guess I should care more and pay less."

"Good point. Strike my last statement."

"So stricken. Can I go now?"

"My client enjoys hunting. It means a great deal to him."

"And his left arm means a lot to us."

"So I suggest a fair compromise."

"What?"

"A bonus. If Sandy doesn't hunt, you agree to pay him twenty thousand dollars at the end of the year."

Laughter. "You're out of your mind."

"Then take that clause out. It's not standard and we don't want it."

Pause. "Five grand. Not a penny more."

"Fifteen."

"Up yours, Myron. Eight."

"Fifteen," Myron said.

"I think you're forgetting how this is played," Bob said. "I say a number a little higher. You say a number a little lower. Then we meet somewhere in the middle."

"Fifteen, Bob. Take it or leave it."

Win opened the door and came in. He sat down silently, crossed his right ankle over his left thigh, and studied his manicured nails.

"Ten," Bob said.

"Fifteen."

The negotiation continued. Win stood, checked his reflection in the mirror behind the door. He was still fixing his hair five minutes later when Myron hung up. Not a blond lock was out of place, but that never seemed to deter Win.

"What was the final number?" Win asked.

"Thirteen five."

Win nodded. He smiled at his reflection. "You know what I was just thinking?"

"What?"

"It must suck to be ugly."

"Uh-huh. Think you can tear yourself away for a second?"

Win sighed. "It won't be easy."

"Try to be brave."

"I guess I can always look again later."

"Right. It'll give you something to look forward to."

With one last hair pat, Win turned away and sat down. "So what's up?"

"The powder-blue Caddy is still following me."

Win looked pleased. "And you want me to find out who they are?"

"Something like that," Myron said.

"Excellent."

"But I don't want you to move in on them without me there."

"You don't trust my judgment?"

"Just don't, okay?"

Win shrugged. "So how was your visit to the Van Slykes' estate?"

"I met Kenneth. The two of us really hit it off."

"I can imagine."

"You know him?" Myron asked.

"Oh yes."

"Is he as big an asshole as I think?"

Win spread his hands wide. "Of biblical proportions."

"You know anything else about him?"

"Nothing significant."

"Can you check him out?"

"But of course. What else did you find out?"

Myron told him about his visits to both the Van Slykes and Jake.

"Curiouser and curiouser," Win said when he finished.

"Yes."

"So what's the next step?" Win asked.

"I want to attack this from several directions."

"Those being?"

"Valerie's psychiatrist, for one."

"Who will throw all kinds of terms like 'doctor-patient confidentiality' at you," Win said with a dismissive wave. "A waste of time. Who else?"

"Curtis Yeller's mother witnessed her son's shooting. She's also Errol Swade's aunt. Maybe she has some thoughts on all this."

"For example?"

"Maybe she knows what happened to Errol."

"And you—what?—expect her to tell you?"

"You never know."

Win made a face. "So basically your plan is to flail about helplessly."

"Pretty much. I will also need to talk to Senator Cross. Do you think you can arrange it?"

"I can try," Win said. "But you're not going to learn anything from him either."

"Boy, you're a bundle of optimism today."

"Just telling it like it is."

"Did you learn anything at the Plaza?"

"As a matter of fact, I did." Win leaned back and steepled his fingers. "Valerie made only four calls in the past three days. All were to your office."

"One to make an appointment to see me," Myron said. "The other three on the day she died."

Win gave a quick whistle. "Very impressive. First you figure out Kenneth is an asshole and now this."

"Yeah, sometimes I even scare myself. Is there anything else?"

"A doorman at the Plaza remembered Valerie rather well," Win continued. "After I tipped him twenty dollars, he recalled that Valerie took a lot of quick walks. He found it curious, since guests normally leave for hours at a time, rather than scant minutes."

Myron felt a surge. "She was using a pay phone."

Win nodded. "I called Lisa at NYNEX. By the way, you now owe her two tickets to the Open."

Great. "What did she find out?"

"On the day before Valerie's murder, two calls were placed from a nearby pay phone at Fifth and Fifty-ninth to the residence of one Mr. Duane Richwood."

Myron felt a sinking feeling. "Shit."

"Indeed."

"So not only did Valerie call Duane," Myron said, "but she went out of her way to make sure no one would know."

"So it appears."

Silence.

Win said, "You'll have to talk to him."

"I know."

"Let it wait until after the tournament," Win added. "Between the Open and the big Nike campaign, there's no reason to distract him now. It will keep."

Myron shook his head. "I'll talk to Duane tomorrow. After his match."

11

FRANÇOIS, THE MAÎTRE D' AT LA RESERVE, flitted about their table like a vulture awaiting death—or worse, a New York maître d' awaiting a very large tip. Since discovering that Myron was a close friend of Windsor Horne Lockwood III's, François had befriended Myron in the same way a dog befriends a man with raw meat in his pocket.

He recommended the thinly sliced salmon appetizer and the chef's special scrod as an entree. Myron took him up on both suggestions. So did the so-far silent Mrs. Crane. Mr. Crane ordered the onion soup and liver. Myron was not going to be kissing him anytime soon. Eddie ordered the escargot and lobster tails. The kid was learning fast.

François said, "May I recommend a wine, Mr. Bolitar?"

"You may."

Eighty-five bucks down the drain.

Mr. Crane took a sip. Nodded his approval. He had not smiled yet, had barely exchanged a pleasantry. Luckily for Myron, Eddie was a nice kid. Smart. Polite. A pleasure to talk to. But whenever Mr. Crane cleared his throat—as he did now—Eddie fell silent.

"I remember your basketball days at Duke, Mr. Bolitar," Crane began.

"Please call me Myron."

"Fine." Instead of reciprocating the informality, Crane knitted his eyebrows. The eyebrows were his most prominent feature—unusually thick and angry and constantly undulating above his eyes. They looked like small ferrets furrowing into his forehead. "You were captain of the team at Duke?" he began.

"For three years," Myron said.

"And you won two NCAA championships?"

"My team did, yes."

"I saw you play on several occasions. You were quite good."

"Thank you."

He leaned forward. The eyebrows grew somehow bushier. "If I recall," Crane continued, "the Celtics drafted you in the first round."

Myron nodded.

"How long did you play for them? Not long, as I recall."

"I hurt my knee during a preseason game my rookie year."

"You never played again?" It was Eddie. His eyes were young and wide.

"Never," Myron said steadily. Better lesson than any lecture he could give. Like the funeral of a high school classmate who died because he was D.U.I.

"Then what did you do with yourself?" Mr. Crane asked. "After the injury?"

The interview. Part of the process. It was harder when you were an ex-jock. People naturally assumed you were dumb.

"I went through rehab for a long while," Myron said. "I thought I could beat the odds, defy the doctors, come back. When I was able to face reality, I went to law school."

"Where?"

"At Harvard."

"Very impressive."

Myron tried to look humble. He almost batted his eyes.

"Did you make Law Review?"

"No."

"Do you have an MBA?"

"No."

"What did you do upon graduation?"

"I became an agent."

Mr. Crane frowned. "How long did it take you to graduate?"

"Five years."

"Why so long?"

"I was working at the same time."

"Doing what?"

"I worked for the government." Nice and vague. He hoped Crane didn't push it.

"I see." Crane frowned again. Every part of him frowned. His mouth, his forehead, even his ears frowned. "Why did you enter the field of sports representation?"

"Because I thought I'd like it. And I thought I'd be good at it."

"Your agency is small."

"True."

"You don't have the connections of some larger agencies."

"True."

"You certainly don't wield the power of ICM or TruPro or Advantage."

"True."

"You don't have too many successful tennis players."

"True."

Crane gave a disapproving scowl. "Then tell me, Mr. Bolitar, why should we choose you?"

"I'm a lot of fun at parties."

Mr. Crane did not break a smile. Eddie did. He caught himself, smothered the smile behind his hand.

"Is that supposed to be funny?" Crane said.

"Let me ask you a question, Mr. Crane. You live in Florida, right?"

"St. Petersburg."

"How did you get up to New York?"

"We flew."

"No. I mean, who paid for the tickets?"

The Cranes shared a wary glance.

"TruPro bought your tickets, right?"

Mr. Crane nodded tentatively.

"They had a limo meet you at the airport?" Myron continued.

Another nod.

"Your jacket, ma'am. It's new?"

"Yes." First time Mrs. Crane had spoken.

"Did one of the big agencies buy it for you?"

"Yes."

"The big agencies, they have wives or female associates who take you around town, show you the sights, do a little shopping, that sort of thing?"

"Yes."

"What's your point?" Crane interrupted.

"That kind of thing is not my bag," Myron said.

"What kind of thing?"

"Ass-kissing. I'm not very good at ass-kissing a client. And I'm terrible at ass-kissing the parents. Eddie?"

"Yes?"

"Did the big agencies promise to have someone at every match?"

He nodded.

"I won't do that," Myron said. "If you need me I'm available twenty-four hours a day, seven days a week. But I'm not physically there twenty-four hours a day, seven days a week. If you want your hand held at every match because Agassi's or Chang's is, go with one of the big agencies. They're better at it than I am. If you need someone to run errands or do your laundry, I'm not the guy either."

The Cranes shared another family glance. "Well," Mr. Crane said. "I heard you speak your mind, Mr. Bolitar. It appears you are living up to your reputation."

"You asked for a contrast between me and the others."

"So I did."

Myron focused his attention on Eddie. "My agency is small and simple. I will do all your negotiations—tournament guarantees, appearances, exhibitions, endorsements, whatever. But I won't sign anything you don't want to. Nothing is final until you look it over, understand it, and approve it yourself. Okay so far?"

Eddie nodded.

"As your father pointed out I am not an MBA. But I work with one. His name is Win Lockwood. He's considered one of the best financial consultants in the country. Win's theory is similar to mine: he wants you to understand and approve every investment he makes. I will insist that you meet with him at least five times a year, preferably more, so that you can set up solid, long-term financial and tax plans. I want you to know what your money is doing at all times. Too many athletes get taken advantage of—bad investments, trusting the wrong people, that sort of thing. That won't happen here because *you*—not just me, not just Win, not just your parents, but *you*—won't let it."

François came by with the appetizers. He smiled brightly while the underlings served. Then he pointed and ordered them about in impatient French, like they couldn't possibly know how to put a plate down in front of a human being without his fretting.

"Is that everything?" François asked.

"I think so."

François sort of lowered his head. "If there is any way I can make your dining experience more pleasurable, Mr. Bolitar, please do not hesitate to ask."

Myron looked down at his salmon. "How about some ketchup?"

François's face lost color. "Pardon?"

"It's a joke, François."

"And a funny one at that, Mr. Bolitar."

François slithered away. Myron the Card strikes again.

"How about the young lady who set up this dinner?" Mr. Crane asked. "Miss Diaz. What's her function at your agency?"

"Esperanza is my associate. My right hand."

"What's her work background?"

"She's currently goes to law school nights. That's why she couldn't join us tonight. She was also a professional wrestler."

That piqued Eddie's interest. "Really? Which one?"

"Little Pocahontas."

"The Indian Princess? She and Big Chief Mama used to be the tag team champs."

"Right."

"Man, she is hot!"

"Yup."

Mrs. Crane nibbled at her salmon. Mr. Crane ignored his onion soup for the moment. "So tell me," Mr. Crane said, "what strategy would you employ for Eddie's career?"

"Depends," Myron said. "There's no set formula. You have two conflicting factors pulling at your son. On the one hand Eddie is only seventeen. He's a kid. Tennis shouldn't consume him to the point where he hates it. He should still have fun, try to do the things seventeen-year-olds do. On the other hand it's naive to think that tennis will still be just a game to him. Or that he'll be a 'normal' kid. This is about money. Big money. If Eddie does it right, if he makes some sacrifices now and works with Win, he can be financially set for life. It's a delicate balance—how many tournaments and exhibitions to play in, how many appearances, how many endorsements."

Crane's eyebrows nodded. They seemed to agree.

Myron turned his attention to Eddie. "You want to score a lot of money early, because you never know what can happen. I'm proof of that. But I don't want you sucked dry. Sometimes the hardest thing in the world is to say no to staggering amounts of money. But in the end it's your decision, not mine. It's your money. If you want to play in every tournament and every exhibition match, it's not my place to stop you. But you can't do it, Eddie. No one can. You're a good kid. You have your head on straight. You were raised right. But if you try to bend too far, you'll break. I've seen it happen too often.

"I want you to make a lot of money. But not every cent out there. I don't want to turn you into a money machine. I want you to have some fun. I want you to enjoy all of this. I want you to realize how lucky you are."

The Cranes listened in rapt silence.

"That's my theory, Eddie, for what it's worth. You may make more money with the big agencies. I can't deny that. But in the long run, with a long and healthy career, with careful planning, I think you'll be wealthier and better off with MB SportsReps."

Myron looked at Mr. Crane. "Anything else you care to know?"

Crane sipped his wine, studied its color, put the glass down. He did the eyebrow mambo again. "You came highly recommended to us, Mr. Bolitar. Or should I say to Eddie."

"Oh?" Myron said. "By whom?"

Eddie looked away. Mrs. Crane put her hand on his arm. Mr. Crane provided the answer. "Valerie Simpson."

Myron was surprised. "Valerie recommended me?"

"She thought you'd be good for Eddie."

"She said that?"

"Yes."

Myron turned to Eddie. He wasn't crying, but he looked on the verge. "What else did she say, Eddie?"

Shrug. "She thought you were honest. That you'd treat me right."

"How did you know Valerie?"

"They met at Pavel's camp in Florida," Crane answered. "She was sixteen when Eddie arrived. He was only nine. I think she looked after him a little."

"They were quite close," Mrs. Crane added. "Such a tragedy."

"Did she say anything else, Eddie?"

Another shrug. Eddie finally looked up. Myron met his gaze, held it steady.

"It's important," Myron said.

"She told me not to work with TruPro," he said.

"Why?"

"She didn't say."

"My theory," Crane added, "is that she blamed them for her downfall."

"What do you think, Eddie?" Myron asked.

Yet another shrug. "Could be. I don't know."

"But you don't think so."

Nothing.

Mrs. Crane said, "I think that's enough for now. Valerie's murder has been very hard on Eddie."

The conversation slowly drifted back to business. But Eddie was silent now. Every once in a while he would open his mouth, then close it again. When they rose to leave, Eddie leaned toward Myron and whispered, "Why do you want to know so much about Valerie?"

Myron opted for the truth. "I'm trying to find out who killed her."

That widened his eyes. He looked behind him. His parents were busy saying good-bye to François. François kissed Mrs. Crane's hand.

"I think you might be able to help," Myron said.

"Me?" Eddie said. "I don't know anything."

"She was your friend. You were close to her."

"Eddie?"

Mr. Crane's voice.

"I have to go, Mr. Bolitar. Thank you for everything."

"Yes, thank you," Crane added. "We have a few more agencies to see, but we'll be in touch."

After they left, François came by with the bill. "Your tie is very becoming, Mr. Bolitar."

The man knew how to kiss ass. "You should have been an agent, François."

"Thank you, sir."

Myron gave him a Visa card and waited. He turned his cell phone back on. A message from Win. Myron called him back.

"Where are you?" Myron asked.

"On Twenty-sixth Street, near Eighth," Win said. "There were two gentlemen—and I use that term in its absolute loosest sense—in the Cadillac. They followed you to La Reserve, sat outside for a while, and left about half an hour ago. They've just entered a drinking establishment of rather questionable repute."

"Questionable repute?"

"It's called the Beaver Hunt. Enough said?"

"Stay on them. I'm on my way down."

12

WIN WAS WAITING ACROSS THE STREET FROM the Beaver Hunt. The block was quiet, the only sound was the faint beat of music coming from inside the bar. A large neon sign said TOPLESS!

"Two of them," Win said. "The driver was a white man, approximately six-three. Overweight but powerfully built. I think you'll like his fashion sense."

"Meaning?"

"You'll see. He is with a black man. Six foot. Big scar on his right cheek. I guess you might describe him as thin and wiry."

Myron looked down the street. "Where did they park?"

"A lot on Eighth Avenue."

"Why not on the street? Plenty of spots."

"I believe our man is quite attached to his charming chariot." Win smiled. "If anything happened to it, I bet he'd be very upset."

"How difficult will it be to break in?"

Win looked insulted. "I'll pretend you didn't ask that."

"Fine, you check the car. I'll go inside."

Win snapped a salute. "Roger, Wilco."

They split up. Win headed for the lot, Myron for the bar. Myron would have preferred it the other way around, especially since the two men obviously knew what Myron looked like, but they needed to play their strengths. Win was far better at breaking into cars or handling anything mechanical. Myron was better at, well, this.

He entered the bar with his head lowered, just in case. No need. No one paid him any attention. There was no cover charge here. Myron looked around. Two words came to mind: major dive. The decor's theme was Early American Beer. The walls were ornamented with neon beer signs. The bar and table were crusted with beer rings. Behind the bar were pyramids of beer bottles from all over the land.

Of course, there were topless dancers. They lazily pranced atop small stages that looked like old stage props from *Wonderama*. Most of the dancers were not attractive. Far from it. The exercise craze had not yet hit the Beaver Hunt. Flesh jiggled. The place looked more like a cellulite test center than a male-fantasy cantina.

Myron moved to a corner table and sat by himself. There were a few suits, but for the most part the clientele was blue-collar. The well-to-do usually got their topless kicks at Goldfingers or Score, where the women were far more aesthetically pleasing, though their body parts were about as real as their inflatable brethren's.

Two men were laughing it up by center stage. One black, one white. They fit Win's description. When the dancers rotated stages, the one in front of them stepped off. Her downtime. The boys began to negotiate with her. In places like Goldfingers and Score, you paid about twenty or twenty-five dollars for a table dance. It was basically just what it sounded like. The girl took off her top and danced at your table for maybe five minutes. No touchy, no feely. At the Beaver Hunt, the order of the day was a recent craze known as the Lap Dance, which took place in discreet corners of the bar. The Lap Dance, known to young adolescents as the Dry Hump, consisted of a dancer gyrating on a man's crotch until he, well, orgasmed. Moral repugnancy aside, Myron had several questions about the technical aspects of such an act. Like after the act, how does a guy go around the rest of the night? Does he bring a change of underwear with him?

So many questions. So little time.

The two men and the dancer headed toward Myron's corner. Myron could now see clearly what Win had been talking about. The white guy did indeed have big arms, but he also had a protruding gut and flabby chest. Some of these flaws could be hidden with proper fashion sense, but the white guy was wearing a tight fishnet shirt. Fishnet. As in a lot of holes. As in practically no shirt at all. His chest hairs—and there were lots of them—were jutting through the holes. The hairs seemed unusually long, coiling around—and indeed getting enmeshed in—the many gold chains that were draped about his neck. As he walked by, Myron got a full view of his back, thank you very much, which was even hairier and somewhat oilier than the front.

Myron felt a little ill.

"Fifteen dollars for the first ten minutes," the girl said. "I can't do better than that."

"Don't jerk us around, whore," Fishnet said. "There's two of us here. Two for one."

"Yeah," the black guy chimed in. "Two for one."

"I can't do that," the girl said. If she seemed insulted by the name calling, it didn't show. Her voice was tired and matter-of-fact, like a diner waitress on the night shift.

Fishnet was not pleased by this. "Listen, bitch, don't get me angry."

"I'll get the manager," she said.

"The fuck you will. You ain't leaving here till I get my rocks off, slut."

"Yeah," the black guy added. "Me too. Slut."

"Look, I charge more for talking dirty," the girl said.

Fishnet looked at her in disbelief. "What did you say?"

"There's a surcharge for talking dirty."

"A surcharge?" Fishnet shouted. He was enraged now. "This might come as a surprise to a stupid whore, but we live in the U.S. of A. Land of the free, home of the brave. I can say whatever I want, slut—or haven't you ever heard of freedom of speech?"

A constitutional scholar, Myron thought. Nice to see a man defending the First Amendment.

"Look," the dancer said, "the price is twelve dollars for five minutes, twenty dollars for ten minutes. Plus tip. That's it."

"How about this," Fishnet said. "You dance on both of us at the same time."

"Huh?"

"Like you're dancing on me but stroking him. How's that sound, pig?"

"Yeah," the black guy said. "Pig."

"Look, fellas, there's no two-for-one deals," the dancer said. "Just let me get another girl. We'll take good care of you."

Myron stepped into view. "Will I do?"

No one moved.

"Gee," Myron said, "they're both so attractive. I just can't choose."

Fishnet looked at the black guy. The black guy looked at Fishnet.

Myron turned to the girl. "Do you have a preference?"

She shook her head no.

"Then I'll take him." Myron pointed to Fishnet. "He likes me. I can tell by the erect nipples."

The black guy said, "Hey, what's he doing here?"

Fishnet shot him a look.

"I mean, who is this guy?"

Myron nodded. "Nice recovery. Very smooth."

"What do you want, mister?" Fishnet asked.

"Actually, I was lying."

"What?"

"About how I knew you liked me. It wasn't just the erect nipples, though they were a noticeable—albeit nauseating—tip-off."

"What the fuck are you talking about?"

"Your following me around the past two days, that's what gave it away. Next time try the secret admirer route. Send flowers without signing for them. A nice Hallmark card. That kind of thing."

"Come on, Jim," Fishnet said to the black guy, "this guy's nuts. Let's get out of here."

The girl said, "No lap dance?"

"No. We gotta go."

"Someone's got to pay for this," the girl said. "Otherwise the manager's going to fry my ass."

"Get lost, whore. Or I'll whack you."

"Whoa, big man," Myron said.

"Look, mister, I don't got no beef with you. Just get out of my way."

"No lap dance for me either?"

"You're crazy."

"I can offer you a special discount," Myron said.

Fishnet's hands tightened into fists. He'd been ordered to follow Myron, not to be found out or get involved in a physical altercation. "Come on, Jim."

"Why have you been following me?" Myron asked.

"I don't know what you're talking about."

"Is it my hypnotic blue eyes? The strong features? The shapely derriere? By the way what do you think of these pants? They're not too tight, are they?"

"Fruitcake." They moved past him.

"Tell you what," Myron said. "You tell me who you're working for and I promise not to tell your boss."

They kept walking.

"Promise," Myron said.

They headed out the door. Another day, another friend. Myron had that knack.

Myron followed them out to the street. Fishnet and Jim hurried west.

Win appeared from the shadows across the street. "This way," he said.

They cut through an alley and arrived at the lot before Fishnet and Jim. It was an outdoor lot. The parking attendant was in a little booth watching a *Roseanne* rerun on a minuscule black-and-white TV. Win pointed out the Cadillac. They ducked behind an Oldsmobile parked two cars away and waited.

Fishnet and Jim approached the booth. They were still looking down the street. Jim was panicking. "How did he find us, Lee? Huh?"

"I don't know."

"What we gonna do?"

"Nothing. We'll change cars. Try again."

"You got another car, Lee?"

"No," Fishnet said. "We'll rent one."

They paid, got a receipt and their keys. Fishnet had insisted on parking the car himself.

"This," Win said, "should be fun."

When they arrived at the Cadillac, Fishnet put his key in the lock. He stopped, looked down, and began screaming.

"Shit! Goddamn fuck!"

Myron and Win stepped out of the shadows.

"Language, language," Myron said.

Fishnet stared down at his car in disbelief. Win had drilled a hole under the lock to break in. He didn't use that particular method when neatness counted, but this was an occasion when he thought it necessary. On top of that, Win's hand had "accidentally" slipped, scratching both driver's-side doors.

"You!" Fishnet shouted. He pointed at Myron, his face red and apoplectic. "You!"

Win turned to Myron. "Quite the vocabulary."

"Yeah, but it's the threads that really make me swoon."

"You!" Fishnet said. "You did this to my car?"

"Not him," Win said. "Me. And may I say you keep the inside lovely. I felt terrible about spilling that maple syrup all over the velour seats."

Fishnet's eyes popped. He looked inside, placed his hand on the inside, and screamed. The scream was deafening. It was so loud, the parking lot attendant almost stirred.

Myron looked at Win. "Maple syrup?"

"Log Cabin."

"I've always been an Aunt Jemima man myself," Myron said.

"To each his own."

"You find anything inside the car?"

"Not very much," Win said. "In the glove compartment were several parking stubs." He handed them to Myron. Myron took a quick glance.

"So," Myron called out, "who are you guys working for?"

Fishnet started walking over. "My car!" he shouted, his face red. "You . . . my car! My car!"

Win sighed. "Can we get past this, please? *Très* dull."

"You motherfucker! You . . ." Fishnet's hands were fists again. He stepped closer, smiling now at Win. It was an ugly smile in every way. "I'm going to break your fucking face, pretty boy."

Win looked at Myron. "Pretty boy?"

Myron shrugged.

Jim stood next to Fishnet. Neither one was armed with a gun, Myron could tell. They might have a blade hidden somewhere, but he wasn't worried.

Fishnet moved to within a yard of Win. Nothing unusual there. The bad guys always honed in on Win. He was smaller than Myron by nearly six inches and thirty-five pounds. Best of all, Win looked like a wimpy rich boy who raised his finger only to call for the butler—everything the discerning bully could want in a punching bag.

Fishnet took one more step and cocked his fist. Whoever had hired these guys had not briefed them well.

The punch whizzed toward Win's nose. He sidestepped it. Sometimes Myron thought Win moved like a cat. But that wasn't accurate. It was more ghostlike. One nanosecond he was there, the next he was two feet to the left. Fishnet tried again. Win blocked it this time. He grabbed Fishnet's fist with one hand and connected with a knife-hand strike to Fishnet's neck. Fishnet backed off, woozy. Jim stepped forward.

"Don't even think about it," Myron said.

Jim ran.

Myron Bolitar. The Intimidator.

Fishnet regained his footing. He charged Win, head lowered, attempting a tackle. Big mistake. Win hated it when an opponent tried to use superior size against him. Win had introduced Myron to tae kwon do during their freshman year at Duke, but he'd been studying it himself since he was five years old. He'd even spent three years in the Far East studying under some of the world's greatest masters.

"Aaaarrrrghhh!" Fishnet shouted.

Again Win stepped to the side, like the smoothest matador against the clumsiest bull. Win connected on a roundhouse kick to the solar plexus and followed up with a palm strike to the nose. There was a sharp crack and blood flowed. Fishnet screamed and went down. He did not get up again.

Win bent down. "Who are you working for?"

Fishnet looked at the blood in his hand. "You broke my nose!" His voice was nasally.

"Wrong answer," Win said. "Let me repeat the question. Who are you working for?"

"I ain't saying nothing!"

Win reached down, gripped the broken nose with two fingers. Fishnet's eyes bulged.

"Don't," Myron said.

Win looked up at him. "If you can't take it, leave." He turned his attention back to Fishnet. "Last chance. Then I start twisting. Who hired you?"

Fishnet said nothing. Win gave the nose a quick squeeze. The small bones grated against one another, making a sound like rain on a skylight. Fishnet bucked in agony. Win stifled his scream with his free hand.

"Enough," Myron said.

"He hasn't said anything yet."

"We're the good guys, remember?"

Win made a face. "You sound like an ACLU lawyer."

"He doesn't have to say anything."

"What?"

"He's a two-bit scum. He'd sell out his mother for a nickel."

"Meaning?"

"Meaning he's more terrified of opening his mouth than the pain."

Win smiled. "I can change him."

Myron held up one of the parking lot stubs. "This lot is at Fifty-fourth and Madison. It's under TruPro's building. Our pal here is working for the Ache brothers. They're the only ones who could put that kind of scare into a guy." Fishnet's face was pure white.

"Or Aaron," Win said.

Aaron.

"What about him?" Myron asked.

"The Aches could be using Aaron. He could put that kind of scare into a guy."

Aaron.

"He isn't working for Frank Ache anymore," Myron said. "At least, that's what I heard."

Win looked down at Fishnet. "The name Aaron mean anything to you?"

"No," he shouted. Quickly. Too quickly.

Myron lowered his head toward Fishnet. "Start talking or I'll tell Frank Ache you told us all about it."

"I didn't say nothing about no Frank Ache!"

"Triple negative," Win said. "Very impressive."

There were two Ache brothers. Herman and Frank. Herman, the elder, was the boss, a sociopath responsible for countless murders and misery. But next to his whacked-out brother Frank, Herman Ache was Mary Poppins. Unfortunately, Frank ran TruPro.

"I didn't say nothing," Fishnet repeated. He was petting his nose like it was an abused dog. "Not a goddamn word."

"But how's Frank to know?" Myron asked. "You see, I'll tell Frank you sang like the tastiest of stool pigeons. And you know what? He'll believe me. How else would I know Frank hired you?"

Fishnet's face went from pale-white to a sort of seaweed-green.

"But if you cooperate," Myron said, "we'll all pretend this never happened. That I never spotted your tail. You'll be safe. Frank will never have to know about your little screwup."

Fishnet didn't have to think too long. "What do you want?"

"One of Ache's men hired you?"

"Yeah."

"Aaron?"

"No. Just some guy."

"What were you hired to do?"

"Follow you. Report wherever you went."

"For what reason?"

"I don't know."

"When did you get hired?"

"Yesterday afternoon."

"What time?"

"I don't remember. Two, three o'clock. I was told you were at the tennis match and to get over there right away."

That would have been almost immediately after Valerie's murder.

"That's all I know. I swear to God. That's it."

"Bull," Win said. But Myron waved him off. Fishnet knew nothing more of any real significance.

"Let him go," Myron said.

13

MYRON WOKE UP EARLY. HE GRABBED SOME cold cereal from the pantry. Something called Nutri-Grain. Yummy name. He read on the back of the box about the importance of fiber. Snore.

Myron longed for his childhood cereals: Cap'n Crunch, Froot Loops, Quisp. Quisp cereal. Who could forget Quisp, the cute alien who competed on TV commercials with some coal-miner loser named Quake? Quisp vs. Quake. Extraterrestrial vs. Mr. Blue-collar. Interesting concept. What happened to those two rivals? Has even lovable Quisp gone the way of the Motels?

Myron sighed. He was far too young for such bouts of nostalgia.

Esperanza had managed to track down an address for Curtis Yeller's mother. Deanna Yeller lived alone in a recently purchased house in Cherry Hill, New Jersey, a suburb outside Philadelphia. Myron made his way to his car. If he started out now, there would be time to drive to Cherry Hill, meet with Deanna Yeller, and get back to New York in time for Duane's match.

But would Deanna Yeller be home? Best to make sure.

Myron picked up the car phone and dialed. A woman's voice—probably Deanna Yeller—answered. "Hello?"

"Is Orson there?" Myron asked.

Warning: Clever deductive technique coming up. Those desiring professional pointers should pay strict attention.

"Who?" the woman asked.

"Orson."

"You have the wrong number."

"I'm sorry." Myron hung up.

Deduction: Deanna Yeller was home.

He pulled up to a modest but modern home on a classic New Jersey suburban street. Every house was more or less the same. Different colors maybe. The kitchen might be on the right instead of the left. But genetically they were clones. Nice. A sprinkling of kids on the street. A sprinkling of multicolored bicycles. Couple of squirrels. A far cry from west Philadelphia. It made him wonder.

Myron walked up the little brick walk and knocked on the door. A very attractive black woman answered, a pleasant smile at the ready. Her hair was tied back in a severe bun, emphasizing the high cheekbones. Age lines around the eyes and mouth, but nothing drastic. She was well dressed, kind of conservative. Anne Klein II. Her jewelry was noticeable but not too flashy. The overall impression: classy.

Her smile seemed to fade when she saw him. "Can I help you?"

"Mrs. Yeller?"

She nodded slowly, as though not sure.

"My name is Myron Bolitar. I'd like to ask you a few questions."

The smile fled completely. "What about?" Her diction was different now. Less suburban civil. More street suspicious.

"Your son."

"I ain't got a son."

"Curtis," Myron said.

Her eyes narrowed. "You a cop?"

"No."

"I ain't got the time. I'm on my way out."

"It won't take long."

She put her hands on her hips. "What's in it for me?"

"Pardon me?"

"Curtis is dead."

"I realize that."

"So what good is talking about it gonna do? He still gonna be dead, right?"

"Please, Mrs. Yeller, if I could just come in for a moment."

She thought about it a second or two, glanced around, then shrugged in tired surrender. She checked her watch. Piaget, Myron noticed. Could be a fake, but he doubted it.

The decor was basic. Lot of white. Lot of pinewood. Torchère lamps. Very Ikea. There were no photographs on the shelves or coffee table. Nothing personal at all. Deanna Yeller didn't sit. She didn't invite Myron to either.

Myron offered up his warmest, most trustworthy smile. One part Harry Smith, two parts John Tesh.

She crossed her arms. "What the hell you grinning at?"

Yep, another minute and she'd be curled up in his lap.

"I want to ask you about the night Curtis died," Myron said.

"Why? What's this got to do with you?"

"I'm investigating."

"Investigating what?"

"What really happened the night your son died."

"You a private eye?"

"No. Not really."

Silence.

"You got two minutes," she said. "That's it."

"According to the police your son drew a gun on a police officer."

"So they say."

"Did he?"

She shrugged. "Guess so."

"Did Curtis own a gun?"

Another shrug. "Guess he did."

"Did you see it that night?"

"I don't know."

"Did you ever see it before that night?"

"Maybe. I don't know."

Boy, was this helpful. "Why would your son and Errol break into the Old Oaks Club?"

She made a face. "You serious?"

"Yes."

"Why you think? To rob the place."

"Did Curtis do that a lot?"

"Do what?"

"Rob places."

Another shrug. "Places, people, whatever." Her tone was matter-of-fact. No shame, no embarrassment, no surprise, no revulsion.

"Curtis didn't have a record," Myron said.

Yet another shrug. Her shoulders would tire soon. "Guess I

raised a smart boy," she said. "Until that night, anyhow." She made a show of looking at her watch again. "I gotta go now."

"Mrs. Yeller, have you heard from your nephew Errol Swade?"

"No."

"Do you know where he went after your son was shot?"

"No."

"What do you think happened to Errol?"

"He's dead." Again matter-of-fact. "I don't know what you want here, but this thing is finished. Finished a long time ago. No one cares anymore."

"How about you, Mrs. Yeller? Do you care?"

"It's done. Closed."

"You were there when the police shot your son?"

"No. I got there right after." Her voice sort of faded away.

"And you saw your son on the ground?"

She nodded.

Myron handed her his business card. "If you remember any-thing else . . ."

She didn't take it. "I won't."

"But if you do . . ."

"Curtis is dead. Nothing you can do can change that. Best to just forget it."

"It's that easy?"

"Been six years. Not like anybody misses Curtis."

"How about you, Mrs. Yeller? Do you miss him?"

She opened her mouth, closed it, opened it again. "Not like Curtis was a good kid or nothing. He was trouble."

"Doesn't mean he should have been killed," Myron said.

She looked up at him, held his gaze. "Don't matter. Dead is dead. Can't change that."

Myron said nothing.

"Can you change that, Mr. Bolitar?" she asked, challenging.

"No."

Deanna Yeller nodded, turned away, picked up her purse. "I have to go now," she said. "Best if you leave now too."

14

H ENRY HOBMAN WAS THE ONLY ONE IN THE players' box.

"Hi, Henry," Myron said.

No one was playing yet, but Henry was still in his coach repose. Without turning away from the court, Henry muttered, "Heard you had a meeting with Pavel Menansi last night."

"So?"

"You unhappy with Duane's coaching?"

"No."

Henry almost nodded. End of conversation.

Duane and his opponent, a French Open finalist named Jacques Potiline, came onto the court. Duane looked himself. No signs of strain. He gave Myron and Henry a big smile, nodded. The weather was perfect for tennis. The sun was out, but a cool breeze gently purled through Stadium Court, staving off the humidity.

Myron glanced around courtside. There was a rather buxom blonde in the next box. She was packed into a white tank top. The word for today, boys and girls, is cleavage. Plenty of men ogled. Not Myron, of course. He was far too worldly. The blonde suddenly turned and caught Myron's eye. She smiled coyly, gave him a little wave. Myron waved back. He wasn't going to do anything about it, but yowzer!

Win materialized in the chair next to Myron. "She's smiling at me, you know."

"Dream on."

"Women find me irresistible," Win said. "They see me, they want me. It's a curse I live with every day of my life."

"Please," Myron said. "I just ate."

"Envy. It's so unattractive."

"So go for it, stud."

Win looked over at her. "Not my type."

"Gorgeous blondes aren't your type?"

"Her chest is too big. I have a new theory on that."

"What theory?"

"The bigger the breasts, the lousier the lay."

"Pardon me?"

"Think about it," Win said. "Well-endowed women—I am referring here to ones with mega-fronts—have a habit of laying back and relying on their, er, assets. The effort isn't always what it should be. What do you think?"

Myron shook his head. "I have several reactions," he replied, "but I think I'll stick with my initial one."

"Which is?"

"You're a pig."

Win smiled, sat back. "So how was your visit with Ms. Yeller?"

"She's hiding something too."

"Well, well. The plot doth thicken."

Myron nodded.

"In my experience," Win said, "there is only one thing that can silence the mother of a dead boy."

"And that is?"

"Cash. A great deal of it."

Mr. Warmth. But in truth the same thought had crossed Myron's mind. "Deanna Yeller lives in Cherry Hill now. In a house."

Win leapt on that one. "A single widow from the dumps of west Philadelphia moving to the 'burbs? Pray tell, how does she afford it?"

"Do you really think she's being bought?"

"Is there another explanation? According to what we know, the woman has no solid means of support. She spent her life in an impoverished area. Now all of a sudden she's Miss Better Homes and Gardens."

"Could be something else."

"For example?"

"A guy."

Win made a scoffing noise. "A forty-two-year-old ghetto woman does not find that kind of sugar daddy. It just doesn't happen."

Myron said nothing.

"Now," Win continued, "add into that equation Kenneth and Helen Van Slyke, the grieving parents of another dead child."

"What about them?"

"I've done a bit of checking. They too have no visible signs of support. Kenneth's family was already destitute when they married. As for Helen, whatever money she had Kenneth lost in his business ventures."

"You mean they're broke?"

"Completely," Win replied. "So pray tell, dear friend, how are they managing to carry on at Brentman Hall?"

Myron shook his head. "There has to be another explanation."

"Why?"

"One mother being bought off by her child's killer I *might* be able to buy. But two?"

Win said, "You have a rather rosy view of human nature."

"And you have a rather dim one."

"Which is why I'm usually correct in these matters," Win said.

Myron frowned. "What about TruPro's connection with this?"

"What about it?"

"Fishnet was hired to follow me immediately after the murder. Why?"

"The Ache brothers know you quite well by now. Perhaps they feared you'd investigate."

"So? What's their interest?"

Win thought a second. "Didn't TruPro used to represent Valerie?"

"But that was six years ago," Myron said. "Before the Ache brothers had even taken over the agency."

"Hmm. Perhaps you are barking up the wrong tree."

"What do you mean?" Myron asked.

"Perhaps there is no connection. TruPro is interested in signing Eddie Crane, correct?"

Myron nodded.

"And Eddie's mentor—this Pavel fellow—is closely associated with TruPro. Perhaps they feel you are moving in on their turf."

"Which the Ache brothers would not like," Myron added.

"Precisely."

A possibility. Myron tried it on and walked around a bit, but it just didn't feel right.

"Oh, one other thing," Win replied.

"What?"

"Aaron is in town."

Myron felt a quick chill. "What for?"

"I don't know."

"Probably just a coincidence," Myron said.

"Probably."

Silence.

Win sat back and steepled his fingers. The match began. Duane's play was nothing short of spectacular. He cruised through the first set 6–2. He stumbled a bit in the second, but came on to win it 7–5. Jacques Potiline had had enough. Duane whipped him in the final set 6–1.

Another impressive victory.

As the players left the court, Henry Hobman stood. His face remained locked on grim. He chewed at the inside of his mouth. "Better," he said tightly. "But not great."

"Stop gushing, Henry. It's embarrassing."

Ned Tunwell sprinted down the steps toward Myron. His arms were flapping like a kid making windmills in the snow. Several other Nike execs followed him. There were tears in Ned's eyes.

"I knew it!" Ned shouted in glee. He shook Myron's hand, hugged him, turned to Win, pumped his hand too. Win pulled his hand back and wiped it on his pants. "I just knew it!"

Myron simply nodded.

"Soon! So soon!" Ned cried. "The promo of the year begins!

Everyone is going to know the name Duane Richwood! He was fantastic, utterly fantastic! I can't believe it. I swear, I don't think I've ever been this excited before!"

"You're not going to come again, are you, Ned?"

"Oh, Myron!" He nudged Win playfully with his elbow. "Is he a kidder or what?"

"A gifted comedian," Win agreed.

Ned slapped Win's shoulder. Win visibly winced but did not break the offending hand. Amazing restraint for Win.

"Look, guys," Ned said, "I'd love to stand here and chat all day. But I gotta run."

Win managed to hide his disappointment.

"Ciao for now. Myron, we'll talk, okay?"

Myron nodded.

"Bye, guys." Ned skipped—actually skipped—back up the stairs.

Win watched him depart with something approaching horror. "What," he asked, "was that?"

"A bad dream. I'll meet you back at the office."

"Where are you going?" Win asked.

"To talk to Duane. I have to ask him about Valerie's call."

"Let it go until after the tournament."

Myron shook his head. "Can't."

15

MYRON WAITED FOR THE PRESS CONFERENCE to end. It took some time. Duane was holding court, firmly in his element. The media had a new darling. Duane Richwood. Cocky but not obnoxious. Confident yet gracious. Handsome. American.

When the hordes of press finally ran out of questions, Myron accompanied Duane back to the dressing room. He sat on a chair next to Duane's locker. Duane took off his sunglasses and put them on the top shelf.

"Some match, huh?" Duane said.

Myron nodded.

"Hey, this win oughta make Nike happy."

"Orgasmic," Myron agreed.

"They going to air the ad during my next match, right?"

"Yep."

Duane shook his head. "Quarterfinal, at the U.S. Open," he said in awe. "I can't believe it, Myron. We're on our way."

"Duane?"

"Yeah?"

"I know Valerie called you," Myron said.

Duane stopped. "What?"

"She called your apartment twice. From a pay phone near her hotel."

"I don't know what you're talking about."

Duane quickly reached for the sunglasses, fumbled them, put them on.

"I want to help you, Duane."

"Nothing to help me with."

"Duane . . ."

"Just leave me the fuck alone."

"I can't do that."

"Look, Myron, I don't need distractions right now. Just drop it."

"She's dead, Duane. That just won't go away."

Duane took off his shirt and began toweling off his chest. "Some stalker killed her," he said. "I saw it on the news. Got nothing to do with me."

"Why did she call you, Duane?"

His hands were clenching and unclenching. "You work for me, right?"

"Right."

"Then drop it or you're fired."

Myron looked at him. "No," he said.

Duane sunk into a chair, his head in his hands. "Shit, I'm sorry, Myron. I didn't mean that. It's just the pressure. What with this tournament and that Dimonte cop accusing me and all. Look, just forget I said anything, okay? Just forget this whole conversation happened."

"No."

"What?"

"Why did she call you, Duane?"

"Man, don't you listen?"

"Not well."

"Just stay out of it."

"No."

"It's got nothing to do with the murder."

"Then you admit she called you?"

Duane stood, turned his back toward Myron, leaned against his locker.

"Duane?"

His words were soft. "Yeah, she called me. So what?"

"Why?"

"Let's just say we were acquainted. Intimately, if you get my drift."

"You and Valerie . . . ?" Myron made futile hand gestures.

Duane nodded slowly. "It was no big thing. Just a few times."

"When did this start?"

"Couple of months ago."

"Where did you meet?"

He looked at Myron, confused. "At a tournament."

"Which one?"

"I don't remember. New Haven, I think. But it was over quick."

"So why did you lie to the police?"

"Why do you think?" he countered. "Wanda was standing right there. I love her, man. I made a mistake. I didn't want to hurt her. Is that so wrong?"

"So why wouldn't you tell me?"

"What?"

"When I asked you just now. Why didn't you tell me the truth?"

"Same reason."

"But Wanda isn't here."

"I was ashamed, okay?"

"Ashamed?"

"I'm not proud of what I did."

Myron watched him. With those sunglasses Duane's face looked sleek and robotic. But something wasn't right here. It was a nice sentiment, but twenty-one-year-old professional athletes, no matter how faithful to their partners, were not this ashamed of letting their agents know about an indiscretion. The excuse might be commendable, but it rang hollow. "If it was over, why was Valerie calling you?"

"I don't know. She wanted to see me again. One last fling, I guess."

"Did you agree to see her?"

"No. I told her we were finished."

"What else did you say?"

"Nothing."

"What else did she say?"

"Nothing."

"Are you sure? Do you remember anything at all?"

"No. Nothing."

"Did she seem distressed?"

"Not that I could tell."

The door opened. Players began to file in, many offering Duane icy congratulations. Rising stars were not big in the locker room. If someone new was joining the ultra-exclusive tennis club known as the "Top Ten," another member had to be thrown out. The way it was. No boardroom was this cutthroat. Everyone was a rival here. Everyone was competing for the same dollars and fame. Everyone was an enemy.

Duane suddenly looked very much alone.

"You hungry?" Myron asked.

"Starved," Duane said.

"You want anything in particular?"

"Pizza," Duane said. "Extra cheese and pepperoni."

"Get dressed. I'll meet you out front."

16

"**M**YRON BOLITAR?"

The car phone. He'd just dropped Duane off at his apartment.

"Yes."

"This is Gerard Courter with the NYPD. Jake's son."

"Oh, right. How's it going, Gerard?"

"Can't complain. I doubt you remember but we played against each other once."

"Michigan State," Myron said. "I remember. And I have the bruises to prove it."

Gerard laughed. Sounded just like his old man. "Glad I was memorable."

"That's a polite word for what you were."

Another Jake-like guffaw. "My dad said you needed info on the Simpson homicide."

"I'd appreciate it."

"You probably heard there's a major suspect. Guy named Roger Quincy."

"The stalker."

"Yeah."

"Is there anything specific tying him to the murder?" Myron asked. "Besides the stalking?"

"He's on the run, for one thing. When they got to Quincy's apartment he was packed and gone. No one knows where he is."

"He might have just been scared," Myron said.

"Good reason to be."

"Why do you say that?"

"Roger Quincy was at the tennis center on the day of the murder."

"You have witnesses?"

"Several."

That slowed Myron down. "What else?"

"She was shot with a thirty-eight. Very close range. We found the weapon in a garbage can ten yards away from the shooting. Smith and Wesson. It was in a Feron's bag. The bag had a bullet hole in it."

Feron's. Another tournament sponsor. They were licensed to sell "official tournament merchandise." Feron's had at least half a dozen stands selling to a zillion people. No way to trace it back. "So the killer walked up to her," Myron said, "shot her through the bag, kept walking, dumped the gun in the garbage, and headed out."

"That's how we see it," Gerard said.

"A cool customer."

"Very."

"Any prints on the gun?" Myron asked.

"Nope."

"Any witnesses to the shooting?"

"Several hundred. Unfortunately all anyone remembers is the sound of the gun, and Valerie toppling over."

Myron shook his head. "The killer took a hell of a chance. Shooting her in public like that."

"Yeah. A major case of brass balls."

"You got anything else?"

"Just a question," Gerard said.

"Shoot."

"Where are our seats for next Saturday?"

17

ESPERANZA HAD NEATLY STACKED TWO PILES OF six-year-old press clippings on Myron's desk. The pile on the right—the taller pile—was made up of articles on the murder of Alexander Cross. The smaller stack was on the hospitalization of Valerie Simpson.

Myron ignored the third stack—the one with his messages—and started sifting through the pile on Valerie. The story was already familiar to him. Valerie's family had claimed she was "taking time off," but a well-placed source leaked the truth to the press: the teen tennis star was actually a patient at the famed Dilworth Mental Health Facility. The family denied it for a few days—until a photograph of Valerie taking a walk on the Dilworth grounds appeared in the papers. A belated statement from the family claimed that Valerie was "resting from exhaustion caused by external pressures," whatever that meant.

The media coverage was only mildly intense. Valerie was already a has-been in the tennis world, ergo the press was interested but not ravenous. Still, rumors surfaced, especially in some of the fringe periodicals. One said that Valerie's breakdown had been the result of a sexual assault. Another said she'd been attacked by a stalker. Still another claimed Valerie had murdered someone in cold blood, though the article didn't bother the reader with mundane details—like the victim's name, how he or she was killed, why the police hadn't arrested Valerie, the little things.

But the most interesting rumor, the one that really snared Myron's attention, appeared in two separate papers. According to several "unnamed sources," Valerie Simpson had gone into hiding to cover up a pregnancy.

Might be something, might be nothing. Pregnancy rumors always surface when a young woman goes into hiding. Still . . .

He moved on to articles on Alexander Cross's murder. Esperanza had limited her search to Philadelphia area periodicals, but the material was still immense. The stories basically followed the police version. Alexander Cross had been at a party at his snooty tennis club. He stumbled across two burglars, Errol Swade and Curtis Yeller. He gave chase, confronted them on the main grass court, and was stabbed by Errol Swade. The blade punctured Alexander's heart. Death was instantaneous.

Senator Cross and his family had not commented on the case. According to the senator's spokesman, the family was "in seclusion" and was "relying on law enforcement agencies and the justice system," whatever that meant.

The press focused on the manhunt for Errol Swade. The police were confident to the point of cocky that Swade would be captured within a matter of hours. But hours turned to days. Editorials harshly criticized the police for not being able to nab one nineteen-year-old drug addict, but the Cross family remained silent. The story provoked the standard public outrage—why, editorials demanded to know, had a lowlife like Errol Swade been let out on parole in the first place?

But the anger fizzled, as it always does in such cases. Other stories began to take precedence. The coverage trickled from front page to back page to oblivion.

Myron checked through the pile again. The police shooting of Curtis Yeller had been neatly glossed over. There was no mention of an internal affairs investigation into the incident. None of the usual reactionaries protested the police "brutality," which was strange. Usually some whacko managed to get himself on television, no matter what the facts, especially in the case of a black teen being gunned down by a white cop. But not this time. Or at least it wasn't covered by the press.

Wait. Hold the phone.

An article on Curtis Yeller. Myron had missed it the first time because it'd been printed the day immediately following the murder. Very early for this kind of piece. Probably sneaked in before Senator Cross put his foot down—but that might just be conspiracy paranoia on Myron's part. Hard to tell.

It was a small article on the bottom corner of page 12 in the metro section. Myron read it twice. Then a third time. The article was not on the shooting in west Philly or even the police's role in said shooting. The article was on Curtis Yeller himself.

It started out like any puff piece: Curtis Yeller was described as an "honor roll student." Not a big deal really. A psychotic child molester with the IQ of a citrus beverage was suddenly dubbed an honor student when killed prematurely. Very *Bonfire of the Vanities*. But this story went a bit further. Mrs. Lucinda Elright, Curtis Yeller's history teacher, described Curtis as her "best pupil" and a boy who "had never even gotten a detention." Mr. Bernard Johnson, his English teacher, said Curtis was "unusually bright and inquisitive," "one in a million," and "like a son to me."

The usual death hyperbole?

Perhaps. But school records backed the teachers up. Curtis had never been on report. He also had the best attendance record in his grade. On top of that, his transcript reported a 3.9 average, his sole B coming in some sort of health class. Both teachers firmly believed that Curtis Yeller was incapable of violence. Mrs. Elright blamed Curtis's cousin Errol Swade, but no specifics were given.

Myron sat back. He stared at a movie still from *Casablanca* on the far wall. Sam was serenading Bogie and Bergman as the Nazis moved in. Here's looking at you, kid. We'll always have Paris. You're getting on that plane. Myron wondered if young Curtis Yeller had ever seen the movie, if he had had the opportunity to behold the celluloid image of Ingrid Bergman with tears in her eyes at a foggy airport.

He picked up the basketball from behind his desk and began spinning it on his finger. He slapped it at just the right angle to increase the speed rotation without dislodging the ball from its axis. He stared at his handiwork as though it were a Gypsy's crystal ball. He saw an alternate universe, one with a younger version of himself hitting a three-pointer at the buzzer on the Boston Garden's parquet floor. He tried not to let himself dwell on this image too long, but there it stayed, front and center, refusing to leave.

Esperanza came in. She sat down and waited in silence.

The ball stopped spinning. Myron put it down and handed her the article. "Take a look at this."

She read it. "A couple of teachers said something nice about a dead kid. So what? Probably misquoted anyway."

"But this is more than just a couple of casual comments. Curtis Yeller had no police record, no school record, a nearly perfect attendance record, and a 3.9 GPA. For most kids that's a hell of a statement. But this was a kid from one of the worst parts of Philadelphia."

Esperanza shrugged. "I don't see the relevance. What difference does it make if Yeller was Einstein or an idiot?"

"None. Except it's just one more thing that doesn't add up. Why did Curtis's mother say he was a no-good thief?"

"Maybe she knew more than his teachers."

Myron shook his head. He thought about Deanna Yeller. The proud, beautiful woman who answered the door. The suddenly hostile, defensive woman at the mention of her dead son. "She was lying."

"Why?"

"I don't know. Win thinks she's being bought off."

"Sounds like a good possibility," Esperanza said.

"What, a mother taking bribes to protect her son's murderer?"

Esperanza shrugged again. "Sure, why not?"

"You really think a mother . . . ?" Myron stopped. Esperanza's face was totally impassive—another one who always believed the worst. "Just look at this whole scenario for a second," he tried. "Curtis Yeller and Errol Swade break into this ritzy tennis club at night. Why? To rob the place? Of what? It was night. It wasn't like they were going to find wallets in the locker room. So what were they going to steal? Some tennis sneakers? A couple of rackets? That's a hell of a long way to go for some tennis equipment."

"Stereo equipment, maybe," Esperanza said. "The clubhouse could have a big-screen TV."

"Fine. Assume you're right. Problem is, the boys didn't take a car. They took public transportation and walked. How were they going to carry the loot? By hand?"

"Maybe they planned on stealing one."

"From the club's valet lot?"

She shrugged. "Could be," she said. Then: "Mind if I change subjects for a second?"

"Go ahead."

"How did it go with Eddie Crane last night?"

"He's a big fan of Little Pocahontas. He said she was 'hot.'"

"Hot?"

"Yup."

She shrugged. "Kid's got taste."

"Nice too. I liked him. He's smart, got his head on straight. Helluva good kid."

"You going to adopt him?"

"Uh, no."

"How about represent him?"

"They said they'll be in touch."

"What do you think?"

"Hard to say. The kid liked me. The parents are worried about me being small-time." Pause. "How did it go with Burger City?"

She handed him some papers. "Prelim contract for Phil Sorenson."

"TV commercial?"

"Yeah, but he has to dress up as a burger condiment."

"Which one?"

"Ketchup, I think. We're still talking."

"Fine. Just don't let it be mayonnaise or pickle." He studied the contract. "Nice work. Good figures."

Esperanza looked at him.

"Very good, in fact." He smiled at her. Widely.

"Is this the part where I get all excited by your praise?" she asked.

"Forget I said anything."

She pointed to the stack of articles. "I managed to track down Valerie's shrink from her days at Dilworth. Her name is Julie Abramson. She has a private office on Seventy-third Street. She won't see you, of course. Refuses to discuss her patient."

"A woman doctor," Myron mused. He put his hands behind his head. "Maybe I can entice her with my rapier wit and brawny body."

"Probably," Esperanza said, "but on the off chance she's not comatose, I went with an alternative plan."

"And that is?"

"I called her office back, changed my voice, and pretended you were a patient. I made an appointment for you to see her tomorrow morning. Nine o'clock."

"What's my psychosis?"

"Chronic priapism," she said. "But that's just my opinion."

"Funny."

"Actually, you've been much better since what's-her-name left town."

What's-her-name was Jessica, which Esperanza knew very well. Esperanza did not care much for the love of Myron's life. A casual observer might offer up jealousy as the culprit, but that'd be way off base. True, Esperanza was extraordinarily beautiful. Sure, there'd been moments of temptation between them, but one or the other had always been prudent enough to douse the flames before any real damage was done. There was also the fact that Esperanza liked a bit of diversity when it came to beaus—diversity that went well beyond tall or short, fat or thin, white or black. Right now, for example, Esperanza was dating a photographer. The photographer's name was Lucy. Lucy. As in a female, for those having trouble catching the drift.

No, the reason for her strong dislike was far simpler: Esperanza had been there when Jessica left the first time. She had seen it all firsthand. And Esperanza held grudges.

Myron returned to his original question. "So what did you tell them was wrong with me?"

"I was vague," she said. "You hear voices. You suffer from paranoid schizophrenia, delusions, hallucinations, something like that."

"How did you get an appointment so fast?"

"You're a very famous movie star."

"My name?"

"I didn't dare give one," Esperanza said. "You're that big."

18

D R. JULIE ABRAMSON'S OFFICE WAS ON THE corner of Seventy-third Street and Central Park West. Ritzy address. One block north, overlooking the park, was the San Remo building. Dustin Hoffman and Diane Keaton lived there. Madonna had tried to move in, but the board decided she was not San Remo material. Win lived a block south, in the Dakota, where John Lennon had lived and literally died. Whenever you entered the Dakota's courtyard you crossed over the spot where Lennon had been gunned down. Myron had walked it a hundred times since the shooting, but he still felt the need to be silent when he did.

There was an ornate, wrought-iron gate on Dr. Abramson's door. Protective or decorative? Myron couldn't decide, but he saw some irony in a psychiatric office being guarded by a "wrought" iron gate.

Okay, not much irony but a little.

Myron pressed a doorbell. He heard the buzzer and let himself in. He was wearing his best pair of sunglasses for the occasion, even though it was cloudy outside. Mr. Movie Star.

The receptionist, a neatly attired man wearing fashionable

spectacles, folded his hands and said, "Good morning," in a supposedly soothing voice that grated like a tortured cat's screech.

"I'm here to see Dr. Abramson. I have a nine o'clock appointment."

"I see." He perked up now, studying Myron's face, trying to guess who the big movie star was. Myron adjusted his sunglasses but kept them on. The receptionist wanted to ask for a name, but discretion got the better of him. Afraid of insulting the big-time celebrity.

"Could you fill out this form while you're waiting?"

Myron tried to look annoyed by the inconvenience.

"It's just a formality," the receptionist said. "I'm sure you understand how these things are."

Myron sighed. "Very well then."

After it was filled out the receptionist asked for it back.

"I'd rather give it directly to Dr. Abramson," Myron said.

"Sir, I assure you—"

"Perhaps I didn't make myself clear." Mr. Difficult. Just like a real movie star. "I will give it to Dr. Abramson personally."

The receptionist sulked in silence. Several minutes later the intercom buzzed. The receptionist picked up the phone, listened for a second, hung up. "Right this way please."

Dr. Abramson was tiny—four-ten, tops, and seventy pounds soaking wet. Everything about her looked shrunken, scrunched up. Except for her eyes. They peered out of the diminutive face like two big, radiant, warm beacons that missed nothing.

She placed her child-size hand in his. Her handshake was surprisingly firm. "Please have a seat," she said.

Myron did. Dr. Abramson sat across from him. Her feet barely reached the ground. "May I have your sheet?" she asked.

"Of course." Myron handed it to her. She glanced down for a brief second.

"You're Bruce Willis?"

Myron gave her a cocky side smirk. Very *Die Hard*. "Didn't recognize me with the sunglasses, huh?"

"You look nothing like Bruce Willis."

"I would have put Harrison Ford, but he's too old."

"Still would have been a better choice." Then studying him a bit more she added, "Liam Neeson would have been better still." Dr. Abramson did not seem particularly upset by Myron's stunt. Then again, she was a trained psychiatrist and thus used to dealing with abnormal minds. "Why don't you tell me your real name."

"Myron Bolitar."

The little face broke open in a smile nearly as radiant as the eyes. "I thought I recognized you. You're the basketball star."

"I wouldn't say 'star' exactly." Blush, blush.

"Please, Mr. Bolitar, don't be so modest. First team all-American three years in a row. Two NCAA championships. One College Player of the Year. Eighth pick overall in the draft."

"You're a fan?"

"And so observant." She leaned back. Like a small child in a big rocking chair. "As I recall, you made the cover of *Sports Illustrated* twice. Unusual for a college player. You were also a good student, an academic all-American, popular with the press, and considered quite handsome. Am I correct?"

"Yes," Myron said. "Except maybe for that 'considered' part."

She laughed. It was a nice laugh. Her whole body seemed to join in. "Now why don't you tell me what this is all about, Mr. Bolitar."

"Please call me Myron."

"Fine. And you can call me Dr. Abramson. Now what seems to be the problem?"

"No, I'm fine."

"I see." She looked skeptical, but Myron sensed that the good doctor was having a little fun at his expense. "So you have a 'friend' with a problem. Tell me all about it."

"My friend," he said, "is Valerie Simpson."

That got her attention. "What?"

"I want to talk to you about Valerie Simpson."

The open face slammed shut. "You're not a reporter, are you?"

"No."

"I thought I read you were a sports agent."

"I am. Valerie Simpson was about to become a client."

"I see."

"When was the last time you saw Valerie?" Myron asked.

Dr. Abramson shook her head. "I can neither confirm nor deny that Valerie Simpson was ever a patient of mine."

"You don't have to confirm or deny it. I know she was."

"I repeat: I can neither confirm nor deny that Valerie Simpson was ever a patient of mine." She studied him for a moment. "Perhaps you can tell me what your interest is in this."

"Like I said before, I was going to represent her."

"That doesn't explain your visiting me incognito."

"I'm investigating her murder."

"Investigating?"

Myron nodded.

"Who hired you?"

"No one."

"Then why are you investigating?"

"I have my reasons."

She nodded. "What are those reasons, Myron? I'd like to hear about them."

Psychiatrists. "You want me to also tell you about the time I walked in on Mommy and Daddy?"

"If you want."

"I don't want. What I want is to know what caused Valerie's breakdown."

Her response was rote. "I can neither confirm nor deny that Valerie Simpson was ever a patient of mine."

"Doctor-patient privilege?"

"That's right."

"But Valerie is dead."

"That doesn't alter my obligation in the slightest."

"She's been murdered. Gunned down in cold blood."

"I understand that. Dramatics will not alter my obligation either."

"But you may know something helpful."

"Helpful in what way?"

"In finding the killer."

She folded the tiny hands in her lap. Like a little girl in church. "And that's what you're attempting to do? Find this woman's killer?"

"Yes."

"What about the police? I understood from news reports that they have a suspect."

"I don't trust authority types," Myron said.

"Oh?"

"It's one of the reasons I want to help."

Dr. Abramson fixed him with the big eyes. "I don't think so, Myron."

"No?"

"You look more like the rescue-complex sort to me. The kind of man who likes to play hero all the time, who sees himself as a knight in shining armor. What do you think?"

"I think we should save my analysis for later."

She shrugged her little shoulders. "Just giving my opinion. No extra charge."

"Fine." *Extra* charge? "I'm not so sure the police have the right man."

"Why not?"

"I was hoping you could help me with that. Valerie must have talked about Roger Quincy's stalking her. Did she think he was dangerous?"

"For the final time, I will neither confirm nor deny—"

"I'm not asking you to. I'm asking about Roger Quincy. You don't have a relationship with him, do you?"

"I also don't know him."

"Then how about one of those quick opinions. Like you did with me."

She shook her head. "I'm sorry."

"There's no way I can convince you to talk to me?"

"About a possible patient? No."

"Suppose I got parental consent."

"You won't."

Myron waited, watched. She was better at this than him. Her face gave away nothing, but the words couldn't be taken back. "How do you know that?" he asked.

She remained silent. Her eyes dropped to the floor. Myron wondered if the faux pas had been on purpose.

"They called you already, didn't they?" Myron said.

"I'm not at liberty to discuss any communications between myself and—"

"The family called. They hushed you up."

"I will neither confirm—"

"The body is barely cold and they're already covering their tracks," Myron went on. "You don't see anything wrong with that?"

Dr. Abramson cleared her throat. "I do not know what you're talking about it, but I will say this: it is not unreasonable in situations such as the one you've described to me for parents to want to protect their daughter's memory."

"Protect her memory"—Myron rose, put on his best lawyer-in-summation glower—"or her murderer?" Mr. High Drama.

"Now you're being silly," she said. "You surely don't suspect the young woman's family."

Myron sat back down. He gave his best anything's-possible head tilt. "Helen Van Slyke's daughter is killed. Within hours the grieving mother calls you to make sure you keep your mouth shut. You don't find that a tad odd?"

"I will neither confirm nor deny that I have ever heard the name Helen Van Slyke."

"I see," Myron said. "So you think this should all be shoved aside. Bottled up. Let the image rule over the reality. Somehow I don't think that sits well with you, Doc."

She said nothing.

"Your patient is dead," Myron continued. "Don't you think your obligation should be to her, not her mother?"

Dr. Abramson's hands tightened into small balls for a moment, then relaxed. She took a deep breath, held it, let it out slowly. "Let us pretend—and just pretend—that I was the psychiatrist for this young woman. Wouldn't I have an obligation not to betray what she told me in the strictest of confidences?

If the patient chose not to reveal any of this while alive, wouldn't I have an obligation to uphold that right for her in death?"

Myron stared at her. Dr. Abramson stared back. Unyielding. "Nice speech," he said. "But maybe Valerie wanted to reveal something. And maybe someone killed her to deny her that right."

The bright eyes blinked several times. "I think you should leave now," she said.

She pressed a button on her intercom. The receptionist appeared at the door. He crossed his arms and tried to look intimidating. The attempt was hardly a rousing success.

Myron rose. He knew he had planted a seed. He would have to give it time to germinate. "Will you at least think about it?" he added.

"Good-bye, Myron."

The receptionist stepped aside, allowing Myron room to pass.

19

OF THE THREE WITNESSES TO THE MURDER OF Alexander Cross—all college chums of the deceased— only one lived in the New York area. Gregory Caufield, Jr., was now a young associate at daddy's law firm of Stillen, Caufield, and Weston, a high-powered, high-profile firm with offices in several states and foreign countries.

Myron dialed, asked for Gregory Caufield, Jr., and was put on hold. A woman came on the line several seconds later and said, "I'll put you straight through to Mr. Caufield."

A click. One ring. Then an enthusiastic voice said, "Well, hi!"

Well, hi?

"Is this Gregory Caufield?"

"Sure is. What can I do for you today?"

"My name is Myron Bolitar."

"Uh-huh."

"And I'd like to make an appointment to see you."

"Sure. When?"

"As soon as possible."

"How about half an hour from now? Will that be okay?"

"That'll be fine, thank you."

"Super, Myron. Looking forward to it."

Click. *Super?*

Fifteen minutes later Myron was on his way. He walked up Park Avenue past the mosque steps where Myron and Win liked to lunch on summer days. Prime woman-watching perch. New York has the most beautiful women in the world, bar none. They wear business attire and sneakers and sunglasses. They walk with cool purpose, with no time to waste. Amazingly, none of the beautiful women checked Myron out. Probably just being discreet. Probably ogling him like crazy from behind those sunglasses.

Myron cut west to Madison Avenue. He passed a couple of electronics stores with the same GOING OUT OF BUSINESS signs they'd had up for at least a year. The sign was always the same— white sign, black letters. A blind man held out a cup. Didn't even give out pencils anymore. His seeing-eye dog looked dead. Two cops were laughing on the corner. They were eating croissants. Not doughnuts. Another cliché blown to hell.

There was a security guard by the elevator in the lobby.

"Yes?"

"Myron Bolitar to see Gregory Caufield."

"Oh yes, Mr. Bolitar. Twenty-second floor." Didn't call up. Didn't check his list. Hmm.

When the elevator opened, a pleasant-faced woman was standing there. "Good afternoon, Mr. Bolitar. If you'd please follow me."

Down a long corridor with an office-pink carpet, white walls, McKnight framed posters. No typewriters clicked, but Myron heard the whir of a laser printer. Someone was dialing a number on a speakerphone. A fax machine screeched its call to another fax machine. When they turned the corner, a second, equally pleasant-faced, woman approached. Plastic smiles all around.

"Hello, Mr. Bolitar," the second woman said. "Nice to see you today."

"Nice to see you too." Every line a lady-slayer.

The first woman handed him over to the second. Tag-team style. "Mr. Caufield is waiting for you in conference room C," the second woman said, her voice low, as if conference room C were a clandestine chamber in the bowels of the Pentagon.

She led him to a door very much like any other except it had a big bronze *C* on it. In a matter of seconds, Myron managed to deduce that the room was conference room C. The Adventures of Sherlock Bolitar. A man opened the door from the inside. He was young with a thick head of Stephanopoulos-like hair. He pumped Myron's hand enthusiastically. "Hi, Myron."

"Hi, Gregory." Like they actually knew each other.

"Please come in. There's someone here I'd like you to meet."

Myron stepped fully into the room. Big walnut table with dark leather chairs, the expensive kind, the kind with those little gold buttons on them. Oil portraits of stern-faced men on the walls. The room was empty, except for one man down the other end of the table. Though they had never met, Myron recognized the man immediately. He should have been surprised, but he wasn't.

Senator Bradley Cross.

Gregory did not bother with introductions. In fact he didn't bother staying. He slipped out the door, closing it behind him. The senator stood. His were a far cry from the classic patrician good looks one usually associates with political families. They say people look like their pets; in that case Senator Bradley

Cross owned a basset hound. His features were long and malleable. His finely tailored suit did nothing to disguise his exaggerated pear build; on a woman, his hips would be called child-bearing. His hair was wispy gray strands that seemed to be suffering from static cling. He wore thick glasses and an off-center smile. Still, it was an endearing smile—indeed, an endearing, trustworthy face. The kind of face you'd vote for.

Senator Cross slowly put out his hand. "I'm sorry for the dramatics," he said, "but I thought we should meet."

They shook hands.

"Please have a seat. Make yourself comfortable. Can I get you something?"

"No, thank you," Myron said.

They sat facing each other. Myron waited. The senator seemed unsure how to begin. He coughed into his fists several times. Each cough made his jowls flap a bit.

"Do you know why I wanted to see you?" he asked.

"No," Myron said.

"I understand you've been asking a lot of questions about my son. More specifically, about his murder."

"Where did you hear that?"

"Around. Here and there. I am not without my sources." He tilted his head the way a basset hound does when he hears a strange sound. "I'd like to know why."

"Valerie Simpson was going to be a client of mine," Myron said.

"So I've been told."

"I'm looking into her murder."

"And you believe there might be a connection between Valerie's murder and Alexander's?"

Myron shrugged.

"My son was killed by a random street thug six years ago near Philadelphia. Valerie was killed almost gangland style at the U.S. Open in New York. What possible connection could there be?"

"Maybe none."

Cross leaned back, fiddled his thumbs. "I want to be up front with you, Myron. I've looked into your background a bit. I know about your past work. Not the details, of course, but your reputation. I'm not trying to apply any influence here. It's not my style. I've never been comfortable at playing the tough guy." He smiled again. His eyes were wet now and there was a discernible quake in his voice. "I'm talking to you now not as a United States senator but as a grieving father. A grieving father who just wants to let his son rest in peace. I'm asking you to please stop what you're doing."

The pain in the man's voice was raw. Myron had not expected this. "I'm not sure I can, Senator."

The senator rubbed his entire face vigorously, using both hands. "You see two young people . . ." he began tiredly. "You see two young people with the whole world in front of them. Practically engaged to one another. And what happens to them? They're murdered in two separate incidents six years apart. The cruel coincidence is too much to fathom. You wonder about that, don't you, Myron?"

Myron nodded.

"So you begin to scrutinize their deaths. You look for something that might explain such a bizarre double tragedy. And in your search you find inconsistencies. You see pieces that just don't add up."

"Yes."

"And those inconsistencies lead you to believe that there is a connection between Alexander's murder and Valerie's."

"Maybe."

Cross glanced up at the ceiling and rested his index finger on his lip. "Will you take my word that those inconsistencies have nothing to do with Valerie Simpson?"

"No," Myron said. "I can't."

Senator Cross nodded, more to himself than Myron. "I didn't suspect you would," he said. "You don't have children, do you, Myron?"

"No."

"It doesn't matter. Even people who have children don't understand. They can't. What happened . . . it's not just the pain. The death is all-consuming. It never lets you go, never gives you a chance to catch your breath. My wife still has to be medicated almost daily. It's like someone scooped out everything inside of her and left behind only a pitiful shell. You can't imagine what it's like to see her like that."

"I don't mean to hurt anyone, Senator."

"But you won't stop either. And no matter how careful you are, someone is bound to get wind of your investigation, just as I did."

"I'll try to be discreet."

"You know that's impossible."

"I can't back away now. I'm sorry."

The senator gave himself the face massage again. He sighed deeply and said, "You leave me no choice. I'll have to tell you what happened. Maybe then you'll let it go."

Myron waited.

"You are an attorney, are you not?"

"Yes," Myron said.

"You're a member of the New York bar?"

"Yes."

Bradley Cross reached into his suit pocket. Sallow skin hung off his face in uneven clumps. He took out a checkbook. "I'd like to hire you as my attorney," he said. "Will a five-thousand-dollar retainer be enough?"

"I don't understand."

"As my attorney, what I'm about to tell you falls under the jurisdiction of attorney-client privilege. You will not be allowed, even in a court of law, to repeat what I am about to tell you."

"You don't need to hire me for that."

"I'd prefer it."

"Fine. Make it a hundred dollars."

Bradley Cross wrote out the check and handed it to Myron.

"My son was on drugs," he said without preamble. "Cocaine mostly. Heroin too, but he'd only just started on it. I knew he was on something, but frankly I didn't think it was serious. I saw him high. I saw the red eyes. But I thought it was just marijuana. Hell, I've tried marijuana. Inhaled even."

Weak smile. Myron returned it, equally weak.

"Alexander and his friends weren't taking a casual stroll around the club grounds that night," he said. "They were going to get high. Alexander was found with a syringe in his pocket. There was cocaine found in the bushes not far from where the murder took place. And, of course, there were traces of both heroin and cocaine in Alexander's body. Not just in his fluids but in his tissue. I'm told that shows he'd been using for a while."

"I thought there was no autopsy," Myron said.

"It was kept secret. Nothing was reported or filed. It didn't matter anyway. A knife wound ended Alexander's life, not drugs. The fact that my son was taking illegal substances was irrelevant."

Maybe, Myron thought, keeping his expression blank.

Cross stared off for a while. After some time had passed he asked, "Where was I?"

"They left the party to get high."

"Right, thank you." He cleared his throat, sat up a little straighter. "The rest of the story is fairly straightforward. The boys stumbled upon Errol Swade and Curtis Yeller on one of the grass courts. The papers talked about how brave Alexander was, how he tried to thwart the evil-doers without concern for his own safety. My spin doctors at their best. But the truth is, he was flying so high he acted irrationally. He swooped in like some kind of superhero. The Yeller boy—the one the police shot—dropped everything and ran. But Errol Swade was a cooler customer. He took out a switchblade and punctured my boy's heart like a balloon. Casually, they say. Nonchalant."

Senator Cross stopped. Myron waited for him to continue. When it was clear he had reached the end of his saga, Myron asked, "Why were they at the club?"

"Who?"

"Swade and Yeller."

Senator Cross looked puzzled. "They were thieves."

"How do you know that?"

"What else would they have been doing here?"

Myron shrugged. "Selling drugs to your son. Dealing. It sounds a lot more plausible than a late-night robbery of a tennis club."

Cross shook his head. "They were carrying items. Tennis rackets. Tennis balls."

"According to whom?"

"According to Gregory and the others. The items were also found at the scene."

"Tennis rackets and balls?"

"There may have been other things, I don't remember."

"That's what they were after?" Myron said. "Some tennis gear?"

"The police believe that my son interrupted them before the robbery was complete."

"But your son stumbled across them *outside*. If they'd already stolen some gear, then they'd already been inside."

"So what are you suggesting?" the senator asked sharply. "That my son was murdered in a drug deal gone bad?"

"I'm just trying to see what sounds most plausible."

"Would a drug deal murder make a connection with Valerie more likely?"

"No."

"So what's your point?"

"No point. Just trying out different theories. What happened next? Directly after the murder?"

He looked off again, this time in the general direction of one of the portraits, but Myron didn't think he was actually seeing it. "Gregory and the other boys came running back into the party," he said in a hollow voice. "I followed them outside. Blood was bubbling out of Alexander's mouth. By the time I reached him he was dead."

Silence.

"You can pretty much figure out the rest. Everything switched over to autopilot. I really didn't do much. Aides did. Gregory's father—he's a senior partner here—helped too. I just stood and nodded numbly. I won't lie to you. I won't tell you I didn't know what was going on. I did. Old habits die hard, Myron. There is no creature more selfish than a politician. We so easily justify our selfishness as the 'common good.' So the cover-up was done."

"And if the truth came out now?"

He smiled. "I'd be destroyed. But I'm not really afraid of that anymore. Or maybe that's a lie too, who knows anymore?" He threw up his hands, lowered them. "But my wife never learned the truth. I don't know what it would do to her, I really don't. Alexander was a good kid, Mr. Bolitar. I don't want his memory ripped to shreds. In the end drugs do not make Errol Swade and Curtis Yeller any less culpable or my son any more guilty. He didn't ask to be stabbed."

Myron waited a beat. Then the left-field question: "What about Deanna Yeller?"

Puzzled. "Who?"

"Curtis Yeller's mother."

"What about her?"

"You have no relationship with her?"

More puzzled. "Of course not. Why would you ask something like that?"

"You never paid to keep her silent?"

"About what?"

"About the circumstances of her son's death."

"No. Why should I?"

"You know there was never an autopsy done on Curtis Yeller either. Strange, don't you think?"

"If you're insinuating that the police did not act strictly within regulations, I can't answer that because I don't know. I don't care either. Yes, I've wondered about the police shooting myself. Perhaps there was a second cover-up that night. If there was, I was not involved in it. And more important, I don't see what possible connection it could have with Valerie Simpson. In fact I don't see any connection in any of this with Valerie."

"She was at the party that night?"

"Valerie? Of course."

"Do you know where she was at the time Alexander was murdered?"

"No."

"Do you remember how she reacted to his death?"

"She was devastated. Her fiancé had just been killed in cold blood. She was distraught and angry."

"Did you approve of their relationship?"

"Yes, very much so. I thought Valerie was a bit troubled. A bit too sad. But I liked her. She and Alexander were good together."

"Valerie's name was never mentioned in connection with your son's murder. Why?"

The jowls were quivering big-time. "You know why," he said. "Valerie Simpson was still something of a celebrity from her tennis days. We felt that there was already enough scrutiny without adding her name to the mix. It wasn't a question of liking or not liking Valerie. We just wanted to minimize the story as much as possible. Keep it off the front pages."

"You got lucky then."

"What do you mean?"

"Yeller was killed. Swade vanished."

Cross blinked several times. "I'm not sure I understand."

"If they were alive there would have been a trial. More media attention. Maybe too much media attention for even your spin doctors to handle."

He smiled. "I see you've heard the rumors."

"Rumors?"

"That I had Errol Swade killed. That the mob did me a favor or some such nonsense."

"You have to admit, Senator, their fates made for a convenient little public relations package. No one to dispute your spin on things."

"I don't cry over the fate of Curtis Yeller, and if Errol Swade was murdered I doubt I'd shed too many tears about that either. But I don't know any mobsters. That may sound silly, but I wouldn't know the first thing about enlisting the mob's help. I did hire a detective agency to look for Swade."

"Did they find anything?"

"No. They believe that Swade is dead. So do the police. He was a punk, Myron. He wasn't on a path that led to a long life even before this incident."

Myron followed up with a few more questions, but there was nothing more to learn. A few minutes later the two men stood.

"Would you mind if I spoke to Gregory Caufield before I leave?" Myron asked.

"I'd prefer it if you didn't."

"If there's nothing to hide—"

"I don't want him knowing I told you this. Attorney-client privilege, remember? He won't speak honestly to you anyway."

"He will if you tell him to."

Cross shook his head. "Gregory's father controls him. He won't talk."

Myron shrugged. The senator was probably right. The only leverage he could apply on Gregory would be what Cross just told him. Cross had neatly arranged it so Myron couldn't do that. He'd have to think of a way to end-run that. Caufield was an eyewitness. He'd be worth a few questions.

The two men shook hands, both making serious eye contact. Was Senator Cross a sweet old codger, a grieving father trying to protect his son's memory? Or had he calculated that this would be the most effective strategy for dealing with Myron? Was he cagey or sympathetic or both?

Cross gave him the endearing off-center smile again. "I hope I've satisfied your curiosity," he said.

He hadn't. Not even close. But Myron didn't bother telling him that.

20

MYRON LEFT THE BUILDING AND STROLLED down Madison Avenue. Traffic was at a standstill. Big surprise in Manhattan. Five lanes were merging into one on Fifty-fourth Street. The other four lanes were blocked by one of those purely New York construction sites with steam pouring up out of the streets. Very Dante. What was with all that steam anyway?

He was about to cut across Fifty-third Street when he felt a sharp stab in his ribs.

"Give me an excuse, asshole."

Myron recognized the voice before seeing the taped nose and the black eyes. Fishnet. He was pressing a gun against Myron's rib cage, using his body to hide the gun from any curious onlookers.

"You're wearing the same shirt," Myron said. "Jesus Christ, you didn't even change."

Fishnet gave him a little gun jab. "You're going to wish you were never born, asshole. Get in the car."

The car—the powder-blue Caddy with thick scratches on the side—pulled alongside of them. Jim, Fishnet's partner, was driving, but Myron barely noticed him. His eyes immediately locked on the familiar figure in the backseat. The figure smiled and waved.

"Hey, Myron," he called out. "How's it going?"

Aaron.

"Bring him here, Lee," Aaron said.

Fishnet Lee gave Myron a nudge with the gun. "Let's go, asshole."

Myron got in the backseat with Aaron. Fishnet Lee joined Jim in the front. The front seats were both covered with plastic where Win had dumped the maple syrup.

Aaron was dressed in his customary garb. Pure-snow-white suit, white shoes. No socks. No shirt. Aaron never wore a shirt, preferring to display his tan pectorals. They gleamed from some sort of oil or grease. He always looked fresh out of the wax salon, his body smooth as a baby's bottom. Aaron was a big man, six-six, two-forty. The weight lifter's build was not merely for show. Aaron moved with a speed and grace that defied the bulk. His black hair was slicked back and tied into a long ponytail.

He gave Myron a game-show-host grin and held it.

Myron said, "Nice smile, Aaron. Lots of teeth."

"Proper dental hygiene. It's a passion of mine."

"You should share your passion with Lee," Myron said.

Fishnet's head spun. "What the fuck did you say, asshole?"

"Turn around, Lee," Aaron said to Fishnet. Fishnet glared a few more daggers. Myron yawned. Jim drove. Aaron sat back. He said nothing, smiling brightly. Every part of him glistened in the sunlight. After two blocks of this Myron pointed at Aaron's cleavage. "Your electrolysis missed a chest hair."

To Aaron's credit he didn't look. "We need to chat, Myron."

"What about?"

"Valerie Simpson. For once I think we're on the same side."

"Oh?"

"You want to capture Valerie Simpson's killer. So do we."

"You do?"

"Yes. Mr. Ache is determined to bring her killer to justice."

"That Frank. Always the Good Samaritan."

Aaron chuckled. "Still the funny man, eh, Myron? Well, I admit it sounds a bit bizarre, but we'd like to help you."

"How?"

"We both know that Roger Quincy killed Valerie Simpson. Mr. Ache is willing to use his considerable influence to help locate him."

"And in return?"

Aaron feigned shock. He put a manicured hand the size of a manhole cover to his chest. "Myron, you wound me. Really. We try to extend the hand of friendship and you slap it away with an insult."

"Uh-huh."

"This is one of those rare win-win situations," Aaron said. "We're willing to help you get your killer."

"And you get?"

"Not a thing." He settled back into his seat. "If the killer is found, the police will move on to other matters. We will move on to other matters. And you, Myron, should also move on to other matters."

"Ah."

"Now, there's no reason to have a problem here," Aaron added. When the sun hit his chest at a certain angle, the reflection dazzled the eyes. "This isn't like some of our past encounters. We both want the same thing. We both want to put this tragic episode behind us. For you, that means finding the killer and bringing him to justice. For us, that means ending the investigation as soon as possible."

"But suppose I'm not convinced Roger Quincy did it," Myron said.

Aaron raised an eyebrow. "Come on now, Myron. You've seen the evidence."

"It's circumstantial."

"Since when has that bothered you? Oh by the way, a new witness has come forward. We just got wind of it."

"What kind of witness?" Myron asked.

"A witness who saw Roger Quincy talking to your beloved Valerie within ten minutes of the murder."

Myron said nothing.

"You doubt my word?"

"Who's the witness, Aaron?"

"Some housewife. She was at the matches with her kids. And to answer your next question we have nothing to do with her."

"So why the big fear?"

"What fear?"

"What's Ache so concerned about? Why hire Starsky and Hutch up there to follow me?"

Fishnet turned around. "What the fuck did you call me, asshole?"

"Turn around, Lee," Aaron said.

"Ah, come off it, Aaron, let me fuck him up a little. You see what the motherfucker did to my car? And look at my fucking nose." Car first, then nose. Priorities. "He and his faggot buddy jumped me. Two on one. When I wasn't looking. Let me teach him a little respect."

"You couldn't, Lee. You and Jim together couldn't."

"Fuck I couldn't. If I didn't have this busted nose—"

"Shut up, Lee," Aaron said.

Immediate silence.

Aaron rolled his eyes at Myron and spread his hands. "Rank amateurs," he said. "Frank is always trying to cut corners. Save a buck here. Save a buck there. In the end it always costs more."

"I thought you stopped working for the Ache brothers," Myron said.

"I work freelance now."

"So Frank just brought you in?"

"As of this morning."

"Must be something big," Myron said. "You don't come cheap."

Aaron gave him the teeth again, adjusted the jacket of his suit. "You want the best, you have to pay."

"So why's Frank so bent out of shape about this?"

"I have no idea. But make no mistake about it: Frank wants your investigation to end. Now. No excuses. Look, Myron, we both know you've been something of a pain in the ass to Frank. He doesn't like you. To be honest he'd like to ace you. That's no bullshit. I'm talking man-to-man here. Friend to friend. We're friends, right? Buddies?"

"Best of chums," Myron added. Shovel, shovel.

"But Frank is showing incredible restraint with you. Generosity even. He knows, for example, that you took Eddie Crane out to dinner. That alone would be reason for Frank to want you roughed up a bit. But he doesn't. In fact he's decided that if Eddie Crane chooses your agency, he won't get in the way."

"Big of him."

"But it *is* big of him," Aaron insisted. "He owns the kid's coach, for crying out loud. By all rights he belongs to TruPro. But Frank is willing to let him go, and he's willing to help you bring in Roger Quincy. Two very big favors. Gifts really. In exchange, you do nothing."

Myron turned his palms up. "How can I pass up a deal like that?"

"Do I sense a whiff of sarcasm?"

Myron shrugged.

"Frank's trying to be fair, Myron."

"Yeah, the man's a prince."

"Don't push him on this. It's not worth it."

"Can I leave now?"

"I'd like your answer first."

"I'll have to think about it," Myron said. "But I'd be much more willing to let go if I knew what Frank was trying to hide."

Aaron shook his head. "Still the same old Myron, huh? You never change. I'm surprised no one has wasted you yet."

"I'm not easy to kill," Myron said.

"Maybe not."

"And I'm also a snazzy dancer. No one likes to kill a snazzy dancer. There're so few us left."

Aaron put his hand on Myron's knee and leaned toward him. "Can we stop the lunatic routine for a moment?"

Myron's eyes flicked down to the knee, then back to Aaron. "Uh, your hand?"

"You know about the carrot and the stick, Myron?"

"The what?"

"The carrot and the stick." The hand was still on Myron's knee.

"Oh. Sure. The carrot and the stick." *What?*

"So far I have shown you only the carrot. I would feel amiss if I did not also show a bit of stick."

In the front seat Fishnet and Jim shared a chuckle.

Aaron's fingers gave the knee a little squeeze. Like a hawk's talons. "Now you know me. I'm not a stick man. I'm the gentle sort. I'm kind. I'm nice. I'm . . ." He looked up as though searching for the word.

"A carrot," Myron finished.

"Right. A carrot."

Myron had seen Aaron kill a man. Snap his neck as though it were a twig. He'd also seen the results of Aaron's work in venues ranging from boxing rings to morgues. Some carrot.

"But nonetheless I need to add a bit of stick. Just for the record, you understand. It's expected. I know it's not necessary in your case. The stick, I mean."

"I'm listening," Myron said.

"Yeah," Fishnet added, "tell him, Aaron." Fishnet and Jim restarted the chuckle. Louder.

"Shut up," Aaron said softly.

Again immediate silence. Like they'd both been shot in the head.

Aaron swung his line of vision to Myron. His eyes were suddenly dark and hard. "There will be no further warnings. We will simply strike. I know you don't scare easily. I explained that to Frank. He doesn't care. He suggested striking places that another man might consider taboo."

"Like?"

"I understand Duane Richwood is playing well. I'd hate to see his career cut short." He gave the knee a harder squeeze. "Or take your beautiful Jessica, for example. Now I know she's out of the country right now. In Athens, in case you don't know. The Grand Bretagne Hotel. Room 207. Frank has friends in Greece."

Myron felt a cold chill. "Don't even think about it, Aaron."

"Not my decision." He finally let go of the knee. "It's Frank. He's adamant about this. He wants you to let go now. You know what they say about grabbing a tiger by the tail."

"If he touches her—"

Aaron waved him off. "Please, Myron, no threats. There's no reason for threats here. You can't win. You know that. The price of victory is too high. You and Win are only two men. Two good men. Two of the best. Worthy adversaries. But Frank has me, for one. And he has others. Many others. As many men as he needs. Men with no scruples. Men who would break into Jessica's room, take turns with her, and then blow her away. Men who would jump Esperanza on her way home from work. Men who would even do unspeakable things to your mother."

Myron stared at Aaron. Aaron did not blink. "You can't win, Myron. No matter how tough you are, you can't stand up to that kind of thing. We both know it."

Silence. The Caddy pulled up to the front of Myron's building.

"Can I have your answer now?" Aaron asked.

Myron tried not to shake as he got out of the car. Without glancing behind him he walked inside.

21

WIN WORKED THE HEAVY BAG. HE WAS SNAP-ping side kicks that bent the eighty-pound bag almost in half. He threw kicks at every level. The opponent's knee. The abdomen. The neck. The face. He struck with his heel, his toes angled down. Myron went though several katas, or forms, concentrating on the precision of his strikes, imagining a person in front of him rather than the air. Sometimes the person was Aaron.

They were at Master Kwon's new downtown location. The *dojang* was divided into two sections. One looked like a dance studio. Hardwood floor and lots of mirrors. The other section had matted floors, dumbbells, a speed bag, a heavy bag, a jump rope. On the shelf were rubber knives and guns to practice take-away techniques. The American flag and Korean flag were hung near the doorway. Each student bowed to them as they entered and left. School rules were listed on a poster. Myron knew them by heart. His favorite was rule number ten. Always finish what you start.

Hmm. Good advice? Hard to say right now.

There were fourteen school rules in all. Every once in a

while Master Kwon added a new one. Number fourteen had been put up two months ago: Do not overeat. "Students too fat," Master Kwon had explained. "Too much put in mouth." In the twenty years since Win had helped Kwon relocate to the United States, Kwon's English had continually degenerated. Myron suspected it was part of his image as a wise old man from the Far East. Playing Mr. Miyagi from the *Karate Kid* movies.

Win stopped. "Here," he said, gesturing to the bag. "You need this more than I do."

Myron began to hit the bag. Hard. He started with some punches. Tae kwon do's fighting stance is simple and practical, not all that different from a boxer's. Anyone who tried that crane-stance bullshit on the streets usually ended up on their ass. Myron followed up with some elbow and knee strikes. Elbows and knees were useful, particularly for fighting in close. Martial arts movies showed lots of spinning kicks to the head, jumping kicks to the chest, stuff like that. But street fighting was far simpler. You aimed for the groin, the knee, the neck, the nose, the eyes. Occasionally the solar plexus. The rest was wasteful. You get in a real life-or-death situation, you twist the guy's balls. You stick your fingers in his eyes. You throw an elbow to his throat.

Win walked over to a full-length mirror. "Let's review what we've learned so far," he said in the mock voice of a kindergarten teacher. He began to play air golf, practicing his swing in the mirror. He did that a lot. "One, the esteemed senator from Pennsylvania wants you off this case. Two, a major mobster from New York wants you off this case. Three, your client, the womanizing Duane Richwood, wants you off this case. Have I left anybody out?"

"Deanna Yeller," Myron said. "And Helen Van Slyke. Kenneth too, don't forget Kenneth. Pavel Menansi." Myron thought a moment. "I think that's it."

"The police officer," Win added. "Detective Dimonte."

"Oh yeah, right. I forgot about Rolly."

Win checked the grip on his imaginary club. "Thus," he continued, "your cause is mustering its customary support—i.e., none."

Myron shrugged, threw a combination. "'Can't please everyone, so you've got to please yourself.'"

Win made a face. "Quoting Ricky Nelson?"

"It's been a long day."

"I would say."

Myron back-kicked. A good countermove to almost any attack. "So why is everyone so afraid of Valerie Simpson? A United States senator sets up a clandestine meeting with me. Frank Ache brings in Aaron. Duane threatens to fire me. Why?"

Win took another air-golf swing in the mirror. He looked up after the shot, squinting, as though following the trajectory of the imaginary ball. He seemed displeased. Golfers.

The door to the *dojang* opened. Wanda peered inside, gave a shy wave.

"Hi," Myron said.

"Hi."

Myron smiled. He was happy to see her—someone who did indeed want him to continue his investigation. She wore a patterned, almost little-girlish summer dress. The dress was sleeveless, revealing her nicely toned arms. She wasn't wearing one of those big summer hats, but she should have been. Her makeup had been applied with a light hand. Gold hoop earrings hung from her lobes. She looked young and healthy and quite beautiful.

A sign beside the door read NO SHOES ALLOWED. Wanda obeyed, slipped her flats off before stepping inside the *dojang*. "Esperanza told me you'd be here," she said. "I'm really sorry about disturbing you outside the office again."

"Don't worry about it," he said. "You know Win."

"Yes," she said, turning to him. She managed a smile. "Nice to see you."

Win gave her an almost indiscernible head tilt. Stoic. Playing Tonto.

Wringing her hands together Wanda asked, "Can we talk for a moment?"

Win did not need prompting. He moved to the door, bowed deeply at the waist, left. They were alone.

She walked toward him deliberately, glancing around like she was on a house tour but not really interested in buying. "Do you come here a lot?" she asked.

"Here or one of Master Kwon's other *dojangs*."

"I thought they were called dojos," she said.

"Dojo is Japanese. *Dojang* is Korean."

She nodded as though this information had some significance in her life. She glanced around a bit more. "Have you studied this for a long time?"

"Yes."

"And Win?"

"Even longer."

"He doesn't look the fighting type," she said. "Except maybe in the eyes."

Myron had heard that before. He waited.

"I just wanted to know if you'd learned anything," she said. Her eyes flicked left, right, up, down.

"Not much," he said. Not exactly the truth, but Myron wasn't about to mention Duane's liaisons with Valerie.

She nodded again. Her hands were in constant motion, searching for something to occupy them. "Duane is acting even stranger," she said.

"How?"

"Just more of the same, I guess. He's on edge all the time. He keeps getting these calls he takes in another room. When I answer the phone the caller hangs up. And he disappeared again last night. Said he needed some air, but he was gone for two hours."

"Do you have any thoughts?" he asked.

She shook her head.

Myron aimed for his gentlest voice. "Could there be someone else?"

Her eyes stopped flicking and flared in his direction. "I'm not some hooker he picked up off the street."

"I know that."

"We love each other."

"I know that too. But I also know a lot of guys in love who still do dumb things." Women too. Jessica, for one. Four years ago with a guy named Doug. It still hurt. Guy named Doug. Go figure.

Wanda shook her head again firmly. Convincing herself or Myron? "It's not like that with us. I know I sound like a gullible idiot, but it's the way it is. I can't explain it."

"No need to. I was just seeing what you thought."

"Duane's not having an affair."

"Okay."

Her eyes were wet. She took a couple of deep breaths. "He's not sleeping at night. He paces. I ask him what's wrong, but he won't tell me. I tried eavesdropping on a call, but the only thing I picked up was your name."

"My name?"

She nodded. "He said it twice, but that's all I heard."

Myron thought a moment. "Suppose I put a tap on your phone."

"Do it."

"You don't have a problem with that?"

"No." The wet eyes broke into tears. She let out two quick sobs, made herself stop. "It's getting worse, Myron. We have to find out what's going on."

"I'll do my best."

She gave him a brief hug. Myron wanted to stroke her hair and say something comforting. He didn't do either. She strode out slowly, head high. Myron watched. As soon as she was out of sight Win returned.

"Well?" Win asked.

"I like her," Myron said.

Win nodded. "Very shapely derriere."

"That's not what I meant. She's a good woman. And she's scared."

"Of course she's scared. Her meal ticket is about to go bye-bye."

The Return of Mr. Warmth. "It's not like that, Win. She loves him."

Win strummed a few notes on an air violin. Couldn't talk to him about stuff like that. He just didn't get it. "What did she want?"

Myron filled him in on the conversation. Win spread his legs, dropping into a full split and then sliding back up. He repeated the move several times, faster and faster. Ladies and gentlemen, the Godfather of Soul, Mr. James Brown.

When Myron finished, Win said, "Sounds like Duane is trying to hide more than a quick fling."

"My thoughts exactly."

"You want me to watch him?"

"We can take shifts."

Win shook his head. "He knows you."

"He knows you too."

"Yes," Win said, "but I am invisible. I am the wind."

"Sure you don't mean passing wind?"

Win made a face. "That was a good one. I'm sure I'll laugh for days."

Truth was, Win could be nestled in your B.V.D.'s for a week and you'd never know. "Can you start tonight?" Myron asked.

Win nodded. "I'm already there."

22

MYRON SHOT BASKETS ON THE BLACKTOP OFF the driveway. The long summer day was finally slipping into darkness, but the basket was illuminated with spotlights. He and his father had installed them when Myron was in the sixth grade. A variety of barbecue smells competed in the still air. Chicken from the Dempseys' house. Burgers from the Weinsteins'. Shish kebab at the Ruskins'.

Myron shot, rebounded, shot again. He got a little rhythm going, the ball back-spinning gently through the basket. Nothing but net. Sweat matted his gray T-shirt to his chest. Myron always did his best thinking out here, but right now his mind was a blank. There was nothing but the ball, the hoop, and the sweet arc after the release. It felt pure.

"Hey, Myron."

It was Timmy from next door. Timmy was ten.

"Bug off, kid. You're bothering me."

Timmy laughed and grabbed a rebound. It was an inside joke. Timmy's mother was convinced that her son was bothering Myron and that Myron should send Timmy home whenever he came over. Didn't stop Timmy. He and his friends always came over when Myron was shooting. Once in a while, when they needed an extra body, the kids would knock on the door and ask his mom if Myron could come out and play.

He and Timmy shot around for a while. They talked about stuff that was important to little boys. A few other kids came by. The Daleys' boy. The Cohens' girl. Others. Bikes were parked at the end of the driveway. They started playing a game. Myron was designated steady passer. No one kept score accurately. Everyone laughed a lot. A few fathers came by and joined in. Arnie Stollman. Fred Dempsey. It'd been a while since they'd done this. A bit too Rockwellian for some, but it felt very right to Myron.

It was nearly ten when mothers started to call out for their children. From their front stoops the mothers smiled brightly and waved at Myron. Myron waved back. The kids "aw, Mom"'d, but they listened.

Summer and school break. Still a touch of innocence. Kids were supposed to be different now. They had to deal with guns and drugs and crime and AIDS. But a summer night in middle-class suburbia was the great generational equalizer, a place far away from people like Aaron and the Ache brothers. A place far away from young women being murdered.

Valerie would have had fun tonight.

Mom opened the back door. "Telephone," she said shortly.

"Who is it?"

Her voice was like a closed fist. "Jessica." She made a face when she said it, like the name tasted bad on her lips.

Myron tried not to sprint. He walk/ran up the back steps and into the kitchen. The kitchen had been completely redone last year. Why, Myron couldn't say. No one in the house cooked, unless you count microwaving Celeste frozen pizzas.

"I'll take it in the basement," he said.

A grunt from Mom. No wisecrack. Like Esperanza, Mom too held grudges. Especially when it came to her little boy.

He closed the door, grabbed the receiver, heard his mother hang up the extension. "Jess?"

"Is this Stallions 'R' Us?"

As usual her voice made him soar. "Why, yes it is. What can we do for you, ma'am?"

"I'm looking for a true stallion."

"You called the right place. Any preference?"

"Well hung," she replied. "But you'll do."

"Nice talk."

There was a lot of noise in the background. "What took you so long to pick up?" she asked.

"I was outside. Playing with Timmy and the kids."

"Did I interrupt?"

"Nope. Game just ended."

"Your mom sounded a tad frosty on the phone."

"She gets that way," Myron said.

"She used to like me."

"She still does."

"And Esperanza?"

"Esperanza never liked you."

"Oh yeah," she said.

"You still at the Grand Bretagne Hotel?" Myron asked. "Room 207?"

Pause. "Were you spying on me?"

"No."

"Then how do you know—"

"Long story. I'll tell you about it when you get home. Where are you?"

"Kennedy Airport. We just landed."

His heart did a quick twirl. "You're home?"

"I will be as soon as I find my luggage." She hesitated. "Will you come right over?"

"I'm on my way."

"Wear something I can easily rip off your bod," she said. "I'll be waiting in the tub with all kinds of exotic oils from overseas."

"Hussy."

There was another hesitation. Then Jessica said, "I love you, you know. I get funny sometimes, but I do love you."

"Never mind that. Tell me more about the oils."

She laughed. "Hurry now."

He put the receiver back in its cradle. He quickly stripped down and showered. A cold shower for the time being. He was whistling "Tonight" from *West Side Story*. He dried himself off and checked out his closet. Something in the easy-to-rip-off family. Found it. Snap buttons. He sprinkled on a little cologne. Myron rarely wore cologne, but Jess liked it. He heard the doorbell ring as he was bounding up the stairs.

"I'll get it," he called out.

Two uniformed police officers were at the door.

"Are you Myron Bolitar?" the taller one asked.

"Yes."

"Detective Roland Dimonte sent us. We would appreciate it if you would come with us."

"Where?"

"Queens Homicide."

"What for?"

"Roger Quincy has been captured. He's a suspect in the murder of Valerie Simpson."

"So?"

The shorter cop spoke for the first time. "Mr. Bolitar, do you know Roger Quincy?"

"No."

"You've never met him?"

"Not to my knowledge." Not to my knowledge. Lawyer talk for *no*.

The officers exchanged a glance.

"You better come with us," the taller cop said.

"Why?"

"Because Mr. Quincy refuses to make a statement until he talks with you."

23

Myron called Jessica's place and left a message that he'd be late.

When they arrived at the precinct, Dimonte greeted Myron at the door. He was chewing a wad of gum or maybe it was spitting tobacco. And he was smiling a whole lot. He wore a different pair of boots this time. Still snakeskin, still hideous. But these were bright yellow with blue fringes.

"Glad you could make it," Dimonte said.

Myron pointed to the boots. "Mug a cheerleader, Rolly?"

Dimonte laughed. This wasn't good. "Come on, smart-guy," he said with something approaching good nature. He led Myron down a corridor, threading between lots of bored-looking cops. Almost every one of them had a cup of coffee in their hands, leaning against a wall or refreshment machine, pleading some pathetic case to a nodding head.

"No press," Myron noted.

"They haven't been told of Quincy's capture yet," Dimonte said. "But it'll leak soon enough."

"You going to leak it?"

He shrugged happily. "The public has a right to know."

"Sure."

"What about you, Bolitar? You want to come clean?"

"Come clean on what?"

He shrugged again. Mr. Carefree. "Suit yourself."

"I don't know him, Rolly."

"Guess he got your name out of the yellow pages, huh?"

Myron stayed silent. No point in arguing now.

Dimonte opened a door into a small interrogation room. Two cops were already in there. Their neckties were loosened low enough to double as a belt. They'd been working Roger Quincy over pretty good, but Quincy did not seem too agitated. In most movies or TV shows a prisoner in a holding cell wear stripes or grays. But in reality they wear loud, fluorescent orange. Better to see them should they opt to flee.

Roger Quincy's eyes lit up when he saw Myron. He was younger than Myron had expected—early thirties, though he probably could have passed for mid-twenties. He was thin, his face pretty in a feminine way. His fingers were graceful and elongated. He looked like a ballet dancer.

From his chair Roger Quincy waved and said, "Thanks for coming, Myron."

Myron looked at Dimonte. Dimonte smiled back. "Don't know him, huh?" He nodded to the other cops. "Come on, guys. Let's leave the two buddies alone."

A few quiet snickers later, the cops were gone. Myron sat in the chair across the table from Roger Quincy.

"Do I know you?" Myron asked.

"No, I don't think so." Quincy extended his hand. "I'm Roger Quincy."

Quincy's hand felt like a small bird. Myron gave it a quick shake. "How do you know my name?"

"Oh, I'm a big sports fan," he said. "I know I don't look the type, but I've been one for years. I don't follow basketball that closely anymore. Tennis is my favorite. Do you play at all?"

"Just a little."

"I'm not very good, but I try." His eyes lit up again. "Tennis is such a magnificent sport when you think about it. A competitive acrobatic dance really. A small ball hurls at you with unearthly velocity and you have to move, set your feet, hit the ball back using a racket. Everything has to be calculated in a matter of moments: the speed of the oncoming ball, the spot it will land, the spin on it, the angle of the bounce, the distance between your hand and the center of the racket head, the stroke you will use, the placement of your return. It's amazing when you think about it."

Two words: Looney Tunes.

"Uh, Roger, you didn't answer my question," Myron said. "How do you know me?"

"I'm sorry." He flashed a shy smile. "I get overexcited sometimes. Some people think it's a flaw. Me, I'd rather be like that than some couch potato. Did I mention that I'm also a basketball fan?"

"Yes."

"That's how I know your name. I saw you play at Duke." He smiled like that explained everything.

"Okay," Myron said, struggling to keep a patient tone. "So why did you tell the police you wanted to talk to me?"

"Because I did. Want to talk to you, that is."

"Why?"

"They think I killed Valerie, Myron."

"Did you?"

His mouth made a surprised little O. "Of course not. What kind of man do you think I am?"

Myron shrugged. "The kind who stalks young girls. The kind who harassed Valerie Simpson, who followed her around, called her repeatedly, wrote her long letters, frightened her."

He waved Myron off with those long fingers. "You're exaggerating," he said. "I courted Valerie Simpson. I loved her. I cared about her well-being. I was merely a persistent suitor."

"She wanted you to leave her alone."

He laughed. "So she turned me down. Big deal. Am I the first man ever rejected by a beautiful woman? I just don't give up as easily as most. I sent her flowers. I wrote her love letters. I asked her out again. I tried different tactics. Do you ever read romance novels?"

"Not really."

"The hero and heroine are always rejecting each other. Through wars or pirate attacks or high society parties, the couple fight and claw and seem to hate each other. But deep down they are in love. They're repressing their true feelings, see? That's how it was with Valerie and me. There was an undeniable tension there. A high-voltage surge between us."

"Uh-huh," Myron said. "Roger, why did you want to see me?"

"I thought you could talk to the police for me."

"And tell them what?"

"That I didn't kill Valerie. That she was in imminent danger from someone else."

"Who?"

"I thought you knew."

"What makes you think that?"

"Valerie told me. Right before she was murdered."

"She told you what exactly?"

"That she was in danger."

"In danger of what?"

"I thought you'd know."

Myron raised his hand. "Slow down a second, okay? Let's start at the beginning. You were at the U.S. Open."

"Yes."

"Why?"

"I go every year. I'm a big fan. I love to watch the matches. They're so mesmerizing—"

"I think we covered that already, Roger. So you went as a fan. Your going had nothing to do with Valerie Simpson? You didn't follow her there?"

"Of course not. I had no idea she'd even be there."

"Okay, so what happened?"

"I was sitting in the stadium watching Duane Richwood demolish Ivan Restovich. Incredible performance. I mean, Duane slaughtered him." He smiled. "But why am I telling you this? You're his agent, right?"

"Yes."

"Can you get me his autograph?"

"Sure."

"Not tonight, of course. Tomorrow maybe?"

"Maybe." Earth to Roger. "But let's stick with Valerie right now. You were watching Duane's match."

"Exactly." His voice grew serious. "I wish I'd known you were Duane Richwood's agent then, Myron. Maybe everything would have been okay then. Maybe Valerie would still be alive and I'd be the hero who saved her and she'd have to stop denying her true feelings and let me into her life and let me protect her forevermore."

Myron remembered a quote from *Man of La Mancha:* "I can see the coo-coo singing in the coo-coo berry tree."

"What happened, Roger?"

"The match was basically over so I checked my program. Arantxa Sanchez-Vicario was about to start her match on court sixteen, so I figured I'd go over there and get a good seat. Arantxa's a wonderful player. Such a hustler. Her brothers Emilio and Javier are pros also. Nice players, but they don't have her heart."

"So you left the stadium," Myron tried

"I left the stadium. I had a few minutes, so I went over to the booth near the front entrance. The one with all the TV monitors giving the scores of the other matches. I saw that Steffi had already won and that Michael Chang had been dragged into a fifth set. I was checking out some doubles matches on the board. Men's doubles, I think. Ken Flach was one of the people. No, it was . . . I can't remember."

"Stay with me, Roger."

"Anyway, that's when I saw Valerie."

"Where?"

"By the front gate. She was trying to get in, but the guard wouldn't let her. She didn't have a ticket. She was very upset, that was clear. You know, the Open is always sold out. Every year. But I still couldn't believe what I was seeing. The guard wouldn't let her in. Valerie Simpson. He didn't even recognize her. So naturally I went to her aid."

Naturally. "What did you do?"

"I got my hand stamped by another guard and walked outside the gate. Then I came up behind her and tapped her on the shoulder. When she turned around I couldn't believe what I saw."

"What?"

"I know Valerie Simpson," he said, his words slower now. "Even you will have to concede that. I've seen every match she ever played in. I saw her at work. I saw her at play. I've seen her on the streets, on the court, at her house, practicing with that slimy coach of hers. I've seen her happy and sad, up and down, in triumph and defeat. I saw her progress from an enthusiastic teenager to a fierce competitor to a despondent, lifeless beauty. My heart has ached for her so many times, I've lost count. But I'd never seen her like this."

"Like what?"

"So scared. She was absolutely terrified."

Little wonder, Myron thought. Daffy Duck here sneaks up behind her and taps her on her shoulder. "Did she recognize you?"

"Of course."

"What did she do then?"

"She asked for my help."

Myron arched a skeptical eyebrow. He'd learned the technique from Win.

"It's true," Roger insisted. "She said she was in danger. She said she needed to get in and see you."

"She mentioned me by name?"

"Yes. I'm telling you, she was desperate. She pleaded with the guard, but he wouldn't listen. So I came up with an idea."

"What was that?"

"Scalp a ticket," he answered. He was clearly pleased with himself. "There were dozens of scalpers hanging around the subway entrance. I found one. A black man. Nice enough fellow. He wanted a hundred and fifty dollars. I told him that was way too much. They always start high. The scalpers, I mean. You have to negotiate with them. They expect it. But Valerie would have none of that. She just accepted his price. That's Valerie. No head for money. If we'd gotten married, I would have had to handle the finances. She's too impulsive."

"Focus with me, Roger. What happened after you bought the ticket?"

His face went soft and dreamy. "She thanked me," he said, like he'd seen a burning bush. "It was the first time she ever opened up to me. I knew then that my patience had won out. After all this time I'd finally cracked the face. Funny, isn't it? For years I tried so hard to make her love me. And then when I least expect it, boom!—love crashed into my life."

I, me, I, me, I, me. Even Valerie's murder he could only see in terms of himself. "What did she do then?" Myron asked.

"I escorted her through the gates. She asked me if I knew what you looked liked. I said, you mean Myron Bolitar the basketball player? She said yes. I said yes, I knew. She said she needed to find you." He leaned forward. Earnest. "You see what I mean? If I had known you were Duane's agent I would have known exactly where you were. I would have led her right to you. Then everything would have been all right. I'd have gotten a bigger thank-you and that priceless Valerie Simpson smile all for me. I'd have saved her life. I would have been her hero." He shook his head for what might have been. "It would have been perfect."

"But instead?" Myron tried.

"We split up. She asked me to cover the outside courts while she searched the Food Court and the stadium area. We were going to meet back by the Perrier booth every fifteen minutes. I took off and began my search. I was anxious. Finding you would have proved my undying love—"

"Yeah, I got that part." This guy must have been gobs of fun for ol' Rolly to interrogate. "What happened next?"

"I heard a gunshot," Quincy continued. "Then I heard screams. I ran back toward the Food Court. By the time I got there a crowd had formed. You were running toward the body. She was on the ground. So still. You bent down and cradled her body. My dreams. My life. My happiness. Dead. I knew what the police would think. They tormented me for courting her. Called me names. Heck, they threatened to put me in jail for asking her out—what were they going to think now? They never understood the bond between us. The attraction."

"So you ran," Myron said.

"Yes. I went to my place and packed a bag. Then I took out the maximum amount on my MAC card. I saw on TV once how the police tracked a guy down by where he used his credit cards, so I wanted to make sure I had enough cash. Smart, huh?"

"Ingenious," Myron agreed. But he felt his heart sink. Valerie Simpson had had no one. She'd been alone. When danger struck she turned to Myron, a man she barely knew. And someone had murdered her. A painful pang consumed him.

"I stayed in crummy motels and used fake names," Quincy rambled. "But someone must have recognized me. Well, you know the rest. When they caught me, I asked for you. I thought you'd be able to explain to them what really happened." Quincy leaned forward, whispered conspiratorially. "That Detective Dimonte can be rather hostile."

"Uh-huh."

"The only time he smiled was when I mentioned your name."

"Oh?"

"I told him you and I were friends. I hope you don't mind."

"Not at all," Myron said.

24

M YRON FACED DIMONTE AND SIDEKICK KRIN-
sky in the adjoining interrogation room. It was identical to the other one in every way. Dimonte was still gleeful.

"Would you care for an attorney?" he asked sweetly.

Myron looked at him. "Your face is positively beaming,
Rolly. New moisturizer?"

The smile stayed. "I'll take that as a no."

"Am I under arrest?"

"Of course not. Have a seat. Care for a drink?"

"Sure."

"What would you like?" Quite the host, that Rolly. "Coke?
Coffee? Orange juice?"

"Got any Yoo-Hoo?"

Dimonte looked at Krinsky. Krinsky shrugged and went to
check. Dimonte folded his hands and put them on the table.
"Myron, why did Roger Quincy ask for you?"

"He wanted to speak to me."

Dimonte smiled. Mr. Patience. "Yes, but why you?"

"I'm afraid I can't answer that."

"Can't," Dimonte said. "Or won't?"

"Can't."

"Why can't you?"

"I think it falls under attorney-client privilege. I have to check."

"Check with who?"

"With whom," Myron said.

"What?"

"Check with whom. Not who, whom. Prepositional phrase."

Dimonte nodded. "So it's going to be like that, is it?"

"Like what?"

His voice was a little rougher now. "You're a suspect, Bolitar. No, check that. You're *the* suspect."

"What about Roger?"

"He's the trigger man. I'm sure of that. But he's too much of a nut job to have done it on his own. Way we figure it, you set the whole thing up. Had him do the dirty work."

"Uh-huh. And my motive?"

"Valerie Simpson was having an affair with Duane Richwood. That's why his phone number was in her book. A white girl with a black guy. How would the sponsors have reacted to that?"

"It's the nineties, Rolly. There's even a mixed marriage on the Supreme Court."

Dimonte put a boot up on a chair and leaned on the raised knee. "Times may change, Bolitar, but sponsors still don't like black boys boffing white chicks." He tickled his chin with two fingers. "Let me run this by you, see how it sounds: Duane is a bit of a coonhound. He sniffs out white meat. He nails Valerie Simpson, but she doesn't fancy the idea of being a one-nighter. We know she's a bit of a fruitcake, spent time in an asylum. Probably a bunny burner to boot."

"Bunny burner?"

"You seen *Fatal Attraction*?"

Myron nodded. "Oh. Bunny burner. Right."

"So like I said, Valerie Simpson is crazy. Her elevator don't stop at every floor. But now she's also pissed off. So she calls up Duane just like it says in her little diary and threatens to go to the press. Duane is scared. Like he was yesterday when I came by. So who does he call? You. That's when you hatch your little scheme."

Myron nodded. "That'll hold up in court."

"What? Greed isn't a good motive?"

"I might as well confess right here."

"Fine, smart-guy. You play it that way."

Krinsky returned. He shook his head. No Yoo-Hoo.

"You want to tell me why Quincy called you first?" Dimonte continued.

"Nope."

"Why the hell not?"

"Because you've hurt my feelings."

"Don't fuck with me, Bolitar. I'll throw your ass into a holding cell with twenty psychos and tell them you're a child molester." He smiled. "He'll like that, won't he, Krinsky?"

"Yeah," Krinsky said, mirroring Dimonte's smile.

Myron nodded. "Right. Okay, now I say, what do you mean? Then you say, a tasty morsel like you will be popular in the slammer. Then I say, please don't. Then you say, don't bend over to pick up the soap. Then you both give me a cop snicker."

"What the fuck you talking about?"

"Don't waste my time, Rolly."

"You think I won't throw your ass in jail?"

Myron stood. "I know you won't. If you thought you could I'd be handcuffed by now."

"Where the fuck do you think you're going?"

"Arrest me or get out of my way. I got places to go, people to see."

"I know you're dirty, Bolitar. That whacko didn't ask for you by accident. He thought you could save him. That's why you've been playing cop with us. Pretending to investigate on your own. You just wanted to stay close, find out what we knew."

"You got it all figured out, Rolly."

"We'll grill him and grill him and grill him until he gives you up."

"No, you won't. As his attorney I am forbidding any interrogation of my client."

"You can't represent him. Ever heard of conflict of interest?"

"Until I find him someone else I'm still his attorney of record."

Myron opened the door and stepped into the corridor. He was surprised to see Esperanza. So were the cops. Every one of them up and down the corridor stared at her hungrily. Probably just being careful, Myron mused, afraid maybe Esperanza had a concealed weapon in her tight jeans. Yeah, that was probably it.

"Win called," she said. "He's looking for you."

"What's up?"

"He followed Duane. There's something he thinks you should see."

25

—————

ESPERANZA AND MYRON SHARED A YELLOW cab to the Chelsea Hotel on Twenty-third Street between Seventh and Eighth. The cab smelled like a Turkish whorehouse, which was an improvement over most.

"Win will be seated in a red chair near the house phones," she told him when they stopped. "It's to the right of the concierge's desk. He'll be reading a newspaper. If he's not reading a newspaper, the coast isn't clear. Ignore him and walk out. He'll meet you at the Billiards Club."

"Win said that?"

"Yes."

"Even that part about the coast not being clear?"

"Yes."

Myron shook his head. "You want to come?"

"Can't. I still have studying to do."

"Thanks for finding me."

She nodded.

Win was seated where advertised. He was reading the *Wall Street Journal* so the coast was clear. Oooo. Win looked exactly like himself, except a black wig covered the blond locks. Dr.

Disguise. Myron sat next to him and whispered, "The white rabbit turns yellow when the black dog urinates on him."

Win continued to read. "You said to contact you if Duane did anything unusual."

"Yep."

"He arrived here about two hours ago. He took the elevator to the third floor and knocked on the door to room 322. A woman answered. They embraced. He entered. The door closed."

"That's not good," Myron said.

Win turned the page. Bored.

"Do you know who the woman is?" Myron asked.

He shook his head. "Black. Five-seven, five-eight. Slim. I took the liberty of booking room 323. The peephole has a view of Duane's door."

Myron thought of Jessica waiting for him. In a warm tub. With those exotic oils.

Damn.

"I'll stay if you want," Win said.

"No. I'll handle this."

"Fine." Win stood. "I'll see you at the match tomorrow, if our boy isn't too tired to play."

Myron took the stairs to the third floor. He peered out into the corridor. No one. With key in hand he hurried down to room 323 and went inside. Win, as usual, was right. From the keyhole he had a good, albeit convex, view of the door to room 322. Now he had to wait.

But wait for what?

What the hell was he doing here? Jessica was waiting for him in a bathtub filled with exotic oils—the thought made his body both sing and ache—and here he was, playing Peeping Tom over . . .

Over what?

What was he after anyway? Duane had explained his connection to Valerie Simpson. They'd briefly been lovers. What was so weird about that? They were both attractive, both in their early twenties, both tennis players. So what was the big deal? The racial thing? Nothing unusual about that anymore. Hadn't he just pointed that out to Dimonte?

So what was Myron doing with his eye pressed against a peephole? Duane was a client, for chrissake, an important client. What right did Myron have to invade his privacy like this? And for what reason—because his girlfriend didn't like the fact that Duane was having affairs? So what? That wasn't Myron's concern. Myron wasn't Duane's social worker, parole officer, priest, shrink—he was his agent. His job was to get the maximum return for his client, not make morality judgments.

On the other hand, what the hell was Duane doing here? Maybe he liked to play the field, fine and dandy, no problem. But tonight of all nights? It's crazy. Tomorrow was the biggest day of Duane's career. Nationally televised match. His first U.S. Open quarterfinal. His first match against a seeded player. The launching of the Nike spots. Kind of a strange night for a romantic tryst in a hotel room.

Duane Richwood, the Wilt Chamberlain of professional tennis.

Myron didn't like it.

Duane had always been a bit of a mystery. In reality Myron knew nothing about his past. He'd been a runaway, or so Duane said, but who knew for sure? Why had he run in the first place?

Where was his family now? Myron had created a spin on the facts—portraying Duane as the poor street kid struggling to escape the shackles of poverty. But was that the truth? Duane seemed like a good kid—intelligent, well-spoken, well-mannered—but could that all be an act? The young man Myron had known would not be spending such an important night screwing in a strange hotel room—which, of course, circled Myron back to the question:

So what?

Myron was his agent. Period. The kid had talent to burn and a terrific court sense. He was good-looking and could make a lot of money in endorsements. In the end, that was all that mattered to an agent. Not a player's love life. The kid was a dream on the court. Who cared what he was like off it? Myron was getting too close to this. He had no perspective anymore. He had a business to run, and spying on one of his biggest clients, invading that client's privacy, was not good business sense.

He should leave. He should go to Jessica and talk to her about it, see what she thought.

Ten more minutes.

He needed only two. He switched eyes just as the door to room 322 opened. Duane appeared, or at least the back of him. Myron saw a woman's arms go around his neck, pulling him down. They embraced. He couldn't see the woman's face, just the arms. Myron thought about Wanda's intuition. She had been so sure of herself, so blind to this possibility. Myron understood. He'd been there. Love has a way of putting on the blinders.

"Putting on the blinders," Myron muttered to himself. "Unbelievable."

After the hug broke, Duane straightened up. The woman's arms dropped out of sight. Duane looked ready to leave. Myron pushed his eye closer to the peephole. Duane spun and looked directly at Myron's door. Myron almost jumped back. For a second it was like Duane was looking right at Myron, like he knew Myron was there.

Once again Myron wondered how he had ended up here. If his job included checking on the promiscuity of every athlete he represented, he would spend his life peering through peepholes. Duane was a kid. Twenty-one years old. He wasn't even married or officially engaged. Nothing Myron was seeing was connected in any way with Valerie Simpson's murder.

Until Duane finally stepped away.

Duane had given the woman one more brief hug. There had been muffled voices, but Myron couldn't make out any specific words. Duane looked left, then right, then moved away. The woman was already starting to close the door, but she glanced out one last time. And that was when Myron saw her.

The woman was Deanna Yeller.

26

THE MORNING.

Myron had not confronted Duane. He'd stumbled to Jessica's in something of a daze. He'd opened the door with his key and said, "I'm sorry. I had to—"

Jessica shushed him with a kiss. Then a bigger kiss. Hungrier kiss. Myron tried to fight off her advances, though some might call his struggle less than valiant.

He rolled over in the bed. Jessica was gently padding across the room. Naked. She slipped into a silk robe. He watched, as he always did, with utter fascination. "You're so hot," he said, "you make my teeth sweat."

She smiled. There is something that happens to men when Jessica looks at them. Shallow breathing. Fluttering stomach. A cruel longing. But her smile raised all those symptoms to the tenth power.

"Good morning," she said. She bent down and kissed him gently. "How are you feeling?"

"My ears are still popping from last night."

"Nice to know I still have the touch," she said.

The understatement of the millennium. "Tell me about your trip."

"Tell me about your murder first."

He did. Jess was a great listener. She never interrupted, except to ask the right question. She looked at him steadily without a lot of that phony head nodding or out-of-context smiling. Her eyes focused in on him as if he were the only person in the world. He felt light-headed and happy and scared.

"This Valerie got to you," Jessica said when he finished.

"She had no one. Her life was in danger and she had no one."

"She had you."

"I only met her once. She wasn't even signed yet."

"Doesn't matter. She knew what you were. If I were in trouble, you'd be the person I'd run to." She tilted her head. "How did you know my room number and hotel?"

"Aaron. He was trying to be intimidating. He succeeded."

"Aaron threatened to hurt me?"

"You, me, my mom, Esperanza."

She hesitated, thinking. "Esperanza would be my choice. I mean, if it has to be one of us."

"I'll tell him." He took her hand. "I'm glad you're home."

"No third degree?"

Myron shook his head.

"But I owe you an explanation."

"I don't want one," he said. "I just want to be with you. I love you. I've always loved you. We are soul mates."

"Soul mates?"

He nodded.

"When did you decide this?" she asked.

"A long time ago."

"So why not tell me before now?"

He shrugged. "I didn't want to scare you off."

"And now?"

"Now it's more important to tell you how I feel."

The room was still. "What am I supposed to say to that?" she asked.

"Nothing."

"I do love you, Myron. You know that."

"I know."

Silence. A long silence.

Jessica crossed the room. She was not self-conscious about her body. Then again, she had no reason to be. "It seems to me," she began, "there are a lot of weird connections with this murder. But there is one overriding constant."

Change of subjects. That was okay. Enough had been said for one day. "What?" Myron asked.

"Tennis," she said. "Alexander Cross is killed at a tennis club. Valerie Simpson is murdered at the National Tennis Center. Valerie and Duane have an affair—both are professional tennis players. Those two kids who supposedly killed Alexander Cross—what's their names?"

"Errol Swade and Curtis Yeller."

"Swade and Yeller," she repeated. "They were both up to no good at a tennis club. The Ache brothers and Aaron are connected to an agency who deals with tennis players. That leaves us with Deanna Yeller."

"What about her?"

"Her sleeping with Duane. It can't just be a coincidence."

"So?"

"So how would she have met Duane?"

"I don't know," Myron said.

"Does she play tennis?"

"What if she does?"

"Keeps things constant." She stopped. "I don't know. I'm ranting. It's just that everything circles back to tennis—except for Deanna Yeller."

Myron thought about it a moment. Nothing clicked, but something did rumble somewhere in the back of his brain.

"Just a thought," she said.

He sat up. "Before you said 'supposedly' killed Alexander Cross. What did you mean?"

"What real evidence do you have that Swade and Yeller murdered the Cross kid?" she asked. "They might have just been convenient scapegoats. Think about it a second. Yeller was conveniently killed by the police. Swade has conveniently fallen off the face of the earth. Who better to take the fall?"

"Then who do you think killed Alexander Cross?" he asked.

She shrugged. "Probably Swade and Yeller. But who knows for sure?"

More rumbling in the brain. But still nothing surfaced. Myron checked his watch. Seven-thirty.

"You in a rush?" she asked.

"A little."

"I thought Duane Richwood doesn't play until one," she said.

"I'm trying to land a kid named Eddie Crane. He's playing in the juniors at ten."

"Can I come along?" she asked.

"Sure."

"What are your chances of landing him?" she asked.

"I think they're pretty good. His father might be a problem."

"The father doesn't like you?"

"I think he'd prefer a bigger agency," Myron said.

"Should I smile sweetly at him?" she asked.

Myron thought a moment. "Flash a little cleavage. I'm not sure this guy's into subtle."

"Anything to get a client," she said.

"Maybe you should practice a little first," he said.

"Practice what?"

"Flashing cleavage. I'm told it's something of an art."

"I see. And on whom should I practice?"

Myron spread his hands. "I'm willing to volunteer my services."

"The sacrifices you make for clients," she said. "It's heroic, really."

"So what do you say?"

Jessica gave him a look. *The* look, actually. Myron felt it in his toes, to name one place. She leaned toward him. "No."

"No?"

She put her lips to his ear. "Let's try out my new oils first."

One word: Yowzer.

27

J ESSICA HADN'T NEED TO FLASH CLEAVAGE.
Both Cranes were immediately entranced. Mrs.
Crane chatted with Jess about her books. Mr. Crane couldn't
stop smiling and sucking in his gut. At the start of the second
set Mr. Crane tried to chew down the commission a half point.
A very good sign. Myron made a mental note to bring Jess to
more business gatherings.

There were other agents there. Lots of them. Most wore
business suits and had their hair slicked back. They ranged in
age, but most looked pretty young. Several tried to approach,
but Mr. Crane shooed them away.

"Vultures," Jessica whispered to Myron as one forced his
card on Mr. Crane.

"Just trying to hustle business," Myron said.

"You're defending them?"

"I do the same thing, Jess. If they're not aggressive they don't
have a chance. You think the Cranes are going to come to
them?"

"But still. You don't hang around like these guys."

"What exactly am I doing now?"

Jessica thought a second. "Yeah, but you're cute."

Hard to argue. Eddie crushed his opponent 6–0, 6–0, but the match was not as close as the score indicated. Eddie lacked finesse. He relied on power. But what power. His racket ripped through the still air like the reaper's scythe. The ball shot off the strings as though from a bazooka. The finesse would come. But for now the awesome power was more than enough.

After the players shook hands Eddie's parents went onto the court.

"Do me a favor," Myron said to Jess.

"What?"

"Get rid of the parents for a couple of minutes. I want to talk to Eddie alone."

She did it with a lunch invitation. Jessica escorted Mr. and Mrs. Crane to the Racquets restaurant overlooking the Grandstand. Myron accompanied Eddie to the locker room. The kid had barely broken a sweat. Myron had exerted himself more just watching. Eddie walked with big, unhurried steps, a towel draped around his neck, completely relaxed.

"I told TruPro I wasn't interested," Eddie said.

Myron nodded. That explained Aaron's generous offer to let Myron represent Eddie. "How did they respond?"

"They were pretty pissed," Eddie said.

"I bet."

"I think I want to go with your agency," he said.

"How do your parents feel?"

"Doesn't matter really. They both know it's my decision."

They walked a few more steps.

"Eddie, I need to ask you about Valerie."

He half smiled. "Are you really trying to find her killer?"

"Yes."

"Why?"

"I don't know. It's just something I have to do."

Eddie nodded. The answer was good enough for him. "Shoot."

"You first met Valerie at Pavel's camp in Florida?"

"Right."

"How did you two become friends?"

"You ever been to Pavel's academy?" Eddie asked.

"No."

"You might not get it." Eddie Crane stopped, brushed the hair from his eyes, continued. "It probably sounds weird—a sixteen-year-old girl and a nine-year-old boy being close friends. That's pretty normal in tennis. You don't make friends with kids your own age. They're the enemy. Val and I were both lonely, I guess. And because of our differences we weren't threats to each other. I guess that's how it started."

"Did she ever mention Alexander Cross?"

"Yeah, a couple of times. They dated or something."

"Did you get the impression they were serious?"

He shrugged. The guard checked their passes and let them enter. "Not really. Tennis was her life. Boyfriends were peripheral."

"Tell me more about Pavel's academy. What was it like for Valerie?"

"What was it like?" Eddie grinned sadly, shook his head. "It was like one big game of King of the Mountain. Every kid is trying to knock off every other kid."

"And Valerie was king of the woman's side?"

Eddie nodded. "The undisputed king."

"Did Pavel and Valerie get along?"

"Yeah. At first anyway. He motivated Val like no one else

could. She would practice for hours with his assistants, and just when you thought she couldn't take one more step Pavel would come out and boom! it was like an energy boost. Val was a great player, but Pavel knew how to get her competitive juices really flowing. When he was there, she blew away everyone else. Diving, stretching, running down every lob. She was incredible."

"So when did things start going wrong?"

Eddie shrugged. "When she started losing." He said it like it was the most natural thing in the world.

"What happened?"

"I don't know." He stopped again, thinking. "She stopped caring, I guess. It happens to a lot of the players. They burn out. Too much pressure too fast."

"What did Pavel do?"

"He tried all his old tricks. You see, Pavel fostered the whole dog-eat-dog atmosphere. It weeded out the weak, he told me. But Valerie wasn't responding anymore. She still beat most of the girls. But when she played against the game's greats—Steffi, Monica, Gabriela, Martina—she didn't have the heart to beat them anymore."

Eddie sat in a chair in front of his locker. Very few people were around. The floor, carpeted in an office-brown, was littered with little pieces of wrap and bandaging. Myron sat down next to him. "You told me you saw Valerie a few days before she died."

"Yeah," Eddie said. "In the lobby of the Plaza." He took off his shirt. The kid was bony. The kind of bony where it appears the chest concaves into the heart. "I hadn't seen her in a long time."

"What did she say to you?"

"She was going to make a comeback. She seemed pretty excited about the idea, kinda like the old Val. Then she gave me your number and told me to stay away from Pavel and TruPro."

"Did she say why you should stay away?"

"No."

"Did she say anything else?"

He paused, his mind flashing back. "Not really. She was kinda in a hurry. She said she had to go out and settle something."

"Settle what?"

"I don't know. She didn't say."

"What day was this?" Myron asked.

"Thursday, I think."

"Do you remember the time?"

"Must have been around six."

Valerie had called Duane's apartment Thursday at six-fifteen. Settle something. Settle what? Settle her relationship with Duane? Or expose it? And what if she did threaten that? Would Duane kill her to stop her? Myron didn't think so, especially in light of the fact that Duane was serving a tennis ball in front of several thousand people when she was shot.

Eddie slipped out of his sneakers and socks.

"I got two tickets to the Yankees for Wednesday night," Myron said. "You want to go?"

Eddie smiled. "I thought you didn't do that."

"Do what?"

"That ass-kissing stuff."

"I do. Every agent does. I'm not above it. But in this case I actually thought it might be fun."

Eddie stood. "Should I be skeptical of your motives?" he asked.

"Only if you're smart."

DUANE LIKED TO be alone before a match. Win had taught him meditation techniques, *sans* the dirty videotapes, and you could usually find him curled up in a corner, sitting in the lotus position with his eyes closed. He didn't like to be disturbed, which was good. Myron wasn't sure he wanted to see him right now anyway. His main responsibility, he knew, was still to help his client perform his best—especially on this, the most important day of Duane's career. Raising the issue of Duane's late-night rendezvous with Deanna Yeller would be a distraction. A major distraction.

It would have to wait.

The crowd was huge. Everyone had been waiting for this match between the upstart American Duane Richwood and the cool Czech Michel Brishny, a former number one player now ranked fifth. Myron and Jessica took their seats in the front row. Jess looked incredible in a simple yellow sundress. Spectators gaped. Nothing new there. Without a doubt, the TV cameras would be getting plenty of shots of the box today. Between Jess's beauty and her fame in the literary world they wouldn't be able to resist.

Myron debated having her hold up one of his business cards. Nah. Too tacky.

A bevy of favorites was already in their seats. Ned Tunwell and other Nike VIPs crowded a corner box. Ned waved like a windmill on LSD. Myron gave a small wave back. Two boxes behind them sat chubby Roy O'Connor, the rotund president of TruPro. Sitting with him was Aaron. Aaron had his face tilted to the sun, soaking up the rays. He was garbed in his usual attire—white suit, no shirt. Across the way Myron also spotted Senator Cross in a box jammed with gray-haired lawyer types—the exception being Gregory Caufield. Myron still wanted to talk to Gregory. Perhaps an opportunity would present itself after the match. The buxom blonde from the other day was back in the same seat. The shapely lass gave Myron another small wave. He didn't wave back.

Myron turned to Jessica. She smiled at him.

"You're beautiful," he said.

"More beautiful than the blonde with the big boobs?" she asked.

"Who?" Myron said.

"The Silicone She-Beast giving you the eye."

"I don't know what you mean." Then: "How do you know they're silicone?"

The players took the court for warm-ups. Two minutes later Pavel Menansi made his grand entrance. There was a smattering of applause. Pavel displayed his gratitude with a circular hand gesture. Very popelike. He wore tennis whites, with a green sweater tied around his neck. The smile was on full blast. Pavel made his way toward the TruPro box. Aaron rose, let him in, then sat back down. Pavel and Roy O'Connor shook hands.

It hit Myron like a shot to the solar plexus. "Oh no," he said.

"What?" Jessica asked.

Myron stood. "I've got to go."

"Now?"

"I'll be back. Make my excuses."

28

THE MATCH WAS ON THE CAR RADIO. WFAN, 66 AM. From the sound of it Duane was not playing well. He had just dropped the first set 6–3 when Myron pulled into a lot off Central Park West in Manhattan.

Dr. Julie Abramson lived in a town house half a block down from her office. Myron rang the bell. There was a buzzing noise and then her voice came over the intercom.

"Who is it?"

"Myron Bolitar. It's urgent."

There were a few seconds of silence. Then: "Second floor." The buzzer sounded again. Myron pushed the door open. Julie Abramson was waiting for him on the stairwell.

"Did you call and hang up on me?" she asked.

"Yes."

"Why?"

"To see if you were home."

He arrived at her door. They stood and faced each other. With their height difference—she well under five feet, he six-four—the sight was almost comical.

She looked up. Way up. "I still can't deny or confirm that Valerie Simpson was ever a patient of mine," she said.

"That's okay. I want to ask you about a hypothetical situation."

"A hypothetical situation?"

He nodded.

"And that couldn't wait until Monday?"

"No."

Dr. Abramson sighed. "Come on in."

She had the television turned on to the match. "I should have known," she said. "The TV keeps flashing to Jessica Culver in the players' box, but never you."

"With her there they wouldn't show me anyway."

"The sportscaster says you two are an item. Is that true?"

Myron shrugged. Noncommittal. "What's the score now?" he asked.

"Your client lost the first set 6–3," she said. "He's down 2–0 in this set." She switched off the television with the remote and signaled to a chair. They both sat. "So tell me about your hypothetical situation, Myron."

"I want to start off with a young girl. Fifteen years old. Pretty. From a well-to-do family, parents divorced, the father absent. She dates a boy from a prominent family. She's also a tennis protégée."

"This isn't sounding too hypothetical," Dr. Abramson said.

"Just bear with me a second. The young girl is such a great tennis player that her mother ships her off to an academy run by a world-famous tennis coach. When this young girl arrives at the academy she finds the competition cutthroat. Tennis is the most individual of sports. There is no team spirit here.

There is no camaraderie. Everybody is vying for the approval of the world-famous coach. Tennis is not conducive to making friends." Echoing Eddie's words. "It isolates. Would you say that's true, Doctor?"

"On the level you're talking about, yes."

"So when this young girl is uprooted from the life she has known and tossed into this rather hostile environment, she is not made to feel welcome. Far from it. The other girls see this new tennis protégée as a threat and when they realize what a magnificent player she is, the threat becomes reality. The other girls shun her all the more. She grows even more isolated."

"Okay."

"Now, this world-famous coach, he's a bit Darwinian. Survival of the fittest and all that. He sort of plays a dual role here. On the one hand this isolation will force the girl to search for an escape, a place where she can thrive."

"The tennis court?" Abramson said.

"Exactly. The young girl begins to practice even harder than before. But at the same time the world-famous coach is nice to her. While everyone else is cruel, the world-famous coach praises her. He spends time with her. He gets the most out of her."

"Which in turn," Dr. Abramson interjected, "isolates her from the other girls all the more."

"Right. The young girl becomes dependent on the coach. She thinks he cares and like any eager student she wants—needs—his approval. She begins to play even harder. She also knows that pleasing the world-famous coach will also please her mother. She tries even harder. The cycle continues."

Dr. Abramson had to see where Myron was going with this, but her face remained blank. "Go on," she said.

"The tennis academy is not the real world. It's a secluded domain ruled by the world-famous coach. But he acts like he cares for the young girl. He treats her like she's something special. The young girl plays even harder, pushing herself more than she could ever imagine—not for herself, but to please him. Maybe he offers her a pat on the back after practice. Maybe he rubs her sore shoulders. Maybe they have dinner one night to discuss her tennis. Who knows how it started?"

"How what started?" Abramson asked.

Myron chose to ignore the question. For now. "The young girl and world-famous coach start touring together," he continued. "She starts playing competitive tennis against women who again treat her as a feared rival. But now the young girl and the world-famous coach are alone. On the road. Staying in hotels."

"More isolation," Abramson offered.

"She plays well. She's beautiful, she's young, she's American. The press begins to swarm. The sudden attention frightens her. But the world-famous coach is there to protect her."

"She becomes more dependent on him."

Myron nodded. "Now let's remember that the world-famous coach is a former world-famous player himself. He is accustomed to the narcissistic lifestyle that goes along with being a professional athlete. He is used to doing as he pleases. And that's exactly what he does with this girl."

Silence.

"Could this happen, Doc? In theory?"

Dr. Abramson cleared her throat. "In theory, yes. Whenever a man yields power and authority over a woman the potential for abuse is high. But in your scenario the potential for abuse is maximized. The man is older, the woman no more than a child.

A teacher or a boss might control their victim for a few hours a day, but in your scenario the coach is both omnipotent and omnipresent."

They looked at each other.

"The girl in my scenario," Myron said softly. "Her play would deteriorate if he abused her?"

"Without question."

"What else would happen to her?"

"Every case is different," Abramson replied as though giving a dissertation. "But the results would invariably be catastrophic. A scenario like yours would probably start out for the young girl as nothing more than a crush. This sophisticated, older man is nice to her when nobody else is. He understands and cares about her. She probably doesn't have to invite his advances—they just sort of happen. The young girl may encourage them at first, but probably not. She may even resist, but at the same time she feels responsible. She blames herself."

Myron felt something in the pit of his stomach open wide. "Which causes more problems."

"Yes. You talked about how the world-famous coach isolates her," Abramson continued. "But in your scenario he does more than that. He dehumanizes her. Her adolescence is turned upside down by her tennis greatness. Her life is not about school and friends and family. It's about money and winning. She's become a commodity. She knows that if she displeases him, the commodity becomes worthless. And her being a commodity makes it easier on him too."

"How?" Myron asked.

"A commodity is far easier to abuse than a human being."

Silence.

"So what happens when it's all over?" Myron asked. "When

the world-famous coach uses up the commodity, what happens to her?"

"The young girl would reach out for something—anything—that she thinks might save her."

"The old boyfriend maybe?"

"Perhaps."

"She might even want to get engaged right away."

"That's possible, yes. She may see the old boyfriend as a return to her innocence. In her mind the boyfriend may be raised to savior status."

"And suppose this boyfriend was murdered?"

"You've pulled out the final block," Abramson replied softly. "The young girl was already in need of serious therapy. Now a complete mental breakdown is a very real possibility. Maybe even a likelihood."

Myron felt his heart crumble.

Dr. Abramson looked away for a moment. "But there are other aspects to your scenario that need to be explored," she said, trying to sound offhanded.

"Like?"

"Like what actually occurred during the abuse. If, as you say, the world-famous coach was a narcissistic man, he would only concern himself with his pleasure. He wouldn't worry about her. He probably wouldn't, for example, wear protection. And since this girl is rather young and probably not sexually active, she wouldn't be using oral contraceptives."

Dread flooded Myron's chest. He remembered the rumors. "He got her pregnant."

"In the realm of your scenario," Abramson said, "that is certainly a possibility."

"What would happen . . . ?" Myron stopped. The answer

was obvious. "The world-famous coach would make her get an abortion."

"I imagine so, yes."

Silence.

Myron felt something well up in his eyes. "What she went through . . ." He shook his head. "Everyone thought Valerie was so weak. But in reality—"

"Not Valerie," Abramson corrected. "A young girl. A theoretical young girl in a theoretical situation."

Myron looked up. "Still trying to protect your ass, Doc?"

"You can't say anything, Myron. It's all hypothetical. I will neither confirm nor deny that Valerie Simpson was ever a patient of mine."

He shook his head, stood, and headed for the door. When he reached it, he turned back toward her. "One more hypothetical question," he said. "The world-famous coach. If he's willing to abuse one child, how likely is it he'll do it again?"

Dr. Abramson did not face him. "Very likely," she said.

29

BY THE TIME MYRON GOT BACK TO STADIUM Court, Duane had dropped the first two sets 6–3, 6–1, and it was 2–2 in the third set. Myron sat between Jessica and Win. Pavel Menansi, he immediately noticed, was no longer in his seat. Aaron was still there. Senator Cross and Gregory Caufield were in their box too. Ned Tunwell still sat with his Nike colleagues. Ned was no longer waving. He was, in fact, crying. The entire Nike box looked like a deflated balloon. Henry Hobman was still as a Rodin.

Myron turned to Jessica. She looked concerned but said nothing. She took his hand and gave it a little squeeze. He squeezed back and gave her a small smile. He noticed that she was now wearing a bright pink Ray•Ban cap.

"What's with the cap?" he asked.

"A guy offered me a thousand dollars to wear it."

Myron was familiar with the old advertising trick. Companies—in this case, Ray•Ban—paid anyone seated in the players' boxes to wear the caps during matches, figuring, of course, that there was an excellent chance the person and hence the hat would show up on television. Relatively cheap and effective exposure.

Myron looked at Win. "What about you?"

"I don't do caps," Win replied. "They muss my hair."

"That," Jessica added, "and the guy only offered him five hundred dollars."

Win shrugged. "Sexual discrimination. It's an ugly thing."

More like smart business. Five hundred dollars was the normal rate. But somebody at Ray•Ban realized Jess was both attractive and a celebrity—ergo, extra exposure.

Duane dropped another game. Down 3–2 after losing the first two sets. Not good. The players collapsed in their chairs on either side of the umpire for the changeover. Duane toweled down his racket. He changed shirts. Some female fans whistled. Duane did not smile. He glanced over at their box. Unlike just about any other sport in the world, tennis players are not allowed to talk to their coaches during the match. But Henry did move. He took his hand off his chin and made a fist. Duane nodded.

"Time," the chair ump said.

That was when Pavel made his return.

He entered through the portal on the right near the grandstand carrying an Evian in his hand. Myron's eyes locked on to him. He felt his pulse quicken. Pavel Menansi was still wearing the sweater tied around his neck. He took his seat behind Aaron. Pavel Menansi. He smiled. He laughed. He sipped a cold Evian. He breathed in and out. He lived. People patted his back. Someone asked for an autograph. A young girl. Pavel said something to her. The young girl giggled behind her hand.

"Burgess Meredith," Win said. He was looking at the court, not Myron.

"What?"

"Burgess Meredith."

More Name the *Batman* Criminal. "Not now," Myron said.

"Now. Burgess Meredith."

"Why?"

"Because you're staring. Aaron will pick it up." Win adjusted his sunglasses. "Burgess Meredith."

He was right. "The Penguin."

"Victor Buono."

"King Tut."

"Bruce Lee."

Jessica leaned over. "Trick question," she said.

"No hints," Win said.

"He played Kato," Myron said. "Green Hornet's sidekick. He guest-starred on one episode. I don't know if you could call him a criminal."

"Correct." Silence. Then Win said: "That bad?"

"Worse."

"The police released Valerie's body," Win said. "The funeral is tomorrow."

Myron nodded. On the court Duane served up an ace. Only his second of the match. Myron said, "It may get ugly now."

"How so?"

"I know why the Ache brothers want us out."

"Ah," Win said. "May I assume the Aches will not want you to disseminate this information to the general public?"

"Correct assumption."

"And may I further assume this information is worth the cost of Aaron and an all-star cast?"

"Another correct assumption."

Win sat back. He was very still. He was also smiling. Myron turned to Jessica. Her hand still held his.

"If you get killed," she whispered, "I'll kill you. Soul mate."

Silence.

On the court Duane hit two more aces and then an over-head to tie the third set at three games apiece. Duane looked over at the box. The reflection of the sun off his sunglasses was blinding, giving him a sleek, robotic look. But something in his face had changed. Duane made the fist again.

Henry spoke for the first time. "He's baaack."

30

HENRY HOBMAN WAS GOOD AS HIS WORD. Duane rallied. He took the third set 6–4. Ned Tunwell stopped crying. The fourth set went to a tiebreaker, which Duane won 9–7, saving three match points. Ned started the windmill wave again. Duane won the fifth set 6–2. Ned had to change his underwear.

Final score of the marathon match: 3–6, 1–6, 6–4, 7–6, (9–7), 6–2. Before the combatants had even left the court the word *classic* was being bantered about.

By the time all the congratulations and news conferences ended it was getting late. Jess borrowed Myron's car to visit her mother. Win dropped him off at the office. Esperanza was still there.

"Big win," she said.

"Yup."

"Duane played like shit in the first two sets."

"He had a long night," Myron said. "What have we got?"

Esperanza handed him a stack of papers. "Prenuptial agreement for Jerry Prince. Final copy."

Ah, the beloved prenup. A necessary evil. Myron hated to

recommend them. Marriage should be about love and romance. A prenup, frankly speaking, was about as romantic as licking a litter box. Still, Myron had an obligation to guard the financial well-being of his clients. Too many of these marriages ended in quickie divorces. Gold-digging, it used to be called. Some mistook his concern for sexism. It wasn't. Well-to-do female athletes should do the same.

"What else?" he asked.

"Emmett Roberts wants you to call. He needs your opinion on a car he's buying."

Myron drove a Ford Taurus, hardly qualifying him as *Motor Trend*'s Man of the Year.

Emmett was a fringe basketball player who bounced between bench-sitting in the NBA and starring in the Continental Basketball Association—a sort of basketball minor league where players do nothing but try to impress NBA scouts. Very few do. There were exceptions. John Starks and Anthony Mason of the Knicks, to name two. But for the most part the CBA gymnasiums were yet another haven of shattered dreams, a bottom rung on the ladder before slipping off altogether.

Myron fingered through his Rolodex. Esperanza was good about keeping it up-to-date and in alphabetical order for him. Raston. Ratner. Rextell. Rippard. Roberts. There. Emmett Roberts.

Myron stopped.

"Where's Duane's card?" he asked.

"What?"

Myron quickly skimmed through the rest of the *R*'s. "Duane Richwood isn't in my Rolodex. Could you have misfiled it?"

She dismissed that possibility with a glare. "Look around. It's probably on your desk someplace."

Not on the desk. Myron tried the *D*'s. No Duane.

"I'll make you up a new one," she said, heading for the door. "Try not to lose it this time."

"Thanks a bunch," he said. Still, the missing card gnawed at him. Another coincidence involving Duane? He dialed Emmett Roberts's phone. Emmett answered.

"Hey, Myron. How's it going?"

"Good, Emmett. What's this about buying a car?"

"I saw this Porsche today. Red. Fully loaded. Seventy Gs. I was thinking about using the play-off bonus money to buy it."

"If that's what you want," Myron said.

"Man, you sound like my mother. I wanted your opinion."

"Buy something cheaper," Myron said. "A lot cheaper."

"But the car is so hot, Myron. If you could just see it . . ."

"Then buy it, Emmett. You're an adult. You don't need my blessing." Myron hesitated. "Did I ever tell you about Norm Booker?"

"Who?"

How soon they forget.

"I was maybe fifteen or sixteen years old," Myron said, "and I was working at this summer camp in Massachusetts. It was a Celtics camp. They used to have their rookie tryouts there. I was basically a towel boy. I met a lot of the draft picks back then. Cedric Maxwell. Larry Bird. But my first year the Celtics had a first-round pick named Norm Booker. I think he was out of Iowa State."

"Yeah, so?"

"Norm was a great player. Six-seven, smooth moves, nice touch. Strong as an ox. And nice guy too. He talked to me. Lot of the guys ignored the towel boys, but Norm wasn't like that. I remember he used to shoot foul shots with his back to the basket. He'd toss the ball over his shoulder. He had such a great touch that he could make better than fifty percent that way."

"So what happened to him?"

"He sat the bench as a rookie. The Celtics cut him the next year. He scrounged around a bit and then he landed with the Portland Trailblazers. He mostly rode the bench, played garbage time, that sort of thing. When the Trailblazers made the play-offs Norm got the usual bonus. He was so excited about it he went out and bought a Rolls-Royce. Dropped every dime he had on that car. But he wasn't worried. There was always next year. And the year after that. Only thing was, Portland cut him. He tried out with a couple of other clubs, but nobody wanted him. Last I heard Norm had to sell the car to feed his family."

Silence.

After some time passed Emmett said, "I also saw this Honda Accord. They had a pretty good lease deal."

"Go for it, Emmett."

They hung up a few minutes later. Myron hadn't thought about Norm Booker in a long time. He wondered what became of him.

Esperanza came back in. She put a new card for Duane Richwood in his Rolodex. "Happy?"

"Yes." He handed her two sheets of paper. "This is a party list for the night Alexander Cross was killed."

"What am I looking for?"

"Heck if I know. A familiar name. Something that leaps out at you."

She nodded. "You know about the funeral tomorrow?"

Myron nodded.

"You going?" she asked.

"Yes."

"I tracked down one of the schoolteachers from the article on Curtis Yeller."

"Which one?"

"Mrs. Lucinda Elright. She's retired now, lives in Philadelphia. She'll see you tomorrow afternoon. You can go right after the funeral."

Myron leaned back. "I'm not sure that's necessary anymore."

"You want me to cancel?"

Myron thought a moment. In light of what he'd learned about Pavel Menansi, the connection between Valerie's murder and what happened to Curtis Yeller seemed more tenuous than ever. The murder of Alexander Cross had not caused Valerie's downfall. It wasn't even the final push. Pavel Menansi had pushed Valerie off the cliff years before. He had watched her slowly plummet, tumbling over jagged rocks on her painful way down. Alexander Cross's death had marked the end of the descent. The ground, if you will. The final crash. Nothing more. Clearly there was no connection between Valerie's death and the events of six years ago. There was also no connection between Duane and Valerie other than what Duane had said—they slept together. No big deal.

Except . . .

Except for last night's rendezvous between Duane and Curtis Yeller's mother.

If not for that—if Myron hadn't seen them together at the hotel—he would be able to dismiss them both entirely. But Duane and Deanna Yeller having an affair—it was too much of a coincidence. There had to be a connection.

"Don't cancel," Myron said.

31

V ALERIE'S FUNERAL WAS STRICTLY COOKIE-
cutter.

The reverend, a porky man with a red nose, hadn't known her with any depth. He listed achievements as though reading from a résumé. He mixed in a few oldies but goodies: loving daughter; so full of life; taken so young; God has a plan. An organ sounded self-righteous indignation. Tacky flowers, like something you'd find draped around a winning horse, adorned the chapel. Stern stain-glass figures peered from above.

The crowd did not linger long. They stopped by Helen and Kenneth Van Slyke, not so much to offer comfort but to be sure they'd been seen and recognized, which was the real reason they'd come in the first place. Helen Van Slyke shook hands with her head high. She did not blink. She did not smile. She did not cry. Her jaw was set. Myron waited in the receiving line with Win. As they got closer they could hear Helen repeat the same phrases—"Good of you to come, thank you for coming, good of you to come, thank you for coming"—in a singsong voice reminiscent of a flight attendant upon disembarkation.

When it was Myron's turn Helen gripped his hand hard. "Do you know who hurt Valerie?"

"Yes." She had said hurt, Myron noted. Not kill.

Helen Van Slyke looked at Win for confirmation. Win nodded.

"Come back to the house," she said. "There's going to be a reception." She turned to the next mourner and hit PLAY on her internal tape recorder. "Good of you to come, thank you for coming, good of you to come . . ."

Myron and Win did as she asked. The mood at Brentman Hall was neither Irish wake–like nor devastating grief. There were no tears. No laughter. Either would have been more welcome than this room completely void of any emotion. "Mourners" milled around like they were at an office cocktail party.

"No one cares," Myron said. "She's gone and no one cares."

Win shrugged. "No one ever does." The eternal optimist.

The first person to approach them was Kenneth. He was dressed in proper black with well-shined shoes. He greeted Win with a back slap and a firm handshake. He ignored Myron.

"How are you holding up?" Win asked. Like he cared.

"Oh I'm doing okay," he said with a heavy sigh. Mr. Brave. "But I'm worried about Helen. We've had to medicate her."

"I'm sorry to hear that," Myron said.

Kenneth turned to him, as though seeing him for the first time. He made a face like he was sucking on a lemon. "Do you mean that?" he asked.

Myron and Win shared a glance. "Yes, I do, Kenneth," Myron said.

"Then do me the courtesy of staying away from my wife. She was very upset after your visit the other day."

"I meant no harm."

"Well, you caused plenty of it, I can tell you. I think it's high time, Mr. Bolitar, you showed some respect. Leave my wife alone. We are grieving here. She's lost her daughter and I've lost my stepdaughter."

Win rolled his eyes.

Myron said, "You have my word, Kenneth."

Kenneth nodded a manly nod and moved away.

"His stepdaughter," Win said in disgust. "Bah."

From across the room Myron caught Helen Van Slyke's eye. She made a gesture toward a door on her right and slipped through it. Like they were meeting for a secret liaison.

"Keep Kenneth away," Myron said.

Win feigned surprise. "But you gave Kenneth your word."

"Bah," Myron said. Whatever that meant.

He ducked through the doorway and followed Helen. She too wore all black, a suit of some sort with the skirt cut just low enough to be sexy yet proper. Good legs, he noticed, and felt like a pig for thinking such a thing at such a time. She led him to a small room down the end of an ornate corridor and closed the door behind them. The room looked like a miniature version of the living room. The chandelier was smaller. The couch was smaller. The fireplace was smaller. The portrait over the mantel was smaller.

"This is the drawing room," Helen Van Slyke explained.

"Oh," Myron said. He'd always wanted to know what a drawing room was. Now that he was in one he still had no idea.

"Would you care for some tea?"

"No thanks."

"Do you mind if I have some?"

"Not at all," he said.

She sat demurely and poured herself a cup from the silver set on the table. Myron noticed that there were two tea sets on the table. He wondered if that was a clue as to the definition of drawing room.

"Kenneth tells me you're on medication," he said.

"Kenneth is full of shit."

Big surprise.

"Are you still investigating Valerie's murder?" she asked. There was almost a mocking quality in her voice. Her words also seemed just a tad slurred, and Myron wondered if perhaps she was indeed being medicated or if she'd added a little home brew to her tea.

"Yes," he said.

"Do you still feel some chivalrous responsibility toward her?"

"I never did."

"Then why do you do it?"

Myron shrugged. "Someone should care."

She looked up, searching his face for a shred of sarcasm. "I see," she said. "So tell me: what have you learned from your investigation?"

"Pavel Menansi abused your daughter."

Myron watched for a reaction. Helen Van Slyke smiled semi-teasingly and put a sugar cube in her tea. Not exactly the reaction he had in mind. "You can't be serious," she said.

"I am."

"What do you mean, abused?"

"Sexual abuse."

"As in rape?"

"You may call it that, yes."

She made a scoffing noise. "Come now, Mr. Bolitar. Isn't that a tad extreme?"

"No."

"It is not as though Pavel forced himself on her, is it? They had an affair. It's hardly unheard of."

"You knew about it?"

"Of course. And frankly, I was quite displeased. Pavel showed poor judgment. But my daughter was sixteen years old at the time—maybe seventeen, I'm not really sure. Anyway, she was certainly of legal age. Calling it rape or sexual abuse, well, I think that's being a tad overdramatic, don't you?"

Maybe both medication and booze. Maybe even mixing them. "Valerie was a young girl," he said. "Pavel Menansi was her coach, a man of nearly fifty."

"Would it have made it any better if he was forty? Or thirty?"

"No," Myron said.

"So why bring up their age difference?" She put down the tea. The smile was again toying with her lips. "Let me ask you a question, Mr. Bolitar. If Valerie was a sixteen-year-old boy and he had an affair with a beautiful female coach who was, let's say, thirty—would you call that sexual abuse? Would you call that rape?"

Myron hesitated for a second. It was a second too long.

"I thought so," she said triumphantly. "You're a sexist, Mr. Bolitar. Valerie had an affair with an older man. It happens all the time." Again the playful smile. "To me even."

"Did you have a breakdown after it was over?"

She raised an eyebrow. "So that's your definition of abuse?" she asked. "A breakdown?"

"You entrusted your daughter to this man," Myron said. "He

was supposed to help her. But he used her instead. He tore her down. He destroyed and discarded her."

"Tore? Destroyed? Discarded? My, my, Mr. Bolitar, we are out for shock effect, aren't we?"

"You don't see anything wrong with what he did?"

She put down her tea and took a cigarette. She lit it, inhaled deeply with her eyes closed, and let it all out. "If it makes you happy to blame me for what happened, fine, blame me. I was a lousy mother. The worst. Is that better?"

Myron watched her calmly smoking her cigarette and sipping her tea. Too calmly. Did she really buy this crap she was peddling? Or was it an act? Was she just deluding herself or . . .

"Pavel bought you off," Myron said.

"No."

"TruPro and Pavel are paying—"

"That's not it at all," she interrupted.

"We know about the money, Mrs. Van Slyke."

"You don't understand. Pavel blames himself for what happened. He took it upon himself to remedy the situation in the only way he could."

"By paying you off."

"By providing us with some of the funds Valerie may have earned had her career continued. He didn't have to do that. The affair wasn't necessarily the cause—"

"It's called hush money."

"Never," she said in a near-hiss. "Valerie was my daughter."

"And you sold her for cash."

She shook her head. "I did what I thought was best for my daughter."

"He abused her. You took his money. You let him get away with it."

"There was nothing I could do," she said. "We didn't want to make it public. Valerie wanted to put it behind her. She wanted to keep it confidential. We all did."

"Why?" Myron said. "It was just an affair with an older man. Happens all the time. To you even."

She bit down on her lip for a moment. When she spoke again her voice was softer. "There was nothing I could do," she repeated. "It was in everyone's best interest to keep it quiet."

"Bullshit," Myron said. He realized he was pushing too hard, but something inside of him wouldn't let him back off. "You sold your daughter."

She was silent for a few moments, concentrating only on her cigarette, watching the ash grow longer and longer. In the distance they could hear the low rumble from the funeral crowd. Glasses clinking. A polite titter.

"They threatened Valerie," she said.

"Who?"

"I don't know. Men who work with Pavel. They made it very clear that if she opened her mouth she was dead." She looked up, pleading. "Don't you see? What option did we have? No good could come from talking. They'd kill her. I was afraid for Valerie. Kenneth—well, I think Kenneth was more interested in the money. Hindsight may be twenty-twenty, but at the time I believed it was the best thing."

"You were protecting your daughter," Myron said.

"Yes."

"But she's dead now."

Helen was puzzled. "I don't understand."

"You don't have to worry about her being hurt anymore. She's dead. You're free to do as you please."

She opened her mouth, closed it, tried again. "I have another daughter," she managed. "I have a husband."

"So then what was all that talk before about protecting Valerie?"

"It . . . I was trying . . ." Her voice churned to a silence.

"You took the hush money," Myron said. He tried to remind himself that the woman who sat before him had buried her daughter today, but not even that fact could slow him down. If anything, it seemed to fuel him. "Don't blame your husband. He's a spineless worm. You were Valerie's mother. You took money to protect a man who abused your daughter. And now you'll keep taking money to protect a man who might have killed her."

"You have no proof Pavel had anything to do with her murder."

"The murder, no. His other crimes against Valerie—that's a different story."

She closed her eyes. "It's too late."

"It's not too late. He's still doing it, you know. Guys like Pavel don't stop. They just find new victims."

"There's nothing I can do."

"I have a friend," Myron said. "Her name is Jessica Culver. She's a writer."

"I know who she is."

He handed her Jess's card. "Tell her the story. She'll write it up. Put it in a major publication. *Sports Illustrated* maybe. It'll be out before Pavel's people even know about it. They're bad men, but they're not wasteful or stupid. Once it's published there'll be no reason to go after your family anymore. It'll end him."

"I'm sorry." She lowered her head. "I can't do it."

She was crumbling. Her whole body was slumped and shaking. Myron watched her, tried to muster up some pity, couldn't do it. "You left her alone with him," he continued. "You didn't look after her. And when you had the chance to help her, you told her to bury it. You took money."

Her body racked. Probably from a sob. Attacking a mother at her own daughter's funeral, Myron thought. What could he do for an encore? Drown newborn kittens in the neighbor's pool?

"Perhaps," he went on, "Valerie wanted to tell the truth. Maybe she needed that to put it all behind her. And maybe that's why she was murdered."

Silence. Then without warning Helen Van Slyke raised her head. She stood and left without saying another word. Myron followed. When he reentered the living room he could hear her voice.

"Good of you to come. Thank you for coming."

32

L UCINDA ELRIGHT WAS BIG AND WARM WITH thick, jiggly arms and an easy laugh. The kind of woman that as a child you feared would hug you too hard and as an adult you wish like hell she would.

"Come on in," she said, shooing several small children away from the door.

"Thank you," Myron said.

"You want something to eat?"

"No thanks."

"How about some cookies?" There were at least ten kids in the apartment. All black, none over the age of seven or eight. Some were using a paint set. Some were building a castle out of sugar cubes. One, a boy about six years old, was sticking his tongue out at Myron. "Not homemade, you understand. I can't cook worth spit."

"Actually, cookies sound good."

She smiled. "I do day care now that I'm retired. Hope you don't mind."

"Not at all."

Mrs. Elright went into the kitchen. The little boy waited

until she was out of the room. Then he stuck his tongue out again. Myron stuck his tongue out back. Mr. Mature. The kid giggled.

"Now sit, Myron. Right over there." She knocked various paraphernalia off the sofa. The plate was full of the classics. Oreos. Chips Ahoys. Fig Newtons.

"Eat," she said.

Myron reached for a cookie. The little boy stood behind Mrs. Elright so he couldn't be seen. He stuck his tongue out again. Without so much as a backward glance Mrs. Elright said, "Gerald, you stick your tongue out one more time, I'll cut it off with my pruning shears."

Gerald rolled his tongue back. "What's pruning shears?"

"Never you mind. Just go over there and play now, you hear? And don't you be causing no trouble."

"Yes, ma'am."

When he was out of earshot Mrs. Elright said, "I like them better at this age. They break my heart when they get a little older."

Myron nodded, pulled apart an Oreo. He didn't lick out the cream. Very adult.

"Your friend Esperanza," Mrs. Elright began, grabbing a Fig Newton. "She said you wanted to talk about Curtis Yeller."

"Yes, ma'am." He handed her the article. "Were you correctly quoted in this article?"

She lifted her half-moon reading glasses from her hefty bosom and scanned the page. "Yes, I said that."

"Did you mean it?"

"This wasn't just talk, if that's what you're getting at. I taught high school for twenty-seven years. I've seen lots of kids go to jail. I've seen lots of kids die in the streets. Never said a word to the newspapers about any of them. See this scar?" She pointed to an immense, fleshy bicep.

Myron nodded.

"Knife wound. From a student. I got shot at once too. I've confiscated more weapons than any damn metal detector." She put her arm down. "That's what I mean when I say I like them younger. Before they get like that."

"But Curtis was different?"

"Curtis was more than just a good boy," she said. "He was one of the best students I ever had. He was always polite and friendly and never caused a lick of trouble. But he wasn't a sissy either, you understand. He was still popular with the other boys. Good at all kinds of sports. I'm telling you, the boy was one in a million."

"What about his mother?" Myron asked. "What was she like?"

"Deanna?" Lucinda sat a little straighter. "Fine woman. Like so many of them young mothers today. Single. Proud. Did whatever she had to to get by. But Deanna was smart. She set rules. Curtis had a curfew. Kids today don't even know what curfew means anymore. Couple nights ago, a ten-year-old boy got shot at three in the morning. Now you tell me, Myron—what's a ten-year-old boy doing out on the streets at three in the morning?"

"I wish I knew."

She waved a hand at the air. "Anyway you don't want to hear no old woman rambling on."

"I got time."

"You're a sweet man, but you're here for a reason. A good reason, I think."

She looked at Myron. He nodded but said nothing.

"Now," she continued, slapping her thighs with her palms, "what were we talking about?"

"Deanna Yeller."

"That's right. Deanna. You know, I think about her a lot too. She was such a caring mother. She came to every open house. She loved parent-teacher conferences. She basked in all that praise we heaped on her boy."

"Did you talk to her after his death?"

"Nope." She shook her head hard and let out a sigh. "Never heard from Deanna again, poor woman. No funeral. No nothing. I called her a couple of times, but nobody ever answered. Like she fell off the face of the earth. But I understood. She'd always had it rough. From the start. She used to be a street girl, you know."

"I didn't know. When?"

"Oh, a long time ago. She doesn't even know who Curtis's father really was. But she quit. Got herself cleaned up. Worked like a dog, any job she could get. All for her boy. And then, just like that . . ." She shook her head. "Gone."

"Did you know Errol Swade?" Myron asked.

"Just enough to know he was trouble. In and out of prison his whole life. He was Deanna's sister's boy. The sister was a junkie. Ended up dying of an overdose. Deanna had to take Errol in. He was family. She was a responsible woman."

"How did Errol get along with Curtis?"

"Actually, they got along pretty good—considering how different they were."

"Well, maybe they weren't so different," Myron said.

"What do you mean?"

"Errol got him to break into that tennis club."

Lucinda Elright watched him a moment before she picked

up a cookie and began to nibble. A small smile toyed with her lips. "Come on, Myron, you know better than that," she said. "You're a smart boy. So was Curtis. What would he want to steal way out there? It don't make sense, robbing a place like that at night. Think about it."

Myron had already. He was glad to see someone else had the same trouble with the official scenario. "So what do you think happened?"

"I've thought a lot about it, but I don't really know. Nothing makes much sense to me about that whole night. But I do think Curtis and Errol were set up. Even if Curtis decided to steal— and even if he was dumb enough to break in to this club— I can't believe he'd shoot at a police officer. A boy can change, but that's like the tiger changing his stripes. It's just too incredible." She sat up, adjusting herself on the couch. "I think some fool thing happened at the rich white club and they needed a couple of black boys to take the fall. Now, I'm not that way. I'm not one of those who think the white man is always plotting against the black man. It's just not in my nature. But in this case I don't know what else could have happened."

"Thank you, Mrs. Elright."

"Lucinda. And Myron, do me a favor."

"What?"

"When you find out what really happened to Curtis, let me know."

33

MYRON AND JESSICA DROVE OUT TO NEW JERsey for dinner at Baumgart's. They ate there at least twice a week. Baumgart's was a strange combination. For half a century it had been a popular soda fountain and deli, the kind of place neighbors went for lunch and Archie took Veronica for an after-school smooch. Eight years ago a Chinese immigrant named Peter Li bought the place and turned it into the best Chinese around—but without getting rid of the old soda fountain. You could still twirl on a stool at the counter, surrounded by chrome and blenders and ice-cream scoops in hot water. You could order a milkshake with your dim sum and have french fries with your General Tso's chicken. When they first lived together, Myron and Jess had come at least once a week. Now that they were back together, the tradition had resumed.

"It's the Alexander Cross murder," Myron said. "I can't stop thinking about it."

Before Jess could answer, Peter Li arrived. Myron and Jess never ordered. Peter chose for them. "Coral shrimp for the beautiful lady," he said, putting down her plate, "and Baumgart's

Szechuan chicken and eggplant for the man not fit to grovel at her feet."

"Good one," Myron said. "Very funny."

Peter bowed. "In my country they consider me a man of great humor."

"Must be a lot of laughs in your country." Myron looked down at his plate. "I hate eggplant, Peter."

"You'll eat it and beg for more," he said. He smiled at Jess. "Enjoy." He left.

"Okay," Jess said, "so what about Alexander Cross?"

"It's not Alexander, per se. It's actually Curtis Yeller. Everyone says he was a great kid. His mom was very involved, loved him like mad, the whole nine yards. Now she acts like nothing happened."

"'There's a grief that can't be spoken,'" Jessica replied. "'There's a pain goes on and on.'"

Myron thought a second. "*Les Mis*?" The ongoing game of Guess the Quote.

"Correct, but what character said it?"

"Valjean?"

"No, sorry. Marius."

Myron nodded. "Either way," he said, "it's a lousy quote."

"I know. I was listening to the tape in the car," she said. "But it might not be that far off the mark."

"A grief that can't be spoken?"

"Yes."

He took a sip of water. "So it make sense to you, the mother acting like nothing happened."

Jessica shrugged. "It's been six years. What do you want her to do—break down and cry every time you come around?"

"No," Myron said, "but I'd think she'd want to know who killed her son."

Before touching her shrimp, Jessica reached across the table and forked a piece of Myron's chicken. Not the eggplant. The chicken. "Maybe she already knows," Jess said.

"What, you think she's being bought off too?"

Jess shrugged. "Maybe. But that's not what's really bugging you."

"Oh?"

Jess chewed daintily. Even the way she chewed food was a thing to behold. "Seeing Duane in that hotel room with Curtis Yeller's mother," she replied. "That's what's got to you."

"You must admit it's a hell of a coincidence," he said.

"Do you have a theory?" she asked.

Myron thought a moment. "No."

Jessica forked another piece of chicken. "You could ask Duane," she said.

"Sure. I could just say, 'Gee, Duane, I was following you around and noticed you're shacking up with an older woman. Care to tell me about it?'"

"Yeah, that could be a problem," she agreed. "Of course, you could approach it from the other direction."

"Deanna Yeller?"

Jessica nodded.

Myron took a taste of his chicken. Before Jess finished the whole thing. "Worth a try," he said. "You want to come along?"

"I'll scare her off," Jess said. "Just drop me off at my place."

They finished eating. Myron even ate the eggplant. It was pretty good. Peter brought them a rich chocolate dessert—the kind of dessert you could gain weight just looking at. Jess dove in. Myron held back. They drove back over the George Washington Bridge to the Henry Hudson and down the west side. He dropped her off at her loft on Spring Street in Soho. She leaned back into the car.

"You'll come by after?" she said.

"Sure. Put on that little French maid's uniform and wait."

"I don't have a French maid's uniform."

"Oh."

"Maybe we can pick one up in the morning," she said. "In the meantime I'll find something suitable."

"Groovy," Myron said.

Jess got out of the car then. She made her way up the stairs to the third floor. Her loft took up half the floor. She turned the key and entered. When she flicked on the lights she was startled to see Aaron lounging on her couch.

Before she could move, another man—a man with a fishnet shirt—came up behind her and put a gun to her temple. A third man—a black man—locked the door and turned the dead bolt. He too had a gun.

Aaron smiled at her. "Hello, Jessica."

34

MYRON'S CAR PHONE RANG.
"Hello."

"*Bubbe,* it's your aunt Clara. Thanks for the referral."

Clara wasn't really his aunt. Aunt Clara and Uncle Sidney were just longtime friends of his parents. Clara had gone to law school with Myron's mom. Myron had set her up to represent Roger Quincy.

"How's it going?" Myron asked.

"My client wanted me to give you an important message," Clara said "He stressed that I, his attorney, should treat this as my number one priority."

"What?"

"Mr. Quincy said you promised him an autograph of Duane Richwood. Well, he'd like it to be an autographed *picture* of Duane Richwood, not just an autograph. *Color* picture, if that's not too much trouble. And he'd like it inscribed to him, thank you very much. By the way, did he tell you he was a tennis fan?"

"I think he might have mentioned it. Fun guy, huh?"

"A constant party. Laughs galore. My sides are aching from all the laughing. It's like representing Jackie Mason."

"So what do you think?" Myron asked.

"In legal terms? The man is a major fruitcake. But is he guilty of murder—and more important, can the D.A. prove it?—that's a different kettle of gefilte."

"What do they have?"

"Circumstantial nothings. He was at the Open. Big deal, so were a zillion other people. He has a weird past. So what, he never made any overt threats that I'm aware of. No one saw him shoot her. No tests link him to the gun or that Feron's bag with the bullet hole. Like I said, circumstantial nothings."

"For what's it worth," Myron said, "I believe him."

"Uh-huh." Clara wouldn't say if she believed him or not. It didn't matter. "I'll speak to you later, doll-face. Take care of yourself."

"You too."

He hung up and dialed Jake.

A gruff voice said, "Sheriff Courter's office."

"It's me, Jake."

"What the fuck do you want now?"

"My, what a charming salutation," Myron said. "I must use it sometime."

"Jesus, you're a pain in the ass."

"You know," Myron said, "I can't for the life of me understand why you're not invited to more parties."

Jake blew his nose. Loudly. Geese in the tristate area scattered. "Before I'm left mortally wounded by your caustic wit," he said, "tell me what you want."

"You still have your copy of the Cross file?" Myron asked.

"Yeah."

"I'd like to meet the coroner on the case and the cop who shot Yeller," Myron said. "Think you can set it up?"

"I thought there was no autopsy."

"Nothing formal, but the senator said someone did some work on him."

"Yeah, all right," Jake said. "But I know the cop who did the shooting. Jimmy Blaine. A good man, but he ain't gonna talk to you."

"I'm not interested in bringing him down."

"That's a big comfort," Jake said.

"I just want some information."

"Jimmy won't see you, I'm sure of it. Why do you need all this anyway?"

"I see a connection between Valerie's murder and Alexander Cross's."

"What connection?"

Myron explained. When he finished, Jake said, "I still don't see it, but I'll call you if I get something."

He hung up.

Myron lucked out and found a spot within two blocks of the hotel. He walked in like he belonged and took the elevator to the third floor. He stopped in front of room 322 and knocked.

"Who is it?" Deanna Yeller's voice was cheerful, singsong.

"Bellhop," Myron said. "Flowers for you."

She flung open the door with a wide smile. Just like the first time they'd met. When she saw no flowers—and more to the point, when she saw Myron—the smile fled. Again, just like the first time.

"Enjoying your stay?" Myron said.

She didn't bother hiding her exasperation. "What do you want?"

"I can't believe you came to town and didn't call me. A less mature man would be insulted."

"I got nothing to say to you." She began to close the door.

"Guess who I just spoke to?"

"I don't care."

"Lucinda Elright."

The door stopped. With Deanna looking slightly dazed, Myron slid through the opening.

Deanna recovered. "Who?"

"Lucinda Elright. One of your son's teachers."

"I don't remember none of his teachers."

"Oh but she remembers you. She said you were a wonderful mother to Curtis."

"So?"

"She also said that Curtis was a wonderful student, one of the best she ever had. She said he had a bright future. She said he never got into trouble."

Deanna Yeller put her hand on her hips. "There a point to all this?"

"Your son had no police record. He had a perfect school record, not so much as a detention. He was one of the top students in his class, if not *the* top student. You were clearly involved in his activities. You were an excellent mother, raising an excellent young man."

She looked away. She might have been looking out the window, except the blinds were drawn. The TV was humming softly. A commercial for men's pickup trucks featuring a soap opera star. Soap opera star, pickup trucks—what advertising genius came up with that combo?

"This is none of your business," she whispered.

"Did you love your son, Ms. Yeller?"

"What?"

"Did you love your son?"

"Get out. Now."

"If you cared about him at all, help me find out what happened to him."

She glared at him. "Don't give me that," she countered. "You don't care about my boy. You're trying to find out who killed that white girl."

"Maybe. But Valerie Simpson's death and your son's are connected. That's why I need your help."

She shook her head. "You don't listen too good, do you? I told you before: Curtis is dead. Can't change that."

"Your son wasn't the type to rob. He wasn't the type to carry a gun or threaten the police with one. That's just not the boy you raised."

"Don't matter," she said. "He's dead. Can't bring him back."

"What was he doing at the tennis club that night?"

"I don't know."

"Where did you suddenly get all your money?"

Pow. Deanna Yeller looked up, startled. The old change-topic attention-getter. Works every time. "What?"

"Your house in Cherry Hill," Myron said. "It was a cash deal four months ago. And your bank account at First Jersey. All cash deposits within the past half year. Where did the money come from, Deanna?"

Her face grew angry. Then suddenly she relaxed and smiled eerily. "Maybe I stole it," she said, "just like my son. You gonna report me?"

"Or maybe it's a payoff."

"A payoff? For what?"

"You tell me."

"No," she said. "I don't have to tell you nothing. Get out."

"Why are you here in New York?"

"To see the sights. Now leave."

"One of those sights Duane Richwood?"

Double pow. She stopped. "What?"

"Duane Richwood. The man who was in your room the other night."

She stared at him. "You were following us?"

"No. Just him."

Deanna Yeller looked horror-stricken. "What kind of man are you?" she said slowly. "You get off on that kind of thing, watching other people and all? Checking their bank accounts? Following them around like a Peeping Tom?" She opened the door. "Don't you have no shame at all?"

The argument was a little too close for comfort. "I'm trying to find a killer," Myron argued, but his tone rang lamely in his own ears. "Maybe the person who killed your son."

"And it don't matter who you hurt to do it, right?"

"That's not true."

"If you really want to do some good, then just drop this whole thing."

"What so you mean by that?"

She shook her head. "Curtis is dead. So is Valerie Simpson. Errol . . ." She stopped. "It's enough."

"What's enough? What about Errol?"

But she kept shaking her head. "Just let it go, Myron. For everyone's sake. Just let it go."

35

JESSICA FELT THE COLD BARREL OF THE GUN against her temple.

"What do you want?" she asked.

Aaron signaled. The man behind her covered her mouth with his free hand. He pressed her hard against him. Jessica could feel hot spittle on her neck. It was hard to breathe. She twisted her head back and forth. Her chest hitched as she scrambled for more air. Panic seized her.

Aaron rose off the couch. The black man moved a step closer, his gun still pointed at her.

"No reason for preliminaries," Aaron said calmly. He took off his white jacket. He wore no shirt underneath, revealing instead the hairless, bodybuilder physique. He flexed a little. His pectoral muscles made ripples, like a stadium crowd doing the wave. "If you can still speak when we're through, make sure you tell Myron it was me." He cracked his knuckles. "I'd hate for my work to go unaccredited."

"Should I break her jaw?" the man with the fishnet asked. "So she can't yell or nothing."

Aaron thought a moment. "No," he said. "I kind of enjoy a good yell now and again."

All three men laughed.

"I go second," the black man said.

"Like hell," the man with the fishnet countered.

"You always go before me," the black man whined.

"All right, we'll flip for it."

"You got a coin? I never carry change."

"Shut up," Aaron said.

Silence.

Jessica struggled feverishly, but the man in the fishnet was too strong. She bit down and managed to skim one of his fingers. He yelped and called her a bitch. Then he bent her head back in a way it was never supposed to go. Pain shot down her spine. Her eyes widened.

Aaron was about to unbutton his pants when it happened.

A gunshot. Or more than one gunshot. It sounded to Jessica like only one, but it had to be more. The hand pressed hard against her mouth slackened and slid off. The gun against her temple dropped to the floor. She turned just enough to see the man behind her no longer had a face or even much of a head. He was dead well before his legs realized it and let him cave onto the floor.

At seemingly the same time, the back half of the black man's head flew across the room. He too fell to the floor in a bloody heap.

Aaron's speed was uncanny. Seemingly before the first bullet even hit its target he had rolled into a crouch and whipped out a gun. Everything—the shots, the men going down, Aaron rolling to safety—had taken less than two seconds. Aaron came up aiming his gun at Win, who aimed his right back. Jessica stood frozen. Win must have come in through the terrace window, though how he could have gotten there and how long he'd been there Jessica could not say.

Win smiled casually and gave a half-nod. "My, my, Aaron, you're looking rather buff."

"I try to stay in shape," Aaron said. "Nice of you to notice."

The two men continued to aim their guns at each other. Neither blinked. Neither stopped smiling. Jessica had not moved. Her body quaked as though from fever. She felt something sticky on her face and realized it was probably brain matter from the man at her feet.

"I have an idea," Aaron said.

"An idea?"

"For how to end this deadlock. One I think you'll like, Win."

"Do tell," Win said.

"We both put our guns down at the same time."

"So far it doesn't sound very appealing," Win said.

"I'm not finished."

"How rude of me. Please continue."

"We've both killed men with our bare hands," Aaron said. "We both know we like it. A lot. We both know there are very few worthy adversaries in this world. We both know we are rarely if ever seriously challenged."

"So?"

"So I'm suggesting the ultimate test." Aaron's grin grew brighter. "You and me. Man-to-man, hand-to-hand combat. What do you say?"

Win chewed on his upper lip. "Intriguing," he said.

Jessica tried to say something, but her tongue would not

obey. She just stood there, stone-faced; the thing that used to wear fishnet shirts bled without a twitch.

"One condition," Win said.

"What's that?"

"No matter who wins, Jessica goes free."

Aaron shrugged. "Doesn't matter. Frank will get her some other time."

"Maybe. But not tonight."

"Fine then," Aaron said. "But she can't leave until it's over."

Win nodded at her. "Wait by the door, Jessica. When the fight ends, run."

"But you have to wait until it's over," Aaron added.

Jessica found her voice. "How will I know when it's over?"

"One of us will be dead," Win said.

She nodded numbly. She couldn't stop shaking. Both men were still pointing the guns at one another.

"You know the drill?" Aaron asked.

"Of course."

Still holding the guns, both men placed their hand on the floor. At the same time, they twisted their weapons so that the barrel was no longer pointing at the other man. They both released their weapons at the same time. They both stood at the same time. They both kicked the weapons into a corner at the same time.

Aaron grinned. "It's done," he said.

Win nodded.

They approached each other slowly. Aaron's grin spread into something fully maniacal. He got into some weird fighting position—dragon or grasshopper or something—and beckoned with his left hand. His body was sleek, all muscle. He towered over Win. "You forgot the basic premise of the martial arts," Aaron said.

"What's that?" Win asked.

"A good big man will always beat a good little man."

"And you forgot the basic premise of Windsor Horne Lockwood III."

"Oh?"

"He always carries two guns."

Almost nonchalantly, Win reached into his leg holster, took out his gun, and fired. Aaron ducked, but the bullet still hit him in the head. The second bullet also hit Aaron's head. So too, Jessica guessed, did the third.

The big man fell to the ground. Win walked over and studied the still figure, tilting his head from side to side like a dog hearing a strange sound.

Jessica watched him in silence.

"Are you okay?" he asked.

"Yes."

Win continued to look down. He shook his head and made a *tsk, tsk* noise.

"What is it?" she asked.

Win turned to her, an almost shy smile toying with his lips. He gave a half-shrug. "I guess I'm not much for fair fights."

He looked back down at the body and started to laugh.

36

JESSICA DIDN'T WANT TO TALK ABOUT IT. SHE wanted to make love. Myron understood. Death and violence do that to a person. The fine line. There was definitely something to that "reaffirming life" stuff after facing down the Grim Reaper.

When they were spent, Jessica lay her head on his chest, her hair a wonderful fan. For a long time she didn't say anything. Myron stroked her back. Finally she spoke. "He enjoys it, doesn't he?"

Myron knew she meant Win. "Yes."

"Do you?" she asked.

"Not like Win."

She lifted her head and looked at him. "That sounded a tad evasive."

"Part of me hates it more than you can imagine."

"And another part of you?" she prompted.

"It's the ultimate test. There's an undeniable rush to that. But it's not like what happens with Win. He craves it. He needs it."

"And you don't?"

"I like to think I loathe it."

"But do you?"

"I don't know," Myron said.

"It was scary," she said. "Win was scary."

"He also saved your life."

"Yes."

"It's what Win does. He's good at it—the best I've ever seen. Everything with him is black and white. He has no moral ambiguities. If you cross the line, there is no reprieve, no mercy, no chance to talk your way out of it. You're dead. Period. Those men came to harm you. Win wasn't interested in rehabilitating them. They made their choice. The moment they entered your apartment they were doomed."

"It sounds like the theory of massive retaliation," she said. "You kill one of ours, we kill ten of yours."

"Colder," Myron said. "Win's not interested in teaching a lesson. He sees it as extermination. They're no more than pestering fleas to him."

"And you agree with that?"

"Not always. But I understand it. Win's moral code is not mine. We've both known that for a long time. But he's my best friend and I'd trust him with my life."

"Or mine," she said.

"Right."

"So what is your moral code?" she asked.

"It's flexible. Let's leave it at that."

Jessica nodded. She lay her head back down on his chest. The warmth of her felt good against his heartbeat. "Their heads," she said. "They just exploded like melons."

"Win doctors the bullets to maximize impact."

"Where did he take the bodies?" she asked.

"I don't know."

"Will they be found?"

"Only if he wants them to be."

A few minutes later Jessica's eyes closed and her breathing grew deep. Myron watched her drift into a sound sleep. She cuddled closer to him, looking small and frail. He knew what would happen tomorrow. She'd still be in some form of shock—not a dazed shock as much as a denial. She'd go about her day as though nothing had happened, straining extra-hard for normalcy but falling just short of achieving it. Everything would be just a little different than yesterday. Nothing drastic, just the little things. Her food would taste a little different. The air would smell a little different. Colors would have an almost indiscernibly different hue.

At six in the morning, Myron got out of bed and showered. When he came back she was sitting up. "Where are you going?" she asked.

"To see Pavel Menansi."

"This early?"

"They'll think Aaron took care of the problem last night. I might catch them off guard."

She pulled the covers over her. "I've been thinking about what you said last night at dinner. About the connection to the Alexander Cross murder."

"And?"

"Suppose you're right. Suppose something else happened that night six years ago."

"Like?"

She sat upright, leaning against the headboard. "Suppose Errol Swade didn't kill Alexander Cross," she said.

"Uh-huh."

"Well, suppose Valerie saw what really happened to Alexander Cross. And suppose that whatever she saw pushed her already battered psyche over the edge. She had already been weakened by what Pavel Menansi did to her. But now suppose whatever she saw was the ultimate cause of her breakdown."

Myron nodded. "Go on."

"And now suppose years pass. Valerie gets stronger. She makes a remarkable recovery. She even wants to play tennis again. But most of all, she wants to face up to her darkest fear: the truth of what really happened that night."

He saw where she was going with this. "She'd have to be silenced," he said.

"Yes."

Myron slipped a pair of pants on. Over the past few months his clothes had begun a slow migration to Jess's loft. About a third of his wardrobe now resided here. "If you're right," he said, "we now have two people who want to silence Valerie: Pavel Menansi and whoever killed Alexander Cross."

"Or someone who wants to protect those two."

He finished dressing. Jess hated his tie and told him to change it. He complied. When he was ready to leave, Myron said, "You'll be safe this morning, but I want to move you someplace out of town for a little while."

"For how long?" she asked.

"I don't know. Few days. Maybe longer. Just until I can get this situation under control."

"I see," she said.

"Are you going to fight me on this?"

She got out of bed and pattered across the room. She wore no clothes. Myron's mouth went a little dry. He stared. He could stare all day. She walked with the ease of a panther. Every movement was supple and marvelous and rawly sensual. She slipped into a silk robe. "I know this is the part where I'm supposed to get all indignant and say that I'm not going to change my life," she said. "But I'm scared. I'm also a writer who could use a few days of solitude. So I'll go. No arguments."

He hugged her. "You're always a surprise," he said.

"What?"

"Being reasonable. Who would have thought?"

"I'm trying to keep the mystery alive," she said.

They kissed. Passionately. Her skin felt wonderfully warm.

"Why don't you stay a little longer?" she whispered.

He shook his head. "I want to get to Pavel before Ache realizes what happened."

"One more kiss then."

He stepped away. "Not unless you want to pack me in ice." He blew her a kiss and left the bedroom area. Clumps of blood were stuck to the exposed brick wall by the door. Courtesy of Fishnet Lee's head.

Outside, Win was nowhere in sight, but Myron knew he was there. Jess would be safe until they moved her.

Pavel Menansi was staying at the Omni Park Central on Seventh Avenue, across the street from Carnegie Hall. Myron would have preferred to go in with backup, but it was better Win wasn't there. There had been a bond between Win and Valerie—more than just the family-friend variety. Myron didn't know what that bond was. Win cared about very few people, but for those select few he would go to any lengths. The rest of the world meant nothing to him. Somehow Valerie had entered that protective circle. Myron would have enough trouble keeping his own rage in check. If Win were here—if Win were to question Pavel about his "affair" with Valerie—it wouldn't be a very pretty sight.

Pavel was staying in room 719. Myron checked his watch. Six-thirty. Not much activity in the lobby. The floor was being mopped. An exhausted family was checking out. Three kids, all whining. The parents looked like they could use a vacation. Myron walked purposefully onto an elevator, like he belonged. He pressed the button for the seventh floor.

The corridor was empty. When Myron reached the door to Pavel's room, he knocked. No answer. He knocked again. Still no answer. He tried once again. Nothing. He was about to go downstairs and try the house phone when a sound made him stop. He listened again. The sound was barely perceptible. He pressed his ear against the door.

"Hello?" he called out.

Crying. Faint. Growing stronger. The cries of a little girl.

Myron pounded the door this time. The crying picked up a little steam now, becoming more a sob. "Are you okay?" Myron asked. More crying, but still no words. A minute or so more of this and Myron began to look for the familiar sight of the maid cart and her passkey. But it was six-thirty in the morning. The maid wasn't on her run yet.

Picking locks was not Myron's forte. Win was a lot better at it. Plus he didn't have the tools. Another cry from the room. "Open the door," he shouted. The only answer was more cries.

To hell with it, he thought.

Leading with his shoulder, Myron pile-drove his body into the door. It stung him pretty good, but the lock gave way. The cries were still muffled, but for a moment Myron forgot about them. Sprawled across the bed was Pavel Menansi. His eyes were wide open but unseeing. His mouth was frozen in a surprised oval. Dried, dark blood was caked on his chest where the bullet had entered.

He was naked.

Myron stared for a few moments before the renewed cries snapped him out of it. He turned to his right. The sound emanated from behind the bathroom door. Myron moved toward it. There was a plastic Feron's bag on the floor. The same kind they used at the U.S. Open. The same kind they found at Val's murder.

The bag had a bullet hole in it.

In front of the bathroom door, jammed under the knob, was a chair. Myron kicked it out of the way and opened the door. A young girl was sitting on the tile, her knees pulled up to her chest. She was huddled in a corner against the toilet. Myron recognized her right away. It was Janet Koffman, Pavel's newest protégée. Fourteen years old.

She too was naked.

Janet looked up at him. Her eyes were large and red and puffy. Her lower lip quivered. "We were just talking tennis," she said in a dead voice. "He's my coach. We were just talking about a match. That's all."

Myron nodded. Janet started to cry again. He bent down and wrapped a towel around her. He reached out, but she shrank away.

"It's okay now," he said, not knowing what else to say. "You're going to be okay."

37

JANET KOFFMAN HAD STOPPED CRYING. SHE was sitting on the love seat by the window. Her back was to the bed and hence Pavel's corpse. From what Myron could get out of her she had been in the bathroom when someone locked her in with the chair and killed Pavel. She hadn't seen a thing. She was still sticking to her other story too: she and her coach had been talking tennis. Myron chose not to probe into the small details—like why, for example, they would have this particular discussion in the nude.

He had called the police. They'd be here any minute now. The question was, what should he do with Janet? On the one hand, he wanted to protect her from all of this; on the other, he knew she had to deal with what she had been through, that she couldn't just pretend nothing had happened to her. So what should Myron do—tamper with a police investigation or expose her to the brutish ways of the cops and worse, the press? What message of shame would hiding the truth send her? Then again, what would happen to this young girl if the story hit the airwaves?

Myron didn't have a clue.

"He was a good coach," Janet said softly.

"You did nothing wrong," Myron said, again realizing how lame he sounded. "Whatever else happens, remember that. You did absolutely nothing wrong."

She nodded slowly, but Myron wasn't sure if she'd even heard him.

Ten minutes later the police arrived, led by Dimonte. Rolly looked like something the proverbial cat had dragged in. He was unshaven. His shirt was untucked and buttoned wrong. His hair was all over the place. He had sleep-buggers in both eyes. Still, the boots were nicely polished. He charged up to Myron. "Returning to the scene of the crime, asshole?"

"Yeah," Myron said, "that's it."

The press rounded the corner. Flashbulbs started strobing. "Keep those assholes downstairs!" Dimonte hollered. Some uniformed cops pushed them back. "Downstairs, I said! No one on this floor."

Dimonte turned back to Myron. Krinsky came in and stood next to him. His pad was out.

"Hey, Krinsky," Myron said.

Krinsky nodded.

"So what the hell happened?" Dimonte demanded.

"I came up to see him. I found him like this."

"Stop fucking with me, asshole."

Myron didn't bother with a retort. Cops were all over the place. The coroner was slitting a hole in Pavel's torso with a surgical scalpel. The liver area, Myron knew. Trying to get a liver temperature reading to find out time of death.

Dimonte spotted the Feron's bag on the floor. "You touch this?"

Myron shook his head.

Dimonte bent down and looked at the bullet hole. "Cute," he said.

"You going to let Roger Quincy go now?"

"Why should I?"

"You didn't have squat on him before. Now you have less than squat."

Dimonte shrugged. "Could just be a copycat. Or"—he snapped his fingers—"or it could be someone who wants to get Quincy off." A smile. "Someone like you, Bolitar."

"Yeah," Myron said, "that's it."

Dimonte stepped closer. He gave Myron the tough-guy glare again. Then, as though suddenly remembering it, he quickly whipped out his toothpick and put it in his mouth. He glared again and gnawed the toothpick.

"I was wrong before," Myron said.

"What?"

"About the toothpick being cliché. It's actually very intimidating."

"Keep it up, funnyman."

"It's too early for this, Rolly."

"Listen, asshole, I want to know what you're doing here."

"I told you. I came to see Pavel."

"Why?"

"To talk about him coaching a player of mine."

"At six-thirty in the morning?"

"I'm an early riser. It's why they call me Mr. Sunbeam."

"They should call you Mister Lying Sack of Shit."

"Ooooo," Myron said. "That hurt."

Dimonte started gnawing on the toothpick with renewed vigor. You could almost hear something churn inside his head. "So tell me, Bolitar," he said with the beginnings of a smile, "you came to the hotel to talk business. You took the elevator up to see our victim here. You knocked on the door. No one answered. Right so far?"

"Yep."

"So then you kicked the door in, right?"

Myron said nothing.

Dimonte turned to Krinsky. "That make sense to you, Krinsky? Kicking in the door like that?"

Krinsky looked up from his pad, shook his head, looked back down.

"You always do that when no one answers a door, asshole? Kick it down?"

"I didn't kick it. I used my shoulder."

"Don't bullshit me, Bolitar. You didn't come here to talk business. And you didn't kick down the door just because no one answered."

The coroner tapped Dimonte on the shoulder. "Bullet to the heart. Clean shot. Death was instantaneous."

"Time of death?" Rolly asked.

"He's been dead six, maybe seven hours."

Dimonte looked at his watch. "It's seven now. That would mean he was killed between midnight and one."

Myron turned to Krinsky. "And he didn't even see you use his fingers."

Krinsky almost smiled.

Dimonte tossed out another glare. "You got an alibi, Bolitar?"

"I was with a lady friend."

"That Jessica Culver?"

"Correct." Myron waited for Krinsky to look up. When he did, Myron said, "Her number is 555-8420."

Krinsky wrote it down.

"All right, Bolitar, now stop busting my balls. Why did you kick down the door?"

Myron hesitated. He looked at Dimonte. Dimonte looked back and said, "Well?"

"Come with me," Myron said in a quiet voice. He began to leave the room.

"Hey, where the fuck do you think you're going?"

"For once, Rolly, don't be an ass. Just shut up and follow me."

To Myron's surprise Dimonte kept quiet. They went down the corridor in silence. Krinsky stayed at the crime scene. Myron stopped in front of a door, took out a key, and opened it. Janet Koffman was sitting on the bed. She was wearing a hotel bathrobe. If she realized they were there, she didn't show it. Janet rocked back and forth, humming to herself.

Dimonte looked a question at Myron.

"Her name is Janet Koffman."

"The tennis player?"

Myron nodded. "The killer locked her in the bathroom before he shot Menansi. I heard her crying when I knocked on the door. That's why I kicked it in."

Dimonte looked at Myron. "You mean she and Menansi were . . . ?"

Myron nodded.

"Christ, how old is she?"

"Fourteen, I think."

Dimonte closed his eyes. "We have someone down at the precinct," he said softly. "A doctor. She's good with this stuff. I'll talk to the Manhattan cop in charge about sneaking her out, see if he can keep the press away. I'll try to keep the victim's name out of the papers for a while."

"Thank you."

"I've seen this kinda thing before, Bolitar. The girl is going to need help."

"I know."

"Any chance she offed him herself? Frankly I wouldn't give a shit but . . ."

Myron shook his head. "She was locked in from the outside with a chair. It couldn't have been her."

Dimonte gave the toothpick a little chew. "Thoughtful killer," he said.

"What do you mean?"

"He didn't want the girl to see what happened. He made sure she had an alibi by locking her in with the chair. And most of all he saved her from going through any more of Menansi's hell." He looked at Myron. "I'd probably pin a medal on the guy if he hadn't also killed Valerie Simpson."

Myron said, "Me too." It made him wonder.

38

THE OFFICE WAS ONLY ABOUT TEN BLOCKS away. Myron decided to walk it. Cars sat completely still on Sixth Avenue, though the lights were green and there was no visible construction. Everyone honked their horns. Like this ever does any good. A well-groomed man got out of a taxi. He wore a pin-striped suit, a gold Tag Heuer watch, and Gucci shoes. He also wore a green pinwheel hat and plastic Spock ears. New York—my kind of town.

Myron ignored the fumes and tried to think the whole thing through. The popular theory—the main theory, if you will— had gone something like this: Valerie Simpson had been abused by Pavel Menansi. Regaining her mental strength, she had decided to expose him. This exposure would have been detrimental to the financial well-being of TruPro and the Ache brothers. So they eliminated her before she could do any damage. It all added up. It all made sense.

Until this morning.

A major monkey wrench had been tossed into the main theory: Pavel Menansi had been murdered too, in a fashion similar to Valerie Simpson. Under the main theory, the murders of Valerie Simpson and Pavel Menansi were at cross-purposes. Why kill Valerie Simpson to protect Pavel Menansi, only to go ahead and kill Pavel Menansi? It didn't mesh. It wasn't profitable for TruPro or the Aches.

Of course, there was the possibility that Frank Ache had decided Menansi was too big a risk, that exposure was imminent and losses might as well be cut right now. But if Frank had wanted Pavel dead, he would have had Aaron do it. Pavel had been murdered between midnight and one. Aaron was dead by midnight. Myron mulled this over a bit and decided that Aaron's being dead made it extremely unlikely he was the killer. And moreover, if Frank had intended to kill Pavel, there would have been no reason to scare Myron off with the attack on Jessica.

On the street in front of him a pale woman with a bullhorn screamed that she had recently met Jesus face-to-face. She stuffed a pamphlet into Myron's hand.

"Jesus sent me back with this message," she said.

Myron nodded, glanced down at the ink smears on the pamphlet. "Too bad he didn't give you a decent printer."

She gave him a funny look and went back to her bullhorn. Myron stuffed the pamphlet into his pocket and continued walking. His mind returned to the problem at hand.

Frank Ache wasn't behind Pavel's murder, he thought. To the contrary, Frank Ache wanted Pavel saved because Pavel meant mucho dinero to TruPro. Frank Ache had even brought Aaron in to protect Pavel. He had ordered Aaron to harm Jessica and to protect Pavel. Killing TruPro's main tennis drawing card would make no sense.

So what did that leave us?

Two possibilities. One, we were dealing with two separate

killers with two separate agendas. Seeing an opportunity, Pavel's killer had left behind a Feron's bag to put the blame on Valerie's killer. Or two, there was some other linkage between Valerie and Pavel, one that was not readily apparent. Myron favored this possibility, and of course it led back to Myron's earlier obsession:

The murder of Alexander Cross.

Both Valerie Simpson and Pavel Menansi had been at the Old Oaks tennis club that night six years ago. Both had been attending the party for Alexander Cross. But so what? Let's suppose Jessica had been right this morning. Suppose Valerie Simpson had seen something that night, maybe even the identity of the real murderer. Suppose she'd been about to reveal the truth. Suppose that was why she'd been killed. How would that tie in to Pavel Menansi? Even if he had seen the same thing, he hadn't opened his mouth in years. Why would Pavel start now? It's not as though he'd come forward to help poor Valerie. So what is the connection? And what about Duane Richwood? How did he fit into this equation, if at all? And Deanna Yeller? And where was Errol Swade? Was he still alive?

He headed east three blocks and then turned down Park Avenue. The majestic (if not ostentatious) Helmsley Palace or Helmsley Castle or Helmsley Whatever sat straight ahead, seemingly in the middle of the street; the MetLife building huddled over it like a protective parent. For eons the MetLife building had been something of a New York landmark known as the Pan Am building. Myron couldn't get used to the change. Every time he turned the corner he still expected to see the Pan Am logo.

Activity was brisk in the front of Myron's building. He headed past the modern sculpture that adorned the entrance.

The sculpture was hideous. It looked very much like a giant intestinal tract. Myron had looked for a name on the sculpture once, but in a typical New York move, someone had pried off the name plaque. What someone did with an ugly sculpture's name plaque was beyond comprehension. Maybe they sold it. Maybe there was an underground market for name plaques from works of art—for those who couldn't afford actual stolen artworks and thus settled for the plaques.

Interesting theory.

He entered the lobby. Three Lock-Horne hostesses sat on stools behind a tall counter, smiling plastically. They wore enough makeup to double as cosmetic counter girls at Bloomies. Of course, they didn't wear the official white lab coat of genuine Bloomie counter girls, so you could tell they weren't professional makeup people. Still, all three were attractive—model wannabes who found this more enjoyable (and put them in touch with more potential bigwigs) than waiting tables. Myron walked past them, smiled, nodded. None gave him the eye. Hmm. They must know how committed he was to Jessica. Yeah, that must be it.

When the elevator opened on his floor, he walked toward Esperanza. Her white blouse was a nice contrast against her dark, flawless skin. She'd have been great on one of those Bain de Soleil commercials. The Santa Fe tan without any sun.

"Hi," he said.

Esperanza cupped the phone against her shoulder. "It's Jake. You want to take it?"

He nodded. She handed him the phone.

"Hey, Jake."

"Some girl did a partial autopsy on Curtis Yeller," Jake said. "She'll see you."

Myron said, "Some girl?"

"Mea culpa for not being politically sensitive," Jake said. "Sometimes I still refer to myself as black."

"That's because you're too lazy to say African American," Myron said.

"Is it African or Afro?"

"African now," Myron said.

"When in doubt," Jake said, "ask a honky."

"Honky," Myron repeated. "Now there's a word you don't hear much anymore."

"Damn shame too. Anyway, the assistant M.E. is Amanda West. She seemed anxious to talk." Jake gave him the address.

"What about the cop?" Myron asked. "Jimmy Blaine?"

"No dice."

"He still with the force?"

"Nope. He retired."

"You have his address?"

"Yes," Jake said.

Silence. Esperanza kept her eyes on her computer screen.

"Could you give it to me?" Myron asked.

"Nope."

"I won't hassle him, Jake."

"I said no."

"You know I can find the address on my own."

"Fine, but I'm not giving it to you. Jimmy is one of the good guys, Myron."

"So am I," Myron said.

"Maybe. But sometimes the innocent get hurt in your little crusades."

"What's that supposed to mean?"

"Nothing. Just leave him alone."

"And why so defensive?" Myron continued. "I just want to ask him a couple of questions."

Silence. Esperanza didn't look up.

Myron continued, "Unless he did something he shouldn't have."

"Don't matter," Jake said.

"Even if he—"

"Even if. Good-bye, Myron."

The phone went dead. Myron stared at it a second. "That was bizarre."

"Uh-huh." Esperanza still stared at her computer screen. "Messages on your desk. Lots of them."

"Have you seen Win?"

Esperanza shook her head.

"Pavel Menansi is dead," Myron said. "Someone murdered him last night."

"The guy who molested Valerie Simpson?"

"Yep."

"Gee, I'm so brokenhearted. I hope I don't lose too much sleep." Esperanza finally flicked a glance away from the screen. "Did you know he was on that party list you gave me?"

"Yeah. You find any other interesting names?"

She almost smiled. "One."

"Who?"

"Think puppy dog," Esperanza said.

Myron shook his head.

"Think Nike," she continued. "Think Duane's contact with Nike."

Myron froze. "Ned Tunwell?"

"Correct answer." Everyone in Myron's life was a game show host. "Listed as E. Tunwell on the list. His real name is Edward.

So I did a little digging. Guess who first signed Valerie Simpson to a Nike deal."

"Ned Tunwell."

"And guess who had plenty of egg on his face when her career took a nosedive."

"Ned Tunwell."

"Wow," she said dryly, "it's like you're clairvoyant." She lowered her eyes back to her computer screen and started typing.

Myron waited. Then: "Anything else?"

"Just a very unsubstantiated rumor."

"What?"

"The usual in a situation like this," Esperanza said, her eyes still on the screen. "That Ned Tunwell and Valerie Simpson were more than friends."

"Get Ned on the phone," Myron said. "Tell him I need—"

"I already made the appointment," she said. "He'll be here at seven tonight."

39

DR. AMANDA WEST NOW WORKED AS CHIEF PA-thologist at St. Joseph Medical Center in Doylestown, not too far from Philadelphia. Myron pulled into the hospital parking lot. On the radio was the classic Doobie Brothers song "China Grove." Myron sang along with the chorus, which basically consisted of saying "Oh, Oh, China Grove" repeatedly. Myron sang it louder now, wondering—not for the first time—what a "China Grove" actually was.

As he took a parking ticket from the attendant the car phone rang.

"Jessica is hidden," Win said.

"Thanks."

"See you at the match tomorrow."

Click. Abrupt, even for Win.

Inside Myron asked the receptionist where the morgue was. The receptionist looked at him like he was nuts and said, "The basement, of course."

"Oh, right. Like on *Quincy*."

He took the elevator down a level. No one was around. He found a door marked MORGUE, and again using his powers of deductive reasoning, quickly realized that this was probably the morgue. Myron the Medium. He braced himself and knocked.

A friendly female voice chimed, "Come in."

The room was tiny and smelled like Janitor-in-a-Drum. The decor theme was metal. Two desks facing each other, both metal, took up half the room. Metal bookshelves. Metal chairs. Lots of stainless steel trays and bins all over the place. No blood in them. No organs. All shiny and clean. Myron had indeed seen plenty of violence, but the sight of blood still made him queasy once the danger passed. He didn't like violence, no matter what he'd told Jessica before. He was good at it, no denying that, but he did not like it. Yes, violence was the closest modern man came to his true primitive self, the closest he came to the intended state of nature, to the Lockean ideal, if you will. And yes, violence was the ultimate test of man, a test of both physical strength and animalistic cunning. But it was still sickening. Man had—in theory anyway—evolved for a reason. In the final analysis, violence was indeed a rush. But so was skydiving without a parachute.

"Can I help you?" the friendly voiced woman asked.

"I'm looking for Dr. West," he said.

"You found her." She stood and extended her hand. "You must be Myron Bolitar."

Amanda West smiled a bright, clear smile, which illuminated even this room. She was blond and perky with a cute little upturned nose—the complete opposite of what he'd expected. Not to be stereotyping, but she seemed a tad too sunny, too upbeat, for someone handling rotting corpses all day. He tried to picture her cheerful face splitting open a dead body with a Y-incision. The picture wouldn't hold.

"You wanted to know about Curtis Yeller?" she asked.

"Yes."

"Been waiting six years for someone to ask," she said. "Come on in. There's more room in the back."

She opened a door behind her. "You squeamish?"

"Uh, no." Mr. Tough-guy.

Amanda West smiled again. "There's nothing to see really. Just that some people get freaked out by all the drawers."

He entered the room. The drawers. There was a wall of huge drawers. Floor to ceiling. Five drawers up. Eight across. That equals forty drawers. Mr. Multiplication Tables. Forty dead bodies could fit in here. Forty dead rotting corpses that used to have lives and families, that used to love and be loved, that once cared and struggled and dreamed. Freaked out? By a bunch of drawers? Surely you jest.

"Jake said you remembered Curtis Yeller," he said.

"Sure. It was my biggest case."

"Pardon me if I sound out of line," Myron said, "but you look awfully young to have been an M.E. six years ago."

"You're not out of line," she said, still smiling sweetly. Myron smiled back with equal sweetness. "I had just finished my residency and worked there two nights a week. The chief M.E. was with the corpse of Alexander Cross. Both bodies came in nearly the same time. So I did the prelim on Curtis Yeller. I didn't get the chance to do anything resembling a full autopsy—not that I needed one to know how he was killed."

"How was he killed?"

"Bullet wound. He was shot twice. Once in the lower left rib cage"—she leaned to the side and pointed at her own—"and once in the face."

"Did you know which one was fatal?"

"The shot to the ribs didn't do much damage," she said. Amanda West was, Myron decided, cute. She tilted her head a lot when she talked. Jess did that too. "But the bullet in Yeller's head ripped off his face like it was Silly Putty. There was no nose. Both cheekbones were barely splinters. It was a mess. The shot was at very close range. I didn't get a chance to run all the tests, but I'd say the gun was either pressed against his face or no more than a foot away."

Myron almost took a step back. "Are you saying a cop shot him in the face at point-blank range?"

Water dripped into a stainless steel sink, echoing in the room. "I'm just giving you the facts," Amanda West said steadily. "You draw your own conclusions."

"Who else knows about this?" he asked.

"I'm not sure. It was a zoo in there that night. I usually worked alone, but there must have been half a dozen other guys with me on this one. None of them worked for the coroner's office."

"Who were they?"

"Cops and government guys," she replied.

"Government guys?"

She nodded. "That's what I was told. They worked for Senator Cross. Secret service or something like that. They confiscated everything—tissue samples, the slugs I extracted, everything. They told me it was a matter of national security. The whole night was crazy. Yeller's mother even managed to get in the room once. She started screaming at me."

"What was she screaming about?"

"She was very insistent that there should be no autopsy. She wanted her son back immediately. She got her wish too. For once the police acquiesced. They weren't interested in having anyone look too closely at this, so it worked out for all concerned." She smiled again. "Funny thing, don't you think?"

"The mother not wanting an autopsy?"

"Yes."

Myron shrugged. "I've heard of parents not wanting autopsies before."

"Right, because they want the body preserved for a decent burial. But this kid wasn't buried. He was cremated." She offered up another smile, this one more saccharine.

"I see," Myron said. "So any evidence of police wrongdoing would have been burned up with Curtis Yeller."

"Right," she said.

"So you think—what—someone got to her?"

Amanda West put her hands up in surrender. "Hey, I said it was a funny thing. Not ha-ha funny, just strange funny. The rest is up to you. I'm just an M.E."

Myron nodded again. "You find anything else?"

"Yes," she said. "And this too I found funny. Very funny."

"Ha-ha funny or strange funny?"

"You decide," she said. She smoothed her lab coat. "I'm no ballistics expert, but I know a little something about bullet slugs. I pulled two slugs from Yeller. One from the rib cage, one from the head."

"Yeah so?"

"The two slugs were of different calibers." Amanda West put up her index finger. All traces of a smile were gone now. Her face was clear and determined. "Understand what I'm telling you, Mr. Bolitar. I'm not just saying two different guns here. I'm talking about different caliber. And here's the funny part: all the officers on the Philadelphia force use the same caliber weapon."

Myron felt a chill. "So one of the two bullets came from someone other than a cop."

"And," she continued, "all those secret service men were carrying guns."

Silence.

"So," she said, "ha-ha funny or strange funny?"

Myron looked at her. "You don't hear me laughing."

40

MYRON DECIDED TO IGNORE JAKE'S ADVICE. Especially after listening to Amanda West.

Finding Officer Jimmy Blaine's current address had not been easy. The man had retired two years ago. Still Esperanza found out he lived alone on some small lake in the Poconos. Myron drove through the wilderness for two hours until he pulled into what he hoped was the right driveway. He checked his watch. He still had plenty of time to see Jimmy Blaine and get back to the office in time for his meeting with Ned Tunwell.

The house was rustic and quaint, about what you'd expect to find nestled away in the Poconos. Gravel driveway. Dozens of small wooden animals guarded a front porch. The air was heavy and still. Everything—the weather vane, the American flag, the rocking chair, all the leaves and blades of grass—stood frighteningly motionless, as if inanimate objects had the ability to hold their breaths. As Myron climbed up the porch stairs, he noticed a modern-looking wheelchair ramp that also led to the front door. The ramp looked out of place here, like a doughnut in a health food store. There was no doorbell, so he knocked.

No one answered. Curious. Myron had called ten minutes

ago, had heard a man answer, and hung up. Could be out back. Myron circled around the house. As he hit the backyard, the lake stared him in the face. It was a spectacular picture. The sun shone off the still—again, frighteningly motionless—water and made Myron squint. Placid. Tranquil. Myron felt the muscles in his shoulders start to unbunch.

Sitting in a wheelchair facing the lake was a man. A Saint Bernard lay by his feet. The dog too was frighteningly motionless. As Myron approached he saw that the man was whittling wood.

"Hi," Myron called out.

The man barely raised his eyes. He wore a red T-shirt and a John Deere cap pulled down over a weathered face. His legs were covered with a blanket, even in this heat. There was a portable phone within reach. "Hi." He went back to whittling. If he was surprised or upset to have company he was certainly taking it all in stride.

"Beautiful day," Myron said. Mr. Engaging Neighbor.

"Yep."

"Are you Jimmy Blaine?"

"Yep."

Even without the wheelchair it was hard to picture this guy working the city bowels of Philadelphia for eighteen years. Then again, it was hard to picture the bowels of Philadelphia, period, when you were out here.

Silence. No birds or crickets or anything but the whittling.

After some time had passed, Myron asked, "Had much rain this year?" Myron Bolitar, Salt of the Earth. Mr. Farmer's Almanac.

"Some."

"This your dog?"

"Yep. Name is Fred."

"Hi, Fred." Myron scratched the dog behind the ears. The dog wagged its tail without moving any other part of its body. Then it farted loudly.

"Great place you have here," Myron tried. Yep, just two good ol' boys shooting the breeze. Eb and Mr. Haney on *Green Acres*. Myron half expected denim overalls to materialize on his body.

"Uh-huh." Whittle, whittle.

"Listen, Mr. Blaine, my name is—"

"Myron Bolitar," Blaine finished for him. "I know who you are. Been expecting you."

He shouldn't have been surprised. "Jake called you?"

Blaine nodded without looking up from his whittling. "He said you were stubborn. Said you wouldn't listen to him."

"I just want to ask you a few questions."

"Nothing I care to say to you though."

"I'm not here to hound you, Mr. Blaine."

He nodded again. "Jake told me that too. Said you were okay. Said you liked to right wrongs, is all."

"What else did he say?"

"That you don't know how to mind your own business. That you're a wiseass. And that you're a major pain in the butt."

"He left out snazzy dancer," Myron said.

For the first time since he arrived Jimmy Blaine stopped whittling. "You trying to right the wrong done to Curtis Yeller?"

"I'm trying to find out who killed him."

"Simple," Blaine said. "Me."

"No, I don't think so."

That stopped him for a brief moment. He gave Myron the once-over and then began whittling again.

"Could you tell me what happened that night?" Myron asked.

"The boy pulled a gun. I shot him. That's it."

"How far away were you when you shot him?"

He shrugged, whittled. "Thirty feet. Maybe forty."

"How many shots did you fire?"

"Two."

"And he just dropped?"

"Nope. He swung around the corner with the other one— that Swade kid, I guess. They disappeared."

"You shot a man in the face and ribs and he kept running?"

"I didn't say they kept running. The two of them were by a corner. They disappeared around it. Didn't know it at the time, but the Yellers lived right there. They must have climbed in a window."

"With a bullet in his skull?"

Jimmy Blaine shrugged again. "The Swade kid probably helped him," he said.

"That's not how it happened," Myron said. "You didn't kill him."

Blaine eyed him and then went back to his whittling. "Second time you've said that," he noted. "You want to explain what you mean?"

"Two bullets hit Yeller."

"I just told you I shot twice."

"But two different caliber slugs were pulled out of him. One of the shots—the one in the head—was from close range. Less than a foot away."

Jimmy Blaine said nothing. He concentrated hard on his whittling. It looked like he was sculpting an animal of some sort, like the ones on the front porch. "Two different calibers, you say?" He aimed for nonchalance, but he wasn't making it.

"Yes."

"That kid I shot didn't have a record," Blaine continued. "You know what the odds are of that? In that part of the city?"

Myron nodded.

"I checked up on him," Blaine continued. "On my own. His name was Curtis Yeller. He was sixteen years old. He did well in school. He was a good kid. He had a chance at a good life until that night."

"You didn't kill him," Myron said.

Blaine whittled with a bit more intensity now. He blinked a lot. "How did you find out about those slugs?"

"The assistant M.E. told me," Myron said. "You never knew?"

He shook his head. "I guess it makes sense though," he said. "Blame me for it. Why not? It's easier. It's a legit shooting. No one questioned it. IAD barely broke a sweat. It didn't hurt my record. Didn't hurt anyone. No harm done, they figured."

Myron waited for him to say more, but he just kept whittling. Two long ears were now evident in the wood. Maybe he was making a rabbit. "Do you know who really killed Curtis Yeller?" Myron asked.

There was a long moment of the same whittle-filled silence. Fred farted again and wagged his tail. Myron's eyes kept going back to the lake. He stared out at the silver water. The effect was hypnotizing.

"No harm done," Jimmy Blaine said again. "That's what they all probably thought. Good ol' Jimmy. We won't let him take the rap. It'll be washed clean from his record. No one will know. Hell, some of the guys will even treat him special—

making a shooting like that. They'll say he saved his partner's life. Good ol' Jimmy will come out of this looking like a hero. Except for one thing."

Myron was tempted to ask what, but he sensed the answer was coming.

"I saw that boy dead," Blaine continued. "I saw Curtis Yeller lying in his own blood. I saw his mother hold him in her arms and cry. Sixteen years old. If he was a street punk or a drug addict or . . ." He stopped. "But he wasn't any of those things. Not this kid. He was one of the good ones. I found out later he never even touched the senator's kid. The other one—the Swade punk—he did the stabbing."

Two ducks splashed madly for a second, then stopped. Blaine put down the whittling, then thinking better of it, picked it back up again. "I replayed that night a lot of times in my head. It was dark, you know. There was barely any light. Maybe the Yeller kid wasn't going to fire the gun. Maybe what I saw wasn't even a gun. Or maybe none of that mattered. Maybe it was a legit shooting, but the pieces still never quite added up. I kept hearing the mother's screams. I kept seeing her press her dead boy's bloody face into her bosom. And I think about it, you know, and thinking ain't always a good thing for a cop to do. And four years later, the next time a kid is pointing a gun at me, I think about seeing another crying mother. I think long and hard. Too long."

He pointed to his legs. "And this is the result." He changed tools and kept whittling. "Nope, no harm done."

Silence.

Myron now understood Jake's attitude on the phone. Jimmy Blaine had gone through enough. If he'd done wrong in the case of Curtis Yeller, he had already paid an enormous price.

Problem was, Jimmy Blaine hadn't done wrong. He hadn't killed Curtis Yeller—legit shooting or not. In the end Jimmy Blaine was yet another victim of that night.

After some time had passed, Myron tried again. "Do you know who killed Curtis Yeller?"

"No, not really."

"But you have a thought."

"A thought maybe."

"You mind telling me?"

Blaine looked down at Fred, as if looking for an answer. The dog maintained his bear-rug pose. "Henry and I—he was my partner—got the call at a little past midnight," he began. "The two suspects had stolen a car from a driveway three blocks from the Old Oaks tennis club. A dark blue Cadillac Seville. We spotted a vehicle matching the description coming off the Roosevelt Expressway twenty minutes later. When we pulled up behind the stolen vehicle, the suspects sped off. We then engaged in a high-speed pursuit."

His voice had changed. He was a cop again, reading from a notepad he had read too many times in the past. "Henry and I followed the vehicle down an alley not far from Hunting Park Avenue, off Broad. The chase then proceeded on foot. At the time we had no identification on the two youths and thus no address. We only had the car. The chase proceeded for several blocks. As we turned a corner, the driver drew a firearm. My partner told him to freeze and drop his weapon. Yeller responded by aiming the firearm at Henry. I then fired two shots. The youth fell or stumbled out of sight beyond the next corner. By the time Henry and I turned the same corner, there was no sign of either youth. We figured that they were hiding in the nearby vicinity and awaited backup before proceeding. We secured the area as best we could. But the cops didn't get there first. The so-called secret service guys did."

"Senator Cross's men?"

Blaine nodded. "They called themselves 'national security,' but they were probably mob guys."

"Senator Cross told me he had no mob connections," Myron said.

Jimmy Blaine raised an eyebrow. "You serious?"

"Yes."

"The mob owns Bradley Cross," Blaine said. "More specifically, the Perretti family. Cross is a major gambler. I know he's also been arrested twice with prostitutes. One of his early opponents—this is back when he was just a congressman—ended up in the river during the primaries."

"And you traced it back to Cross?"

"Nothing anyone could prove. But we knew."

Myron considered this for a moment. Clearly, the beloved senator had lied to him. Big surprise. He had played Myron for a sucker. Another big surprise. Win was right. Myron always went astray when he believed the best about people. "So what happened next?"

"The senator's hoods were at the scene almost immediately. Been monitoring our radio. We'd been told over the air to cooperate with them one hundred percent. A real community effort finding these two kids. I'm surprised we spotted them first. Mob goons are usually better at this stuff than we are, you know?"

Myron knew. The mob had all the advantages over the police. They were closer to the city's underbelly. They could pay top dollar. They didn't have to worry about rules or laws or constitutional rights. They could inspire genuine fear.

"So what happened?" Myron asked.

"We started combing the area with flashlights, checking garbage Dumpsters, the whole bit. Cops and goons hand in hand. We found nothing for a while. Then we heard some gunshots. Henry and I ran to some dumpy apartment adjacent to where I'd shot Yeller. But Senator Cross's men were already there."

Blaine stopped. He leaned and gave Fred a good ear scratch. Fred still didn't move except for the thumping tail. Still scratching his dog, Blaine said, "Well, you know what we found." His voice was low and dead. "Yeller was dead. His mother was cradling him in her arms. She went through all these stages. First she just kept calling out his name over and over. Sweetly sometimes. Like she was trying to wake him up for school. Then she stroked the back of his head and rocked him and told him to go back to sleep. We all stood around and watched. Even the goons didn't bother her."

"What about the other gunshots?" Myron asked.

"What about them?"

"Didn't you wonder where they had come from?"

"I guess I did," he replied. "But I figured the security guys had shot after Swade. I didn't think they'd be dumb enough to admit it, but that's what I thought."

"It never crossed your mind they might have shot Yeller?"

"No."

"Why not?"

"I told you the mother went through stages."

"Right."

"Once she realized her boy wasn't waking up again, she started pointing fingers and screaming. She wanted to know who had shot her boy. She wanted to look the killer in the eyes, the murderer who had shot her son on the street in cold blood.

She said that Swade had dragged her boy in like that. Already shot up and dead."

"She said all that? That Swade dragged him in and that he was already shot?"

"Yes."

Silence. No water rippling. No birds chirping. Not even whittling. Several minutes passed before Blaine looked up and squinted. Then he said, "Cold."

"What?" Myron asked.

"That mother. If she was lying about who killed her boy. I always wondered why there were no repercussions. The mother never made a fuss. She didn't go to the newspapers. She didn't press charges. She didn't demand an explanation." He shook his head. "But what could have made her do that to her own flesh and blood? How could they have gotten to her so fast? With money? With threats? What?"

"I don't know," Myron said.

Jimmy Blaine finished whittling. It was a rabbit. Pretty good one too. A bird finally chirped, but it wasn't a pretty sound. More like a caw than a melody. Blaine spun his wheelchair around. "You want something to eat?" he asked. "I'm about to make lunch."

Myron looked at his watch. It was getting late. He had to get back to the office for his meeting with Ned Tunwell. "Thanks, but I really have to get going."

"Some other time then. When you're all done with this."

"Yes," Myron said.

Blaine blew the wood dust off the rabbit. "Still don't get it," he said.

"What?"

He stared at his finished handiwork, turning the rabbit over in his hand, studying it from every angle. "Could the mother have really been that frosty?" he asked. "How much money did they offer her? How much fright did they put into her? Hell, is there enough money or frights in the world for a mother to do that to her son?" He shook his head, dropped the wooden rabbit into his lap. "I just don't get it."

Myron didn't get it either.

41

MYRON GOT BACK INTO HIS FORD TAURUS AND headed east. He drove several miles without seeing a car. Mostly he saw trees. Lots of trees. Yes, the great outdoors. Myron was not an outdoors kind of guy. He didn't hunt or fish or do any of that. The appeal seemed clear, but it just wasn't for him. Something about being alone in the woods always reminded him of Ned Beatty in *Deliverance*. He needed people. He needed movement. He needed noise. City noise—as opposed to squeal-like-a-pig noise.

He now knew a lot more about the deaths of both Alexander Cross and Curtis Yeller than he'd known twenty-four hours ago, but he still didn't know if any of it was relevant to what happened to Valerie Simpson. And that was what he was after. Digging into a sensational six-year-old murder might be fun, but it was beside the point. He wanted Valerie Simpson's murderer. He wanted to find the person who had decided to snuff out that young, tortured life. Call it righting a wrong. Call it having a rescue or hero complex. Call it chivalry. Didn't matter. It was far simpler to Myron: Valerie deserved better.

The roads were still abandoned. The foliage on both sides of the road blurred into green walls. He started putting together what he knew. Errol Swade and Curtis Yeller had been spotted by Jimmy Blaine and his partner. A chase had ensued. Leaving aside the question of whether it was a legitimate shooting or not, Jimmy Blaine fired at Curtis Yeller. One of Blaine's bullets probably hit Curtis Yeller in the ribs, but the key fact is that somebody else shot Yeller in the head at close range. Somebody who was using a different caliber gun. Somebody who was not a cop.

So who shot Curtis Yeller?

The answer now seemed fairly obvious. Senator Cross's men—thugs or security forces or whatever they were—had been carrying firearms. Both Amanda West and Jimmy Blaine had confirmed that. They certainly had the opportunity. They certainly had the motive. It didn't matter if Cross had lied to Myron or not. Either way it would be in the senator's best interest for Curtis Yeller and Errol Swade to end up dead. Live suspects could talk. Live suspects could tell tales of drug use. Live suspects could counter the claim that Alexander Cross had died a hero. Dead men tell no tales. More important, dead men do not dispute spin doctors.

As for Errol Swade—the mysterious "escapee"—he'd almost assuredly been killed, probably in that gunfire Jimmy Blaine heard. The senator's men could have hid the body and dumped it later. Not definite, but again most likely. Errol Swade had a lot working against him. He was no genius. He was six-four. Myron knew from personal experience it was difficult to hide when you were that big. The odds of Swade eluding the police dragnet for so long—not to mention the mob's underworld army—were, as they say, statistically insignificant.

The sun was beginning to lower. The beams were now positioned in that one spot high enough to be in Myron's eyes but still low enough to avoid the sun visor. Myron squinted and slowed. His mind shifted gears again, this time to the aftermath of the Yeller shooting. Somehow Curtis Yeller ended up in his mother's arms, and somehow somebody got to her. Through either money or fear of reprisal—probably a combination of both—Deanna Yeller had been convinced to let the death of her son slide.

There were problems with this scenario, of course. For example, the money. Deanna Yeller's son had been murdered six years ago—yet the first big deposit in her account had occurred five months ago. Why the time lapse? She could have been biding her time, hiding the money under a mattress or something. But that didn't feel right. On the other hand, if the money was indeed new, the questions became more focused: why, all of a sudden, was Deanna getting this money? Why, all of a sudden, had Valerie been murdered? And how did Pavel fit in?

Good questions. No answers yet, but good questions. Maybe Ned Tunwell would know something useful.

Something caught Myron's eye. He glanced up. A car grew suddenly large in the rearview mirror. A big car. Black with a tinted windshield so you couldn't see inside. The license plate was New York.

The black car moved to its right, disappearing from the rearview mirror and appearing in the passenger-side mirror. Myron watched its progress. The imprint in the mirror reminded him that objects may be closer than they appear. Thanks for the clue. The black car picked up a little speed. As it came alongside of him, Myron could see it was a stretch limousine. A Lincoln Continental stretch. Extra-long stretch. The side windows too were tinted so you couldn't look in. It was like staring into a pair of giant aviator sunglasses. Myron could see himself in the reflection. He smiled and waved. His reflection smiled and waved back. Handsome devil.

The limo was dead-even with Myron's car now. The back window on the driver's side began to slide open. Myron half expected an elderly man to stick his head out and ask for Grey Poupon. Imagine his surprise when, instead, a gun appeared.

Without warning the gun fired twice, hitting the front and back tires on the passenger side of Myron's car. Myron swerved. He fought to regain control. The car veered off the road. Myron twisted the wheel and skidded away from a tree. The Ford Taurus came to a stop with a thud.

Two men jumped out of the limousine and headed toward him. Both wore blue suits. One also wore a Yankees cap. Business suit, baseball cap—an interesting fashion combo. They also carried guns. Their faces were stern and ready. Myron felt his heart in his throat. He was unarmed. He didn't like carrying guns, not for some moral reason but because they were bulky and uncomfortable and he so rarely ever used one. Win had warned him, but who listens to Win on a subject like this? But Myron had been careless. He was pissing off some powerful people and he should have been better prepared. He should have at least kept one in the glove compartment.

A little late for self-admonishments. Then again he might never have the chance again.

The two men approached. Not knowing what else to do, Myron ducked out of sight. He started dialing the car phone.

"Get your ass out of the car," one of the men barked.

Myron said, "Take another step and I'll drop you where you stand." Mr. Bluff.

Silence.

Myron dialed furiously and hit the send button. At that exact moment, he heard a sound like a twig breaking and then static. The goon with the Yankees cap had snapped off his antenna. This wasn't good. Myron kept himself low. He opened the glove compartment and reached inside. Nothing but maps and registration. His eyes searched the floor anxiously for some sort of weapon. The only thing he saw was the car cigarette lighter. Somehow he doubted that it would be effective against two armed goons. Maps, registration card, cigarette lighter. Unless Myron suddenly became MacGyver, he was in serious trouble.

He could hear footsteps shuffling about now. Myron's mind raced for an answer. Nothing came to him. Then he heard the car door of the limo open again. A quiet curse followed. Sounded like "Shit." Then a deep sigh.

"Bolitar, I ain't here to play no fucking games."

The voice sent a chill through Myron. Something hardened in his chest. New York accent. More specifically, a Bensonhurst accent. Frank Ache.

This was not good.

"Get the fuck out of the car now, ass-wipe. I ain't here to kill you."

"Your men just shot out my tires," Myron called back.

"Right, and if I wanted you dead, they would have shot out your fucking head."

Myron mulled that one over. "Good point," he said.

"Yeah, how about this one? I got two AK's sitting in the back here. If I wanted you dead, I could have Billy and Tony spray-paint this piece of shit you call a car with them."

"Another good point," Myron said.

"Now get the fuck out here," Frank barked. "I don't got all goddamn day. Ass-wipe."

Myron didn't really have a choice. He opened the car and stood. Frank Ache ducked back into the backseat. Billy and Tony scowled at him.

"Get in here," Frank called out.

Myron walked to the car. Billy and Tony blocked his path. "Give me your gun," the one with the Yankees cap said.

"Are you Billy or Tony?"

"The gun. Now."

Myron squinted at the baseball cap. "Wait a second, I get it. Plugs, right?"

"What?"

"Wearing a baseball cap with a suit. You're covering up new hair plugs."

The two men exchanged a glance. *Bingo,* Myron thought.

"Now, ass-wipe," the cap man said. "The gun."

Ass-wipe. The goon word of the week. "You didn't say please."

Frank's voice came from inside the car. "Jesus Christ, Billy, he don't have no piece. He was just yanking your hardware."

Billy's scowl grew angrier. Myron smiled, turned his palms to the sky, shrugged.

Tony opened the door. Myron slid into the backseat. Tony and Billy moved into the front. Frank pressed a button and a partition slid up, separating the back compartment from the front seats. The limo had a wet bar and television with VCR. The inside was sort of a royal red, blood-red actually, which, knowing Frank's history, probably helped cut down on the cost of cleanings.

"Nice wheels, Frank," Myron said.

Frank wore his customary garb—a velour sweat suit a couple of sizes too small. This one was green with yellow trim. The front zipper was down midway, like those guys in the seventies wore at discos. His gut was enormous enough to be mistaken for a multiple gestation. He was bald. He stared at Myron for several seconds before he spoke.

"You enjoy crawling up my ass crack, Bolitar?"

Myron blinked. "Gee, Frank, there's an appetizing thought."

"You're a crazy fuck, you know that? Why you always trying to piss me off? Huh?"

"Hey, I'm not the one who sent goons to rape his girlfriend," Myron said.

Frank pointed his finger at Myron's chest. "And what—you didn't have that coming? You didn't ask for that?"

Myron remained still. Stupid to raise Jessica with this man. Impossible as it seemed, you couldn't let it get personal. You had to separate, to stop thinking of Frank as the man who tried to do grievous harm to the love of your life. To think such thoughts would be at best counterproductive. At worst, suicide.

"I warned you," Frank continued. "I even sent Aaron so you'd know I was serious. You know what Aaron costs per day?"

"Not much anymore," Myron said.

"Ho, ho, I'm dying of laughter," Frank countered, but he wasn't laughing. "I tried to be reasonable with you. I let you have that Crane kid. And how do you thank me? By fucking around with my business."

"I'm trying to find a killer," Myron said.

"And I'm supposed to give a rat's ass? You want to go play

fucking Batman, fine, do it without costing me any money. Once you cost me money, you cross the line. Pavel meant money to me."

"Pavel also slept with underage girls," Myron said.

Frank held up his hands. "Hey, what a guy does in the privacy of his own bedroom, that don't concern me."

"You're so progressive, Frank. You voting Democratic now?"

"Look, ass-wipe, you want to hear I knew about Pavel? Fine, I knew. I knew Pavel fucked kiddies. So what? I work with guys who make Pavel Menansi look like Mother Teresa. I can't go picking and choosing in my line of work. So I ask myself one simple question: Is the guy making me money? If the answer is yes, then that's it. That's my rule. Pavel was making me money. End of story."

Myron said nothing. He was waiting for Ache to get to the point, which he sincerely hoped was not a bullet in the skull.

Frank took out a packet of chewing gum. Dentyne. He popped one in his mouth. "But I ain't here to get in no philosophy talk with you. Fact is, Pavel is dead. He's not making me money anymore, so my rule don't apply no more. You see?"

"Yes."

"I'm a simple businessman," Frank went on. "Pavel can't make me money no more. That means you and me don't have a beef no more. So you get to live. Wasting you would no longer be profitable to me. You understand?"

Myron nodded. "Are we having a tender moment, Frank?"

Frank leaned forward. His eyes were small and black. "No, ass-wipe, we're not. Next time I ain't gonna fuck around. Hiding your girlfriend won't help you. I'll find her. Or I'll waste someone else instead. Your mommy, your daddy, your friends—hell, even your fucking barber."

"His name is Pierre. And he prefers the term 'beauty technician.'"

Frank looked him square in the eye. "You fucking joking with me?"

"You just threatened my parents," Myron said. "What's the proper way to respond?"

Frank nodded slowly and sat back. "It's over. For now." He pressed a button and the partition slid down.

Billy said, "Yes, Mr. Ache?"

"Call a towing service for Bolitar's car."

"Yes, Mr. Ache."

Frank turned back to Myron. "Get the fuck out of my car."

"No hug first?"

"Out."

"Can I ask you one quick question?"

"What?"

"Did you have Valerie killed to protect Pavel?"

Frank grinned with bad, ferretlike teeth. "Get out," he said. "Or I'll use your nuts for snack foods."

"Right, thanks. Nice chatting with you, Frank, stay in touch." He opened the door and got out.

Frank slid across the seat and leaned his head through the open door. "You tell Win we talked, okay?"

"Why?"

"None of your business why. You just tell Win. Got it?"

"Got it," Myron said.

Frank closed the door. The limo drove away.

42

TRIPLE A GOT THERE PRETTY QUICKLY. MYRON reached his office at six-thirty. Ned wasn't there yet. Esperanza handed him his messages. He went into his office and returned calls.

Esperanza buzzed. "The bitch. Line three."

"Stop calling her that." He picked up the phone. "You're back at the loft?"

"Yes," Jessica said. "That didn't take long."

"I work fast," he said.

"And yet I never complain," she said.

"Ouch."

"So what happened?" she asked.

"Someone murdered Pavel Menansi. There's nothing for Ache to protect anymore."

"It's that simple?"

"It's business. Business with these guys is very simple."

"No profit, no kill."

"The cardinal rule," Myron said.

"Will you come over tonight?" she asked.

"Yes."

"But one rule of our own," she said.

"Oh?"

"No talking about Valerie Simpson or murder or any of this. We forget it all."

"What will we do instead?" Myron asked.

"Screw each other's brains out."

Myron said, "I guess I can live with that."

Esperanza leaned her head in and said, "He's heeeeeere."

He nodded at Esperanza and said to Jessica, "I'll call you later."

Myron put the phone back in the cradle. He stood and waited. An evening alone with Jessica. Sounded perfect. It also sounded scary. Things were moving too fast. He had no control. Jess was back and things appeared to be better than ever. Myron wondered about that. Mostly he wondered if he could survive another crash like last time, if he could go through the pain again. He also wondered what he could do to protect himself, realized the answer was nothing, and wished he was better at putting up defenses.

Ned Tunwell practically leaped into his office, hand extended—like an enthusiastic late-show guest coming through a curtain. Myron half expected him to wave to the crowd. He pumped Myron's hand. "Hey, Myron!"

"Hi, Ned. Have a seat."

Ned's smile dropped at Myron's tone. "Hey, there's nothing wrong with Duane, is there?"

"No."

Still standing but his voice was panicky. "He's not hurt?"

"No, Duane is fine."

"Great." The smile was back. Tough to keep a good man down. "That match yesterday—he was fantastic. Fantastic,

Myron. I tell you, the way he came back—it's all anyone's talking about. The exposure was awesome. Simply awesome. We couldn't have scripted it better. I practically wet myself."

"Uh-huh. Sit down, Ned."

"Sure." Ned sat. Myron hoped he wouldn't leave a stain on the seat. "Just a few hours away, Myron. The big day. The Saturday Semis. Big live crowd, huge TV audience. You think Duane's got a shot against Craig? Papers don't seem to think so."

Thomas Craig, the second seed and the game's premier serve-and-volley player, was currently playing his career-best tennis. "Yes," Myron said. "I think Duane's got a shot."

Ned's eyes were bright. "Wow. If he could somehow pull it off . . ." He stopped and just shook his head and grinned.

"Ned?"

He looked up. Wide-eyed. "Yes?"

"How well did you know Valerie Simpson?"

Ned hesitated. The eyes dulled a bit. "Me?"

Myron nodded.

"A little, I guess."

"Just a little?"

"Yeah." He flashed a nervous smile, struggled to hold it. "Why, what's up?"

"I heard differently."

"Oh?"

"I heard you were the one who got Nike to sign her. That you handled her account."

He squirmed a bit. "Yeah, well, I guess so."

"So you must have known her pretty well then."

"Maybe, I guess. Why are you asking me this, Myron? What's the big deal?"

"Do you trust me, Ned?"

"With my life, Myron. You know that. But this subject is painful for me. You understand?"

"You mean her dying and all?"

Ned made a lemon-sucking face. "No," he said. "I mean her career plummet. She was the first person I signed for Nike. I thought she'd launch me to the top. Instead she set me back five years. It was painful."

Another Mr. Sensitive.

"When she flopped," Ned continued, "guess who took the fall? Go ahead, guess."

Myron thought the question was rhetorical, but Ned waited with that expectant face of his. Myron finally said, "Would that be you, Ned?"

"Damn straight, me. I was thrown to the bottom. Just dumped there. I had to start climbing up all over again. Because of Valerie and her collapse. Don't get me wrong, Myron. I'm doing okay now—knock wood." He rapped his knuckles on the desk.

Myron knocked wood too. The sarcasm was lost on Ned. "Did you know Alexander Cross?" Myron asked.

Both Ned's eyebrows jumped. "Hey, what's the deal here?"

"Trust me, Ned."

"I do, Myron, really, but come on. . . ."

"It's a simple question: Did you know Alexander Cross?"

"I may have met him once, I don't remember. Through Valerie, of course. They were something of an item."

"How about you and Valerie?"

"What about me and Valerie?"

"Were you two an item?"

He put his hand out in a gesture of *stop*. "Hey, hold up. Look, Myron, I like you, I really do. You're an honest Joe. A straight shooter just like me—"

"No, Ned, you're not a straight shooter. You're jerking me around. You knew Alexander Cross. In fact you were at the Old Oaks tennis club the night he was murdered."

Ned opened his mouth but no sounds came out. He managed to shake his head no.

"Here." Myron stood and handed him the party guest list. "In yellow highlighter. E. Tunwell. Edward né Ned."

Ned looked down at the paper, looked up, looked down again. "This was a long time ago," he said. "What does this have to do with anything?"

"Why are you lying about it?"

"I'm not lying."

"You're hiding something, Ned."

"No, I'm not."

Myron stared down at him. Ned's eyes scattered, searching for safe haven and finding none. "Look, Myron, it's not what you think."

"I don't think anything." Then: "Did you sleep with her?"

"No!" Ned finally looked up and held a steady gaze. "That damn rumor almost ended my career. It's a lie that slimeball Menansi made up about me. It's a lie, Myron, I swear."

"Pavel Menansi told people that?"

Ned nodded. "He is a sick son of a bitch."

"Was."

"What?"

"Pavel Menansi is dead. Someone killed him last night. Shot in the chest. Very similar to what happened to Valerie." Myron waited two beats. Then he pointed his finger at Ned. "Where were you last night?"

Ned's eyes were two golf balls. "You can't think . . ."

Myron shrugged. "If you've got nothing to hide . . ."

"I don't!"

"Then tell me what happened."

"Nothing happened."

"What aren't you telling me, Ned?"

"It was nothing, Myron. I swear—"

Myron sighed. "You admit Valerie Simpson severely damaged your career. You admit you're still 'pained' by what she did. You've also told me that Pavel Menansi spread rumors about you. In fact you referred to a recent murder victim as—and I quote—'a sick son of a bitch.'"

"Hey, come on, Myron, that was just talk." Ned tried to smile his way out of it, but Myron kept his face stern. "It didn't mean anything."

"Maybe, maybe not. But I wonder how your superiors at Nike are going to react to the publicity."

The smile stayed in place, but there was nothing behind it. "Hey, you can't be serious. You can't go around spreading rumors like that."

"Why?" Myron asked. "You going to kill me too?"

"I didn't kill anyone!" Ned shouted.

Myron feigned fear. "I don't know . . ."

"Look, Valerie took me outside that night, okay, that's all. We kissed, but it went no further, I swear."

"Whoa, back up a second," Myron said. "Start at the beginning. You were at the party."

Ned slid to the tip of his chair, his words came fast now.

"Right, I was at the party, okay? So was Valerie. We arrived together. She was very excited because Alexander was going to announce their engagement. But when he backed out, she got really pissed off."

"Why did he back out?"

"His father. He made Alexander call it off."

"Senator Cross?"

"Uh-huh."

"Why?" Myron asked.

"How the hell am I supposed to know? Valerie told me the man was a major prick. She hated him. But when Alexander bowed to his whim like that, she blew her stack. She wanted revenge. A little payback."

"And you were handy?"

Ned snapped his fingers. "Right, exactly, I was handy. That's all. It wasn't my fault, Myron. I was at the wrong place at the wrong time. You understand, right?"

"So you two went outside," Myron prompted.

"We went outside and found a spot behind a shed. We only kissed, I swear. Nothing more. Just kissed. Then we heard some noise, so we stopped."

Myron sat back down. "What noise?"

"First it was just someone hitting tennis balls. But then we heard raised voices. One of them was Alexander's. Then we heard this awful scream."

"What did you do?" Myron asked.

"Me? Nothing at first. Valerie screamed too. Then she broke into a run. I followed her. I lost her for a second. Then I came around a bend and saw her up ahead just standing there. When I got to her I saw what she was staring at. Alexander was bleeding all over the grass. His friends were starting to run away. The big black guy was standing over the body. He had a tennis racket in one hand, a big knife in the other."

Myron leaned forward. "You saw the murderer?"

Ned nodded. "Up close and personal."

"And he was a big black guy?"

"Yep."

"How many of them were there?"

"Two. Both black."

So much for the setup theory. Unless Ned was lying, which Myron doubted. "So what happened next?"

Ned paused for a second. "You ever see Valerie in her prime? On the court, I mean."

"Yes."

"You ever see that look in her eyes?"

"What look?"

"Certain athletes get it. Larry Bird used to. Joe Montana. Michael Jordan. Maybe you used to too. Well, Val had it, and she had it now. The smaller black guy started screaming at the big one, saying stuff like, 'Look what you did,' 'Are you crazy,' stuff like that. Then they started to run. They ran right toward us. Me, I ran. I'm no fool. But not Val. She just stood there and waited. When they got close she let out this big scream and dove at the little guy. I couldn't believe it. She tackled him like a linebacker. They both ended up on the ground. The little guy whacked her with his tennis racket and managed to pull away."

"Did you get a good look at them?"

"Pretty good, I guess."

"Did you ever see pictures of Errol Swade?"

"Yeah, sure, his picture was on the news every day for a while."

"Was it the same guy you saw?"

"Definitely," he said without hesitation. "No question about it."

Myron mulled this over. They'd been there that night. At the Old Oaks Club. Myron had been wrong. Lucinda Elright had been wrong. Swade and Yeller were not just casual fall guys. "So what did you two do then?" Myron asked.

"Hey, her career was in enough trouble. We didn't need this kind of press. So I brought her back to the party. Didn't say anything to anyone about it. Val was out of it anyway—in a real funk, but that wasn't any surprise. I mean, think about it. She takes me outside to cheat on her boyfriend at the exact moment he's getting murdered. Weird, huh?"

Myron nodded. "Very."

And, Myron thought, the kind of thing that would push a troubled soul over the final ledge.

43

MYRON AND JESSICA KEPT THEIR PROMISE. They did not talk about the murders. They snuggled and watched *Strangers on a Train* on AMC while eating Thai takeout. They made love. They snuggled and watched *Rear Window* while downing some Häagen-Dazs. They made love again.

Myron felt light-headed. For one night he actually forgot all about the world of Valerie Simpson and Alexander Cross and Curtis Yeller and Errol Swade and Frank Ache. It felt good. Too good. He started thinking about the suburbs and the hoop in the driveway and then he made himself stop thinking such thoughts.

Several hours later the morning sunlight drop-kicked him back into the real world. The escape had been paradise and for a fleeting moment, as he lay in bed with Jessica, he considered wrapping his arms around her and not going anywhere. Why move? What was out there that could come close to this?

He had no answer. Jessica hugged him a little tighter, as though reading his thoughts, but it didn't last long. They both dressed in silence and drove to Flushing Meadows. Today was the big match. The last day of the U.S. Open. The women's finals sandwiched by the men's semifinals. First match of the day featured the number-two seed, Thomas Craig, vs. the tournament's biggest surprise, Duane Richwood.

After they passed through the gate Myron gave Jessica a ticket stub. "I'll meet you inside. I want to talk to Duane."

"Now?" she said. "Before the biggest match of his career?"

"Just for a second."

She shrugged, gave him a skeptical eye, took the ticket.

He hurried over to the players' lounge, showed his ID to the guard at the gate, and entered. The room was fairly unspectacular, considering that it was the players' lounge for a Grand Slam event. It reeked of baby powder. Duane sat alone in a corner. He had his Walkman on and his head tilted back. Myron couldn't tell if his eyes were opened or closed because, as always, Duane had on his sunglasses.

When he approached, Duane's finger switched off the music. He tilted his face up toward Myron. Myron could see himself in the reflection of the sunglasses. It reminded him of the windows in Frank's limo.

Duane's face was a rigid mask. He slowly slid the headphones off his ears and let them hang around his neck like a horseshoe. "She's gone," Duane said slowly. "Wanda left me."

"When?" Myron asked. The question was stupid and irrelevant, but he wasn't sure what else to say.

"This morning. What did you tell her?"

"Nothing."

"I heard she came to you," Duane said.

Myron said nothing.

"Did you tell her about seeing me at the hotel?"

"No."

Duane changed tapes in the Walkman. "Get out of here," he said.

"She cares about you, Duane."

"Funny way of showing it."

"She just wants to know what's wrong."

"Nothing's wrong."

The sunglasses were disconcerting. He looked straight up at Myron; it appeared as though they were making eye contact, but who knew? "This match is important," Myron said, "but not like Wanda."

"You think I don't know that?" he snapped.

"Then tell her the truth."

Duane's chiseled face smiled slowly. "You don't understand," he said.

"Make me understand."

He fiddled with the Walkman, popping the tape out, pushing it back in. "You think telling the truth will make it better, but you don't know what the truth is. You talking like 'The truth will set you free' when you don't even know the truth. The truth don't always set you free, Myron. Sometimes the truth can kill."

"Hiding the truth isn't working," Myron said.

"It would if you'd let it lie."

"Someone was murdered. That's not something you can just let lie."

Duane put the Walkman's headphones back on his ears. "Maybe it should be," he said.

Silence.

The two men stared dares. Myron could hear the faint din coming from the Walkman. Then he said to Duane, "You were there the night Alexander Cross was murdered. You were at the club with Yeller and Swade."

The stares continued. Behind them, Thomas Craig lined up by the door. He carried several tennis rackets and what looked like an overnight bag. Security was there too with walkie-talkies and earplugs. They nodded toward Duane. "Showtime, Mr. Richwood."

Duane stood. "Excuse me," he said to Myron. "I have a match to play."

He walked behind Thomas Craig. Thomas Craig smiled politely. Duane did likewise. Very civil, tennis. Myron watched them leave. He sat there for a few minutes in the abandoned locker room. In the distance he heard the cheers as both men entered the court.

Showtime.

Myron found his way to his seat. It was during the match—in the fourth set actually—when he finally figured out who murdered Valerie Simpson.

44

STADIUM COURT WAS PACKED BY THE TIME Myron sat down. Duane and Thomas Craig were still warming up, each taking turns lofting easy lobs for the other to slam away. The fans floated and mingled and socialized and made sure they were seen. The usual celebs were there: Johnny Carson, Alan King, David Dinkins, Renee Richards, Barbra Streisand, Ivana Trump.

Jake and his son Gerard came down to the box.

"I see you got the tickets okay," Myron said.

Jake nodded. "Great seats."

"Nothing's too good for my friends."

"No," Jake said, "I meant yours."

Ever the wiseass.

Jake and Gerard chatted a moment with Jessica before moving up to their seats, which were by any stretch of the imagination excellently situated. Myron scanned the crowd. A lot of familiar faces. Senator Bradley Cross was there with his entourage, including his son's old chum Gregory Caufield. Frank Ache had shown up wearing the same sweat suit Myron had seen him in yesterday. Frank nodded toward Myron. Myron did not nod back. Kenneth and Helen Van Slyke were there too—surprise, surprise. They were sitting a few boxes over. Myron tried to catch Helen's eye, but she was trying very hard to pretend she didn't see him. Ned Tunwell and Friends (not to be confused with Barney and Friends, though the confusion would be understandable) were in their usual box. Ned too was doing his utmost not to see Myron. He seemed less animated today.

"I'll be right back," Jessica said.

Myron sat. Henry Hobman was already in game mode. Myron said, "Hi, Henry."

"Stop messing with his head," Henry said. "Your job is to keep him happy."

Myron didn't bother responding.

Win finally showed up. He wore a pink shirt from some golf club, bright green pants, white bucks, and a yellow sweater tied around his neck. "Hello," Win said.

Myron shook his head. "Who dresses you?"

"It's the latest in sophisticated wear."

"You clash with the world."

"Pardon *moi,* Monsieur Saint Laurent." Win sat down. "Did you talk to Duane?"

"Just a little pep talk."

Jessica returned. She greeted Win with a kiss on the cheek. "Thank you," she whispered to him.

Win said nothing.

They stood for the national anthem. When it was over, the English-accented voice on the loudspeaker asked everyone to lower their heads for a moment of silence to remember the great Pavel Menansi. Heads lowered. The crowd hushed. Someone sniffled. Win rolled his eyes. Two minutes later the match began.

The play was incredible. Both men were power hitters, but no one expected anything like this. The pace was like something from another planet. A far faster planet. The IBM serve speedometer drew constant "Ooo"s from the crowd. Rallies didn't last very long. Mistakes were made, but so were incredible shots. This was serve and volley in the old tradition taken to the tenth power. Duane was unconscious. He whacked at the ball with uncommon fury, as though the ball had personally offended him. Myron had never seen either man play better.

Win leaned over and whispered, "Must have been some pep talk."

"Wanda left him."

"Ah," Win said with a nod. "That explains it. The shackles are off."

"I don't think that's it, Win."

"If you say so."

Myron didn't bother. It was like talking colors with a blind man.

Duane won the first set 6–2. The second set went into a tie-breaker, which Thomas Craig won. As the third set opened, Win said, "What have you learned?"

Myron filled him in, trying to keep his voice down. At one point, Ivana Trump shushed him. Win waved a hand in her direction. "She digs me. Big-time."

"Get real," Myron said.

During a change of sides in the third set, Win said, "So first we believed that Valerie was eliminated because she knew something harmful about Pavel Menansi. Now we believe that she was eliminated because she saw something the night Alexander Cross was killed."

"A possibility," Myron said.

During the next change of sides, Myron felt a tap on his shoulder. He looked down—way down—and was surprised. "Dr. Abramson," he said.

"Hello, Myron."

"Nice to see you, Doc."

"Nice to see you too," she said. "Your client is playing very well. You must be pleased."

"I'm sorry," Myron said. "I can neither confirm nor deny that Duane Richwood is a client of mine."

She didn't smile. "Was that supposed to be funny?"

"Guess not," Myron said "I didn't know you were a tennis fan."

"I come every year." She spotted Win. "Hello, Mr. Lockwood."

Win nodded. "Dr. Abramson."

"This is my friend Jessica Culver," Myron said.

The two women shook hands and exchanged polite smiles. "A pleasure," Dr. Abramson said. "Well, I don't want to keep you. I just wanted to say a quick hello."

"Can we talk a little later?" Myron asked.

"No, I don't think so. Good-bye."

"Did you know that Kenneth and Helen Van Slyke are here?"

"Yes. And I also know they just stepped out for a moment."

Myron looked toward their seats. Empty. He smiled. "You crafty shrink. Coming over to say hello when they weren't looking."

"And to say good-bye," she said, returning the smile. She turned away and left. The match started up again. During the next change of sides, the Van Slykes returned. Myron leaned over to Win. "How do you know Dr. Abramson?"

"I visited Valerie," he said.

"Often?"

Win didn't answer. He might have shrugged, might not. Either way it told Myron to mind his own business. Myron looked at Jessica. She shrugged too.

On the court Duane was growing more erratic, but he was still hitting enough winners to maintain the edge. He won the third set 7–5. He was up two sets to one—one set away from the U.S. Open finals. The Nike box was animated. Hands were slapping Ned's back. Even Ned seemed to be perking up now. Hard to keep a good man down.

Senator Cross watched in silence. No one talked to him, and he talked to no one. Not even during breaks. He had met Myron's eyes only once. He stared for a long time, but did not move. Helen and Kenneth Van Slyke spoke to the people around them, but they both looked uncomfortable. Frank Ache adjusted his crotch and jabbered with Roy O'Connor, the president of TruPro. Frank looked comfortable. Roy looked like he wanted to puke. Ivana Trump glanced about her surroundings. Every time she looked near Win, he blew her kisses.

It was during a serve in the third set when Myron finally began to see it. It started small, a statement made by Jimmy Blaine that did not compute. Something about the foot chase in Philadelphia. The rest sort of tumbled into place. When the final piece clicked, he sat up.

Win and Jessica traded glances. Myron stared off.

"What is it?" Jessica asked.

Myron turned to Win. "I need to talk to Gregory Caufield."

"When?"

"Right away, next break. Can you get him alone?"

Win nodded. "Done."

45

IN THE TOURNAMENT'S FIRST FEW ROUNDS IT was not uncommon for fifteen or more matches to be going on at the same time. The biggest names usually stayed on Stadium Court or the Grandstand, while other matches took place in smaller venues, some with no seating. Today those courts were so barren, Myron half expected a tumbleweed to blow through. He waited by court sixteen, a semimajor court. It had the most seating next to the Stadium and Grandstand, though less than most high school gyms.

He sat on an aluminum bench in the front row. The sun had gained strength and was now at its most potent. Every once in a while he heard cheers erupt from the Stadium's crowd a hundred yards or so away. Sometimes tennis fans sounded like they were having an orgasm during particularly brilliant points. It sort of built up slowly with a low oh-oh-oh, and then increased Oh-Oh, and finally the big OH-OH-OH, followed by a loud sigh and clapping.

Weird thought.

Distracting thought too.

He heard Gregory Caufield well before he saw him. That same creepy, money accent that Win possessed said, "Windsor, where on earth are we going?"

"Just over here, Gregory."

"Are you sure this couldn't wait, old boy?"

Old boy. Neither one of them was thirty-five yet and he was using the term *old boy*.

"No, Gregory, it can't."

They rounded the corner. Gregory's eyes widened a bit when he saw Myron, but he recovered fast. He smiled and stuck out his hand. "Hello, Myron."

"Hi, Greg."

His face flinched for a second. He was Gregory, not Greg.

"What's this all about, Windsor? I thought you had something private to tell me."

Win shrugged. "I lied," he said. "Myron needs to speak with you. He needs your cooperation."

Gregory turned to Myron and waited.

"I want to talk to you about the night Alexander Cross was murdered."

"I know nothing about it," Gregory said.

"You know plenty about it, but I just have one question for you."

"I'm sorry," Gregory said. "I must be getting back now." He turned to leave. Win blocked his path. Gregory looked puzzled.

"Just one question," Myron said.

Gregory ignored him. "Please move out of my way, Windsor."

Win said, "No."

Gregory could not believe what he was hearing. He half smiled and put a hand through his unruly hair. "Are you prepared to use force to keep me here?"

"Yes."

"Please, Windsor, this is no longer amusing."

"Myron needs your cooperation."

"And I am not prepared to give it to him. Now I insist you move."

Win did not move. "Are you telling me you will not cooperate, Gregory?"

"That is precisely what I am telling you."

Win's palm shot out and hit the solar plexus. The wind gushed from Gregory. He collapsed to one knee, his face pale and shocked. Myron shook his head at Win, but he understood what he was doing. To people like Gregory—actually, to most people—violence is abstract. They read about it. They see it in movies and in the newspapers. But it never really touches them. It simply doesn't exist in their world. Win had shown Gregory how quickly that can change. Gregory had now experienced physical pain from the hands of a fellow human being. He would be different now. Not just here, not just today.

Gregory held his chest. He was on the verge of tears.

"Do not make me strike you again," Win said.

Myron stepped toward him but did not help him up. "Gregory, we know all about that night," he said. "I have just one question. I don't care what you were doing out there. I don't care if you were snorting or shooting illegal substances. That doesn't interest me in the least. What you say will in no way incriminate you—unless you lie to me."

Gregory looked up at him. His face was completely void of any color.

"They weren't robbing the club, were they?" Myron asked.

Gregory did not answer.

"Errol Swade and Curtis Yeller hadn't broken into the club to rob it," Myron said. "And they weren't there selling drugs either. Am I right? If I am, just nod."

Gregory looked at Win, then back to Myron. He nodded.

"Tell me what they were doing," Myron said.

Gregory didn't say anything.

"Just say it," Myron continued. "I already know the answer. I just need you to say it. What were they doing there that night?"

Gregory's breathing was returning to normal now. He reached out his hand. Myron took it. He stood up and looked Myron straight in the eye.

"What were they doing?" Myron asked. "Tell me."

And then Gregory Caufield said exactly what Myron had expected. "They were playing tennis."

46

MYRON RAN TO HIS CAR.
Duane was ahead two sets to one, 4–2 in the fourth set. He was two games away from reaching the U.S. Open finals, but that no longer seemed like such a big deal. Myron now knew what happened. He knew what happened to Alexander Cross and Curtis Yeller and Errol Swade and Valerie Simpson and maybe even Pavel Menansi.

He picked up the car phone and began placing calls. His second call was to Esperanza's house. She picked up.

"I'm with Lucy," she said. Esperanza had been dating a woman named Lucy for a couple months now. They seemed serious. Of course, Myron thought Esperanza was serious with a guy named Max just a few months earlier. Dating a Max, then a Lucy. Never a dull moment.

"Do you have the appointment book?" Myron asked.

"I got a copy on my computer here."

"The last day Valerie Simpson was in our office, who had the appointment right before her?"

"Give me a second." He heard her clack some keys. "Duane."

As he thought. "Thanks."

"You're not at the match?"

"No."

"Where are you?"

"In my car."

"Is Win with you?" she asked.

"No."

"How about the witch?"

"I'm alone."

"Swing by and pick me up then. Lucy's leaving anyway."

"No."

He hung up and switched on the radio. Duane was up 5–2. One game away. He dialed the home number of Amanda West, M.E. Then he called Jimmy Blaine. It all checked out. Myron felt something very cold caress his spine.

His hand actually trembled when he called Lucinda Elright. The old teacher answered on the first ring.

"Can you see me today?" Myron asked.

"Yes, of course."

"I should be there in a couple of hours."

"I'll be here," Lucinda said. She asked no questions, wanted no explanations. She simply said, "Good-bye."

Duane won the final set 6–2. He was in the finals of the U.S. Open, but the postgame wrap-up was short for several reasons. First, the women's finals came up right on the heels of Duane's impressive win. Second, the colorful Duane Richwood had run out without doing any interviews. The radio broadcasters seemed surprised.

Myron was not.

He reached Lucinda Elright's apartment in less than two hours. He stayed less than five minutes, but the visit was the final confirmation Myron needed. There was no longer any doubt. He took the book and got back in his car. Half an hour later he parked in the driveway. Myron rang the doorbell. No smile this time when the door opened. No surprise this time either.

"I know what happened to Errol Swade," Myron said. "He's dead."

Deanna Yeller blinked. "I told you that the first time you came by."

"But," Myron said, "you didn't tell me you killed him."

47

MYRON DIDN'T WAIT FOR AN INVITATION. HE pushed past her. Again he was struck by the impersonal feel of this house. Not one picture. Not one remembrance. But now he understood why. The TV was tuned on the tennis match. No surprise there. The women were midway through the first set.

Deanna Yeller followed him.

"It must torture you," he said.

"What?"

"Watching Duane on TV. Instead of in person."

"It was just a fling," she said in a monotone. "It didn't mean anything."

"Duane was just a one-nighter?"

"Something like that."

"I don't think so," Myron said. "Duane Richwood is your son."

"What are you talking about? I only had one son."

"That's true."

"And he's dead. They killed him, remember?"

"That's not true. Errol Swade was killed. Not Curtis."

"I don't know what you're talking about," she said. But there wasn't much conviction in her voice. She sounded tired, like she was going through the motions—or maybe she just realized that Myron was beyond buying the lies.

"I know now." Myron showed her the book in his hand. "Do you know what this is?"

She looked at the book, her face blank.

"It's the yearbook from Curtis's high school. I just got it from Lucinda Elright."

Deanna Yeller looked so frail, a stiff breeze would send her crashing into the wall. Myron opened the yearbook. "Duane has had a nose job since then. Maybe some other surgery too, I can't be sure. His hair is different. He's gotten a lot more muscular, but then again, he's not a skinny sixteen-year-old anymore. Plus he always wears sunglasses in public. Always. Who would recognize him? Who would even imagine Duane Richwood was a murder suspect killed six years ago?"

Deanna stumbled over to a table. She sat down. She pointed weakly to the chair across from her. Myron took it.

"Curtis was a great athlete," Myron continued, fingering through the pages. "He was only a sophomore, but he was already starting varsity football and basketball. The high school he went to didn't have a tennis team, but Lucinda told me that didn't stop him. He played as often as he could. He loved the game."

Deanna Yeller remained still.

"You see, from the beginning I never bought the robbery angle," Myron said. "You were quick to call your son a thief, Deanna, but the facts didn't back it up. He was a good kid. He had no record. And he was smart. There was nothing to steal out there. Then I thought maybe it was a drug deal gone bad.

That made the most sense. Alexander Cross was a user. Errol Swade was a seller. But that didn't explain why your son was there. I even thought for a while that Curtis and Errol had never gone to the club, that they were just scapegoats. But a fairly reliable witness swears he saw them both. He also said he heard tennis balls being hit at night. He also saw Curtis and Errol each carrying one tennis racket. Why? If you're robbing the place, you carry as many rackets as you can. If you're doing a drug deal, you don't carry any rackets. The answer was obvious in the end: they were there to play tennis. They jumped the fence not to rob the place, but because Curtis wanted to play tennis."

Deanna lifted her head up. She was hollow-eyed. Her movements were sparse and slow. "It was a grass court," she said. "He'd watched Wimbledon on TV that week. He just wanted to play on a grass court, that's all."

"Unfortunately Alexander Cross and his buddies were outside getting high," Myron went on. "They heard Curtis and Errol. What happened next is not exactly clear, but I think we can probably take Senator Cross's word on this one. Alexander, high as a kite, created a conflict. Maybe he didn't like the idea of a couple of black kids playing on his court. Or maybe he really thought they were there to rob the club. It doesn't matter. What does matter is that Errol Swade took out a knife and killed him. It might have been self-defense, but I doubt it."

"He just reacted," Deanna said. "Stupid kid saw a bunch of white boys, so he stabbed. Errol didn't know any different."

Myron nodded. "They ran away then, but Curtis got tackled in the bushes by Valerie Simpson. They struggled. Valerie got a good look at Curtis. A very good look. When you are fighting with someone you believed killed your fiancé, you don't forget the face. Curtis managed to break away. He and Errol jumped the fence and ran down the block. They found a car in a driveway. Errol had been arrested several times already for stealing cars. Breaking in and hot-wiring one was no problem for him. That's what first gave it to me. I talked to the officer who supposedly shot your son. His name is Jimmy Blaine. Jimmy said he shot the *driver* of the car, not the passenger. But Curtis wouldn't have been driving. That wouldn't make any sense. The driver was the experienced thief, not the good kid. So then it dawned on me: Jimmy Blaine didn't shoot Curtis Yeller. He shot Errol Swade."

Deanna Yeller sat still as a stone.

"The bullet hit Errol in the ribs. With Curtis's help they managed to round the corner and crawl in through the fire escape. They made their way to your apartment. By now sirens were sounding all over the place. They were closing in on all of you. Errol and Curtis were probably in a state of panic. It was pandemonium. They told you what happened. You knew what this meant—a rich white boy stabbed at a fancy rich white club. Your son was doomed. Even if Curtis had only been standing there—even if Errol told the police that it was all his fault—Curtis was finished."

"I knew more than that," Deanna interjected. "It'd been almost an hour since the murder. The radio already said who the victim was. Not just a rich white boy, but the son of a United States senator."

"And," Myron continued, "you knew Errol had a long record. You knew it was his fault. You knew he was going away for good this time. Errol's life was over, and he had no one to blame but himself. But Curtis was innocent. Curtis was a good boy.

He'd done everything right, and now because of the stupidity of his cousin, his life was about to be flushed away."

Deanna looked up. "But that was all true," she insisted, sparking up just a bit. "Can't deny any of that, can you? Can you?"

"No," Myron said. "I guess I can't. What you did next probably didn't take much thought. You'd heard the police fire two bullets. You saw only one in Errol. Most important, Curtis didn't have a record. His mug shot wasn't on file. His description wasn't on file." He stopped. Her eyes were clear and on him. "Whose gun was it, Deanna?"

"Errol's."

"He had it with him?"

She nodded.

"So you took the gun. You pressed it against Errol's cheek. And you fired."

She nodded again.

"You blew his face right off," Myron continued. "I wondered about that too. Why would someone shoot him up close in the face? Why not in the back of the head or the heart? The answer is, you didn't want anyone to see his face. You wanted him to be an unrecognizable lump. Then you put on your big act. You cradled him in your arms and cried while the police and the senator's hoods came crashing in. It was so simple really. I asked the medical examiner how they identified Curtis's body. She scoffed at such a ridiculous question. The usual way, she told me. The next of kin. You, Deanna. The mother. What else did they need? Why question that? The cops were thrilled you didn't want to make a big deal over it, so they didn't look too closely. And just to cement your plan, you were smart enough to have the body cremated immediately. Even if someone wanted to go back and check, the evidence was ashes.

"As for Curtis, his escape was easy. A nationwide manhunt began for Errol Swade, a six-foot four-inch man who looked nothing like your son. No one was looking for Curtis Yeller. He was dead."

"It wasn't quite that easy," Deanna said. "Curtis and I were careful. Powerful men were in this. The police scared me, sure, but not as much as those men who worked for the senator. And then the papers all made that Cross boy out to be a hero. Curtis knew the truth. If the senator ever got a hold of my boy . . ." She shrugged away the obvious.

Myron nodded. He'd thought the same thing too. Dead men tell no tales. "So Curtis spent the next five years underground?" he asked.

"I guess you could call it that," Deanna said. "He roamed around, scraped by on whatever he could. I sent him money when I had some, but I told him to never come back to Philadelphia. We'd arrange times to talk on public phones and stuff. He grew up on his own. He lived on the streets, but he was well-spoken enough to get some decent jobs. He worked for three years at a tennis club near Boston. He played all the time, even hustled a few games. I saved up enough for him to get a little plastic surgery done. Just some little touches, you know, in case he ran into someone he knew. Like you said, he got a lot bigger. He grew an inch and put on thirty pounds. He also wore those sunglasses, though I always thought that was going a little too far. No one's gonna recognize him, I thought. Not anymore. It'd been too long. Worst thing happen, someone might think he resembles a dead boy they used to know. I mean, five years passed. We thought he was safe."

"That's why you started getting money recently," Myron said. "It wasn't a payoff. The money came from Duane's turning pro. He bought you this house."

She nodded.

"And when I saw you two at the hotel that night, I immediately jumped to the conclusion that you were lovers. But it was actually a son visiting his mother. The embrace I saw when he left your room—it wasn't the embrace of lovers, but a mother hugging her son good-bye. In fact Duane hadn't slept around at all. That was an act on his part. Wanda was right all along. He loved her. He never cheated on her. Not with you. And not with Valerie Simpson."

She nodded again. "He loves that girl. He and Wanda are good together."

"Everything was going just fine until Valerie spotted Duane in my office," Myron continued. "His sunglasses were off. She saw him up close, and like I said before, you don't forget the face of the man you think killed your fiancé. She recognized him. She stole his card from my Rolodex and called. What happened next, Deanna? Did she threaten to expose him?"

"There's some stuff we left out," Deanna said. "I just want to be clear, okay?"

Myron nodded.

"Curtis didn't know I was going to kill Errol that night," she said. "I just told him to hide in the basement. There was a closed-off tunnel down there. I knew he'd be safe for a while. I told Errol to stay with me, I'd fix his ribs. When Curtis was out of the room, I shot Errol."

"Did Curtis ever learn the truth?"

"He figured it out later. But he didn't know then. He had nothing to do with it."

"So what about Valerie? Was she going to talk?"

"Yes."

Their eyes met.

"So you killed her," Myron said.

For a few moments Deanna said nothing. She stared down at her hands, as though looking for something. "She wouldn't listen to reason," she said softly. "Duane told me that Valerie called him. He tried to convince her she had the wrong man, but she wouldn't hear it. So I met up with her at the hotel. I tried to persuade her too. I told her he'd done nothing wrong, but she just kept talking this nonsense about not hiding things anymore—how she'd buried too many things and it had to all come out." Deanna Yeller closed her eyes and shook her head. "The girl left me no choice. I watched her hotel. I saw her rush out. I saw her rush to the matches, and I knew she was scared and I knew she was going to say something and I knew I couldn't wait anymore, that I had to stop her now or . . ." She sat still. Then she moved her hands off the table and folded them on her lap. "I had no choice."

Myron remained quiet.

"I did the only thing I could," she said. "It was her life or my son's life."

"So for the second time you chose your son."

"Yes. And if you turn me in, it'll all be for nothing. The truth will come out, and they'll kill my boy. You know they will."

"I'll protect him," Myron said.

"No, that's my job."

Tires squealed in the driveway. Myron rose and looked out the window. It was Duane. He threw the car in park and leaped out.

"Keep him out," Deanna said, suddenly out of her chair. "Please."

"What?"

She ran to the door and threw the dead bolt. "I don't want him to see."

"See what?"

But now Myron did see. She turned toward him. She had a gun in her hand. "I've already killed twice to save him. What's a third?"

Myron looked for a safe place to dive, but for the second time in this case he'd been careless. He was out in the open. It would be impossible to miss. "Killing me won't make it go away," he said.

"I know," she replied.

There was a pounding at the door. Duane shouted, "Open up! Don't say anything to him!" More pounding.

Deanna's eyes welled with tears. "Don't tell anyone, Myron. No need to say anything anymore. The guilty will have all been punished."

She placed the barrel of the gun against her head.

"Don't," Myron whispered.

From outside the door, Duane shouted, "Mama! Open up, Mama!"

She turned toward the voice. Myron tried to reach her in time, but he had no chance. She pulled the trigger and made one final sacrifice for her son.

48

TIME PASSED. MYRON HAD TO PERSUADE Duane to leave his mother alone. It was what she would have wanted, Myron reminded him. When they were both far enough away, Myron placed an anonymous call to the Cherry Hill police. "I think I heard a gunshot," he said. He gave the address and hung up.

They met up at a stop along the New Jersey Turnpike. Duane was no longer crying.

"Are you going to tell?" Duane asked.

"No," Myron said.

"Not even Valerie's mother?"

"I don't owe her anything."

Silence. Then Duane started tearing again.

"Did the truth set you free, Myron?"

He ignored the question. "Tell Wanda," Myron said. "If you really love her, tell her everything. It's the only chance you have."

"You can't be my agent anymore," Duane said.

"I know," Myron said.

"There was no other way for her. She had to protect me."

"There was another way."

"What? If it was your kid, what would you have done?"

Myron didn't have the answer. He only knew that killing Valerie Simpson was not it. "Are you going to play tomorrow?"

"Yes," he said. He climbed back in his car. "And I'm going to win."

Myron did not doubt it.

IT WAS LATE when he got back to New York. He parked the car at the Kinney lot and headed past the ugly intestinal sculpture and into the building. The security guard greeted him. It was Saturday night. Practically no one was there. But even on street level Myron had seen the light on.

He took the elevator to the fourteenth floor. The customary hubbub of activity at Lock-Horne Securities was absent. The floor was dark. Most of the computers had been turned off and covered with plastic, though a few were left on, the bizarre screen savers dancing streaks of lights across the desk. Myron walked toward the light in the corner office. Win was sitting at his desk, reading a book in Korean. He looked up when Myron entered.

"So tell me," Win said.

Myron did. The whole story.

"Ironic," Win said when he'd finished.

"What?"

"We kept wondering how a mother could care so little for her son when in reality the problem was just the opposite. She cared too much."

Myron nodded.

Silence.

Then Win said, "You know?"

"Yes."

"How?"

"Dr. Abramson," Myron said. "Your visiting Valerie enough for her to know your name. It got me thinking."

Win nodded. "I was going to tell you."

"You didn't have to kill him," Myron said.

"You're a child sometimes," Win said. "I did what had to be done."

"You didn't have to kill him."

"Frank Ache would have killed us," Win said. "The only reason he chose to back off was because Pavel Menansi was dead—ergo the profit was gone. By eliminating Pavel, I took away his motive. Our options were clear: we could have taken on the mob and eventually gotten killed, or we could exterminate a vermin. In the end, sacrificing scum saved our lives."

"What else did you do to Ache?" Myron asked.

"What do you mean?"

"Frank didn't show up in the woods just to call off a hit. Something had scared him. He told me to mention our meeting to you."

"Oh," Win said, "that." He stood and grabbed his putter. He dropped a few golf balls on the floor. "I sent him a little package."

"What package?"

"One containing Aaron's right testicle. That, added together with Pavel's death, was enough to convince him that it would be in all of our interests to drop the matter."

Myron shook his head. "What separates you from Deanna Yeller?"

"Just one thing," Win said. He lined up a putt and sank it. "I don't fault her for what she did the night Alexander Cross was murdered. It was practical. It made sense. She didn't trust the justice system. She didn't trust a United States senator. In both cases, she was undoubtedly right. And what did she sacrifice? Her lowlife nephew who would have spent his life behind bars anyway. No, in that case we were the same."

He lined up over the next putt and checked the lie. "Where we differ, however, is that she killed an innocent person the second time around. I did not."

"You're drawing a pretty thin line," Myron said.

"The world is made up of thin lines, my friend. I was there. I visited Valerie every week in the institution. Did you know that?"

Myron shook his head. He was probably closer to Win than anyone, and he hadn't known that. He hadn't even known he knew Valerie Simpson.

Win took another putt. "From the first moment I saw her in that godforsaken place I wanted to know what changed her. I wanted to know what monstrosity had deadened the spirit that had soared so. You were the one who figured it out. Pavel Menansi did that to her, just as he would have done it to Janet Koffman if I hadn't stopped him." Win looked over at Myron. "You already know this, but I'll say it just the same: the fact that killing Pavel helped us with Frank Ache was just a bonus. I would have killed him anyway. I really didn't need any justification."

"There were other ways to make him pay," Myron said.

"How?" Win scoffed. "By arresting him? No one would press charges. And even if all was revealed as per your plan, what would happen to him? He'd probably write a book and go on *Oprah*. He'd tell the world how he'd been abused as a child or some such nonsense. He'd be an even bigger celebrity." Win took another putt. Another make. "We're not the same, you and I. We both know that. But it's okay."

"It's not okay."

"Yes, it is. If we were the same it wouldn't work. We'd both be dead by now. Or insane. We balance each other. It's why you're my best friend. It's why I love you."

Silence.

"Don't do it again," Myron said.

Win did not reply. He lined up another putt.

"Did you hear me?"

"It's time to move on," Win said. "This incident is in the past. You know better than to try to control the future."

More silence. Win sank another putt.

"Jessica is waiting," Win said. "She told me to remind you about her new oils."

Myron turned and left then. He felt unclean and unsure. But he knew Win was right: it was over. It would just take a bit of time for things to feel normal again. He would recover.

And, Myron thought as he headed into the elevator, what better way to start the healing process than with Jessica's oils?

Acknowledgments

The author wishes to thank the following:
my friends and college roommates James Bradbeer Jr.
and Lawrence Vitale; David Pepe of Pro Agents Inc.;
Peter Roisman of Advantage International;
my editor and friend Jacob Hoye;
Natalie Ayars, M.D.; E. W. Count;
the AOL Writers Club;
and, of course, Dave Bolt.

If you enjoyed *Drop Shot*,
read on for a thrilling preview of
the next Myron Bolitar novel,

FADE AWAY

Available now from Dell

1

_____

"**J**UST BEHAVE."

"Me?" Myron said. "I'm always a delight."

Myron Bolitar was being led through the corridor of the darkened Meadowlands Arena by Calvin Johnson, the New Jersey Dragons new general manager. Their dress shoes clacked sharply against the tile and echoed through empty Harry M. Stevens food stands, Carvel Ice Cream carts, pretzel vendors, souvenir booths. The smell of sporting-event hot dogs—that sort of rubbery, chemically, yet nostalgically delicious aroma—wafted from the walls. The stillness of the place consumed them; there is nothing more hollow and lifeless than an empty sports arena.

Calvin Johnson stopped in front of a door leading to a luxury box. "This may all seem a bit strange," he said. "Just go with the flow, okay?"

"Okay."

Calvin reached for the knob and took a deep breath. "Clip Arnstein, the owner of the Dragons, is in there waiting for us."

"And yet I'm not trembling," Myron said.

Calvin Johnson shook his head. "Just don't be an ass."

Myron pointed to his chest. "I wore a tie and everything."

Calvin Johnson opened the door. The luxury box faced mid-court. Several workers were putting down the basketball floor over the hockey ice. The Devils had played the night before. Tonight was the Dragons' turn. The box was cozy. Twenty-four cushioned seats. Two television monitors. To the right was a wood-paneled counter for the food—usually fried chicken, hot dogs, potato knishes, sausage and pepper sandwiches, that sort of stuff. To the left was a brass cart with a nicely stocked bar and minifridge. The box also had its own bathroom—this so the corporate high rollers would not have to urinate with the great unwashed.

Clip Arnstein faced them, standing. He wore a dark blue suit with a red tie. He was bald with patches of gray over both ears. He was burly, his chest still a barrel after seventy-some-odd years. His large hands had brown spots and fat blue veins like garden hoses. No one spoke. No one moved. Clip glared hard at Myron for several seconds, examining him from head to toe.

"Like the tie?" Myron asked.

Calvin Johnson shot him a warning glance.

The old man made no movement toward them. "How old are you now, Myron?"

Interesting opening question. "Thirty-two."

"You playing any ball?"

"Some," Myron said.

"You keep in good shape?"

"Want me to flex?"

"No, that won't be necessary."

No one offered Myron a seat and no one took one. Of course the only chairs in here were the spectator seats, but it still felt weird to stand in a business setting where you're supposed to sit. Standing suddenly became difficult. Myron felt antsy. He didn't know what to do with his hands. He took out a pen and held it, but that didn't feel right. Too Bob Dole. He stuck his hands in his pockets and stood at a weird angle, like the casual guy in the Sears circular.

"Myron, we have an interesting proposition for you," Clip Arnstein said.

"Proposition?" Always the probing interrogatory.

"Yes. I was the one who drafted you, you know."

"I know."

"Ten, eleven years ago. When I was with the Celtics."

"I know."

"First round."

"I know all this, Mr. Arnstein."

"You were a hell of a prospect, Myron. You were smart. You had an unbelievable touch. You were loaded with talent."

"I coulda been a contenda," Myron said.

Arnstein scowled. It was a famous scowl, developed over some fifty-plus years in professional basketball. The scowl had made its first appearance when Clip played for the now-defunct Rochester Royals in the forties. It grew more famous when he coached the Boston Celtics to numerous championships. It became a legendary trademark when he made all the famous trades ("clipping" the competition, ergo the nickname) as team president. Three years ago Clip had become majority owner of the New Jersey Dragons and the scowl now resided in East Rutherford, right off Exit 16 of the New Jersey Turnpike. His voice was gruff. "Was that supposed to be Brando?"

"Eerie, isn't it? Like Marlon's actually in the room."

Clip Arnstein's face suddenly softened. He nodded slowly,

giving Myron the doelike, father-figure eyes. "You make jokes to cover the pain," he said gravely. "I understand that."

Dr. Joyce Brothers.

"Is there something I can do for you, Mr. Arnstein?"

"You never played in a single professional game, did you, Myron?"

"You know very well I didn't."

Clip nodded. "Your first preseason game. Third quarter. You already had eighteen points that game. Not bad for a rookie in his first scrimmage. That was when fate took over."

Fate took the form of big Burt Wesson of the Washington Bullets. There had been a collision, a searing pain, and then nothing.

"Awful thing," Clip said.

"Uh huh."

"I always felt bad about what happened to you. Such a waste."

Myron glanced at Calvin Johnson. Calvin was looking off, arms crossed, his smooth black features a placid pool. "Uh huh," Myron said again.

"That's why I'd like to give you another chance."

Myron was sure he'd heard wrong. "Pardon?"

"We have a slot open on the team. I'd like to sign you."

Myron waited. He looked at Clip. Then he looked at Calvin Johnson. Neither one was laughing. "Where is it?" Myron asked.

"What?"

"The camera. This is one of those hidden camera shows, right? Is this the one with Ed McMahon? I'm a big fan of his work."

"It's not a joke, Myron."

"It must be, Mr. Arnstein. I haven't played competitive ball in ten years. I shattered my knee, remember?"

"All too well. But as you said, it was ten years ago. I know you went through rehabilitation to rebuild it."

"And you also know I tried a comeback. Seven years ago. The knee wouldn't hold up."

"It was still too early," Clip said. "You just told me you're playing again."

"Pickup games on weekends. It's a tad different than the NBA."

Clip dismissed the argument with a wave of his hand. "You're in shape. You even volunteered to flex."

Myron's eyes narrowed, swerving from Clip to Calvin Johnson, back to Clip. Their expressions were neutral. "Why do I have the feeling," Myron asked, "that I'm missing something here?"

Clip finally smiled. He looked over to Calvin Johnson. Calvin Johnson forced up a return smile.

"Perhaps I should be less"—Clip paused, searched for the word—"opaque."

"That might be helpful."

"I want you on the team. I don't much care if you play or not."

Myron waited again. When no one continued, he said, "It's still a bit opaque."

Clip let loose a long breath. He walked over to the bar, opened a small hotel-style fridge, and removed a can of Yoo-Hoo. Stocking Yoo-Hoos. Hmm. Clip had been prepared. "You still drink this sludge?"

"Yes," Myron said.

He tossed Myron the can and poured something from a decanter into two glasses. He handed one to Calvin Johnson. He signaled to the seats by the glass window. Exactly midcourt. Very nice. Nice leg room too. Even Calvin, who was six-eight, was able to stretch a bit. The three men sat next to one another, all facing the same way, which again felt weird in a business setting. You were supposed to sit across from one another, preferably at a table or desk. Instead they sat shoulder to shoulder, watching the work crew pound the floor into place.

"Cheers," Clip said.

He sipped his whiskey. Calvin Johnson just held his. Myron, obeying the instructions on the can, shook his Yoo-Hoo.

"If I'm not mistaken," Clip continued, "you're a lawyer now."

"I'm a member of the bar," Myron said. "I don't practice much law."

"You're a sports agent."

"Yes."

"I don't trust agents," Clip said.

"Neither do I."

"For the most part, they're bloodsucking leeches."

"We prefer the term 'parasitic entities,'" Myron said. "It's more PC."

Clip Arnstein leaned forward, his eyes zeroing in on Myron's. "How do I know I can trust you?"

Myron pointed at himself. "My face," he said. "It screams trustworthiness."

Clip did not smile. He leaned a little closer. "What I'm about to tell you must remain confidential."

"Okay."

"Do you give me your word it won't go any farther than this room?"

"Yes."

Clip hesitated, glanced at Calvin Johnson, shifted in his seat. "You know, of course, Greg Downing."

Of course. Myron had grown up with Greg Downing. From the time they had first competed as sixth graders in a town league less than twenty miles from where Myron now sat, they were instant rivals. When they reached high school, Greg's family moved to the neighboring town of Essex Fells because Greg's father did not want his son sharing the basketball spotlight with Myron. The personal rivalry then began to take serious flight. They played against each other eight times in high school, each winning four games. Myron and Greg became New Jersey's hottest recruits and both matriculated at big-time basketball colleges with a storied rivalry of their own—Myron to Duke, Greg to North Carolina.

The personal rivalry soared.

During their college careers, they had shared two *Sports Illustrated* covers. Both teams won the ACC twice, but Myron picked up a national championship. Both Myron and Greg were picked first-team All-American, both at the guard spots. By the time they both graduated, Duke and North Carolina had played each other twelve times. The Myron-led Duke had won eight of them. When the NBA draft came, both men went in the first round.

The personal rivalry crashed and burned.

Myron's career ended when he collided with big Burt Wesson. Greg Downing sidestepped fate and went on to become one of the NBA premier guards. During his ten-year career with the New Jersey Dragons Downing had been named to the All-Star team eight times. He led the league twice in three-point shooting. Four times he led the league in free-throw percentage and once in assists. He'd been on three *Sports Illustrated* covers and had won an NBA championship.

"I know him," Myron said.

"Do you talk to him much?" Clip Arnstein asked.

"No."

"When was the last time you spoke?"

"I don't remember."

"Within the last few days?"

"I don't think we've spoken in ten years," Myron said.

"Oh," Clip said. He took another sip. Calvin had still not touched his drink. "Well, I'm sure you heard about his injury."

"Something with his ankle," Myron said. "It's day to day. He's in seclusion working on it."

Clip nodded. "That's the story we gave the media anyway. It's not exactly the truth."

"Oh?"

"Greg isn't injured," Clip said. "He's missing."

"Missing?" Again the probing interrogatory.

"Yes." Clip took another sip. Myron sipped back, not an easy task with Yoo-Hoo.

"Since when?" Myron asked.

"Five days now."

Myron looked at Calvin. Calvin remained placid but he had that kind of face. During his playing days, his nickname had been Frosty because he never displayed emotion. He was living up to his name now.

Myron tried again. "When you say Greg is missing—"

"Gone," Clip snapped. "Disappeared. Into thin air. Without a trace. Whatever you want to call it."

"Have you called the police?"

"No."

"Why not?"

Clip gave him the wave-off again. "You know Greg. He's not a conventional guy."

The understatement of the millennium.

"He never does the expected," Clip said. "He hates the fame. He likes to be on his own. He's even disappeared before, though never during a playoff drive."

"So?"

"So there's a good chance he's just being his usually flaky self," Clip continued. "Greg can shoot like a dream, but let's face facts: the man is a couple of sandwiches short of a picnic. You know what Downing does after games?"

Myron shook his head.

"He drives a cab in the city. That's right, a goddamn Yellow taxi cab in New York City. Says it keeps him close to the common man. Greg won't do appearances or endorsements. He doesn't do interviews. He doesn't even do the charity thing. He dresses like something out of a seventies sitcom. The man is a nut job."

"All of which makes him immensely popular with the fans," Myron said. "Which sells tickets."

"I agree," Clip said, "but that just underlines my point. If we call the cops it could damage both him and the team. Can you imagine the media circus if this got out?"

"It would be bad," Myron admitted.

"Exactly. And suppose Greg is just hanging out in French Lick or whatever hickville town he goes to in the off-season, fishing or something? Christ, we'd never hear the end of it. On the other hand, suppose he's up to something."

"Up to something?" Myron repeated.

"Hell, I don't know. I'm just talking here. But I don't need a goddamn scandal. Not now. Not with the playoffs coming up, you know what I'm saying?"

Not really, but Myron decided to let it go for now. "Who else knows about this?"

"Just the three of us."

The work crew rolled in the baskets. Two extras were kept in storage in case someone pulled a Darryl Dawkins and shattered a backboard. They then began putting down additional seats. Like most arenas, the Meadowlands holds more seats for basketball than hockey—in this case around a thousand more. Myron took another sip of Yoo-Hoo and let it roll around his tongue. He waited until it slid down his throat before he asked the obvious question. "So how do I fit in?"

Clip hesitated. His breathing was deep, almost labored. "I know something of your years with the FBI," he said finally. "No details, of course. Not even vagaries really, but enough to know you have a background in this kinda stuff. We want you to find Greg. Quietly."

Myron said nothing. His "undercover" work for the feds, it seemed, was the worst kept secret in the continental United States. Clip sipped his drink. He looked at Calvin's full glass, then at Calvin. Calvin finally took a sip. Clip turned his attention back to Myron. "Greg's divorced now," Clip went on. "He's basically a loner. All his friends—hell, all his acquaintances—are teammates. They're his support group, if you will. His family. If anyone knows where he is—if anyone's helping him stay hidden—it's got to be one of the Dragons. I'll be honest with you. These guys are a major pain in the ass. Spoiled, pampered prima donnas who think our purpose in life is to serve them. But they all have one thing in common: They see management as the enemy. Us against the world and all that crap. They won't tell us the truth. They won't tell reporters the truth. And if you approach them as some, uh, 'parasitic entity,' they won't talk to you either. You have to be a player. It's the only way to get on the inside."

"So you want me to join the team so I can find Greg."

Myron heard the echoes of hurt in his voice. It was unintentional, but he saw that both men heard it too. His face flushed in embarrassment.

Clip put a hand on his shoulder. "I meant what I said, Myron. You could have been great. One of the greatest."

Myron took a deep swig of his Yoo-Hoo. No more sipping. "I'm sorry, Mr. Arnstein. I can't help you."

The scowl was back. "What?"

"I have a life. I'm a sports agent. I have clients to tend to. I can't just drop it all."

"You'll get the players' minimum prorated. That's two hundred thousand dollars less whatever. And there's only a couple of weeks left until the playoffs. We'll keep you on till then no matter what."

"No. My playing days are over. And I'm not a private investigator."

"But we need to find him. He could be in danger."

"I'm sorry. The answer is no."

Clip smiled. "Suppose I sweeten the pot."

"No."

"Fifty-thousand-dollar signing bonus."

"I'm sorry."

"Greg could show up tomorrow and you'd still get to keep that. Fifty grand. Plus a share of playoff money."

"No."

Clip sat back. He stared at his drink, dipped his finger into it, stirred. His voice was casual. "You say you're an agent, right?"

"Yes."

"I'm very friendly with the parents of three guys that will go in the first round. Did you know that?"

"No."

"Suppose," Clip said slowly, "I guarantee you that one of them signs with you."

Myron pricked up. A first round draft pick. He tried to keep his expression cool—to do like Frosty—but his heart was thumping. "How can you do that?"

"Don't worry about how."

"It doesn't sound ethical."

Clip made a scoffing noise. "Myron, don't play choirboy with me. You do me this favor and MB SportsReps gets a first round draft pick. Guaranteed. No matter how this thing with Greg plays out."

MB SportsReps. Myron's company. Myron Bolitar, ergo MB. Representing sports people, ergo SportsReps. Add it together: MB SportsReps. Myron came up with that name on his own but still no offers came in from major advertising companies to use his services.

"Make it a hundred-thousand-dollar signing bonus," Myron said.

Clip smiled. "You've learned well, Myron."

Myron shrugged.

"Seventy-five thousand," Clip said. "And you'll take it so don't bullshit a bullshitter."

The two men shook hands.

"I have a few more questions about the disappearance," Myron said.

Using both armrests Clip rose and stood over Myron. "Calvin will answer all your questions," he said with a nod toward his general manager. "I have to go now."

"So when do you want me to start practicing?"

Clip looked surprised. "Practicing?"

"Yeah. When do you want me to start?"

"We have a game tonight."

"Tonight?"

"Of course," Clip said.

"You want me to suit up tonight?"

"We're playing our old team, the Celtics. Calvin will make sure you have a uniform by game time. Press conference at six to announce your signing. Don't be late." Clip headed toward the door. "And wear that tie. I like it."

"Tonight?" Myron repeated, but Clip was already gone.

© PIP COWLEY

HARLAN COBEN is the #1 *New York Times* bestselling author of numerous suspense novels, including *Don't Let Go, Home, Fool Me Once, Run Away, The Boy from the Woods, Win, The Match,* and *I Will Find You,* as well as the multi-award-winning Myron Bolitar series. He has more than eighty million copies in print worldwide, he is now published in forty-six languages around the globe, and his books have been #1 bestsellers in more than a dozen countries. Several Netflix series, including *The Stranger, Stay Close,* and the #1 global hit *Fool Me Once,* have been adapted from his novels. Harlan Coben lives in New Jersey.

harlancoben.com
Facebook.com/harlancobenbooks
X: @HarlanCoben
Instagram: @harlancoben

About the Type

This book was set in Minion, a 1990 Adobe Originals typeface by Robert Slimbach. Minion is inspired by classical, old-style typefaces of the late Renaissance, a period of elegant and beautiful type designs. Created primarily for text setting, Minion combines the aesthetic and functional qualities that make text type highly readable with the versatility of digital technology.